When The Music Ends

When The Music Ends

Hearts in Winter Book 1

Simone Beaudelaire

Copyright (C) 2013 Simone Beaudelaire
Layout design and Copyright (C) 2019 by Next Chapter
Published 2019 by Liaison – A Next Chapter Imprint
Cover art by http://www.thecovercollection.com/
This book is a work of fiction. Names, characters, places, and incidents are the product of the author's imagination or are used fictitiously. Any resemblance to actual events, locales, or persons, living or dead, is purely coincidental.
All rights reserved. No part of this book may be reproduced or transmitted in any form or by any means, electronic or mechanical, including photocopying, recording, or by any information storage and retrieval system, without the author's permission.
Author's web site: http://simonebeaudelaireauthor.weebly.com
Author's email: simonebeaudelaireauthor@hotmail.com

*For Sandra, Reed, Guy, Jill, Cary and Lin.
I couldn't have done it without you.*

Part I

Chapter 1

October 2001

"Hello?" Sean Murphy called as he entered the century-old white colonial house in which he had grown up. The age-darkened door slammed shut behind him in a gust of chilly October wind. He stepped into the silent living room. *Home looks the same as always; rose-printed sofa, two maroon armchairs, and an antique wooden rocker flanking the brick and brass fireplace. It's too quiet, though. Mom and Dad must be out,* he thought. *I bet Mom left something delicious in the fridge. That will keep me busy until dinner.*

A muffled greeting interrupted his refrigerator piracy scheme. "Hi, Sean, can you come here, please?"

Smiling to himself, he climbed the stairs to Sheridan's bedroom and opened the door, unsurprised to discover his seventeen-year-old sister wasn't alone. Sheridan's best friend Erin James sprawled with her on the pink and lace canopy bed. *It's interesting to see them together,* Sean reflected. *They couldn't be more opposite.* Sheridan, tall and curvy, resembled sunshine brought to life. She had fair but slightly golden skin, masses of blond curls, and a cheerful demeanor. Small and pale, with dark hair and eyes, Erin's serious face reflected her intense personality.

Sheridan jumped from the bed and ran to her brother.

"Hey, sis, what did you need?" Sean asked as he received his sister's exuberant hug. From the corner of his eye, he saw Erin sit up, her cheeks flaming at the sight of him.

"Your timing is perfect, Sean," Sheridan gushed. "I need you to take Erin to the homecoming dance."

"Huh?" Sean turned from his sister to Erin and saw her fair cheeks had darkened even further.

"Yeah," Sheridan blurted, a flood of words seeming to erupt from her all at once. "This stupid guy has been messing with her, making her think he would take her, but he really just wanted her to help him study. Today we found out that he was going to the dance with Lindsey Jones, that tramp. We know what he wants, and no loss there, but now Erin doesn't have a date and the dance is tomorrow. Would you take her?"

"Danny, please," Erin said, softly interjecting into the rapid gush, "I don't need this. I don't care about homecoming and you know I can't dance. I'll just stay home and practice for that audition."

"No way, you *have to* go," Sheridan insisted. "I won't have a bit of fun without you. I'm so sick of Jake. I may just ditch him."

The mention of his sister's boyfriend aroused Sean's protective instincts. *That punk rubs me the wrong way every time I see him.* "It's about time you ditched that dickhead,' he commented, making both girls giggle. "He's nowhere near good enough for you, Danny. Why don't you forget about him and you and Erin go together? That would be better, wouldn't it?"

"Come on, Sean." Sheridan waved her brother's words away with a careless gesture. "It's not nice to dump someone just before a dance, especially since he's nominated for homecoming king. Oh, don't worry; I'll break up with him. I just think it would be politer to do it after, and after the SATs next week too, so he's not distracted, but that still leaves Erin. She can't come with the two of us. It's too pathetic. Erin deserves better than to be the third wheel. But think, Sean, if she comes with a man instead of one of those little boys." She waved at him again, this time indicating his work-hardened muscles, currently straining the sleeves of a red plaid shirt and a pair of ratty blue jeans.

Sean heaved a heavy breath and took a moment to consider. *A date... with Erin?* His eyes traced the delicate lines of her face. Wide brown eyes that always seemed tinged with sorrow. Long yet elegant nose. Pale rosebud lips. High cheekbones. Her collarbones peeped from the scooped neckline of a navy long-sleeved tee shirt that hugged her slender frame. *There's nothing wrong with her looks, certainly. She's pretty, and as she's been Sheridan's friend since kindergarten, I know her well. I know she's nice. In fact, if I hadn't known her all her life, I might just ask someone like her out.* He stared at the familiar face for long moments, watching the heat in her cheeks fade, and the pale lip slip between teeth that had only recently lost their braces. He shook his head. *Someone like her, but not her.* "Yeah, I know what will happen. I'll be arrested. Sheridan, I'm twenty-three. What do I care about homecoming?" he demanded, raising one eyebrow at his sister.

"Probably nothing," she admitted, "but do you care about Erin?"

"Of course," Sean replied. *She's practically a member of the family. How could I not care?* Again, he considered the proposition, considered how Erin must feel. Already shy and not inclined to date, for her to be toyed with and then dropped – even by a loser – must have played hell with her self-confidence. *But imagine what a coup if she did show up with someone like... me. Someone like me, but not me, right?* But if not him, there was no one. He turned his attention to Erin, whose face lit up like a Fourth of July firework the moment their eyes met. *She likes the idea, even if she's too shy to admit it.* "You know what, Erin, come here a minute. I think we should talk about this without Danny for a while."

"Okay." She rose from the bed and stepped out into the hallway with him, close to his side, but not letting her body brush against his. He led her into the room that used to be his, still decorated with all his old high school memorabilia. Sean couldn't help grinning. *My sentimental mother. She'll never turn this into a storage room or rent it out to college students.*

Erin moved to stand near him, leaning against the thick footboard, biting one short fingernail. "I hope you know," she said earnestly, "that I didn't ask her to do that."

"Of course not," he replied, patting her shoulder. *If she blushes any harder, her face will burst into flame.* "I can smell a Sheridan Murphy plot a mile away. She's my sister, don't forget. However, she is right about one thing. You do need a date; that is, if you really want to go. Tell the truth, Erin. Do you really want to stay home and practice?"

"No, I would like to go," she whispered as if admitting a shameful secret. "I really can't dance, though."

"Come on," he urged, "you're a musician. I can't believe you have no rhythm."

Her dark eyes met his at last, her discomfort pinching the corners. "It's not a question of rhythm but of self-confidence. I always feel silly dancing in front of a room full of people."

"How about if you have someone confident leading the way, kind of like a director?" he offered, pantomiming an invitation with one hand extended.

"That might help." She looked down and as if that were not enough, swept her long, dark lashes over her eyes.

I hope I'm doing the right thing. Her crush on me is kind of sweet… in an embarrassing sort of way. She is still in high school, after all. Sean didn't know what to say next. Her shyness overpowered his attempts at conversation. *To the point, Murphy.* "Okay then, let's do it. At least we can show that douchebag what he's missing."

"Are you sure? Don't you have plans?" Her eyes pleaded with him.

Oh boy. "Nah. Just boring stuff, you know, like laundry. So, Erin, will you let me take you to homecoming?"

She gave him an intense look, her dark eyes glowing with eagerness as she said, "Yes," in a voice so tiny he almost couldn't hear her. He gave her a brotherly hug around the shoulders. She squeaked and fled the room.

Well, one thing I didn't expect was to go to a high school dance. Maybe it will be fun. Then he recalled his own high school dances; awkward, loud and smelling faintly of B.O. *Maybe not, but at least I'll have done a good deed and made my sister and her friend happy.*

Chapter 2

The following night, Sean arrived at Erin's house dressed in a fitted green button up shirt and some dark slacks, trying to appear as mature as possible.

He drove into her prestigious neighborhood near The University of the Lakes, their local institute of higher learning. Elegant, narrow homes, over a century in age, crowded cheek by jowl along the street, the view of their bright colors and gingerbread trim obscured by oak and maple trees, formally attired in their colorful autumn leaves. As he scanned the house numbers, he realized he knew the area, had renovated at least two of the nearby structures. "2107," he muttered, trying to make out the numbers in the semi-darkness. "2107 Water Street." He passed 2103 and knew he must be nearly there. Two houses down, he frowned at the smallest one on the block. Short and squat, it looked like a troll crouching between the two and three-story giants all around it. *Huh. Ritzy area. If this is the best an investment banker and a commercial artist can afford, yikes.* He shook his head. The miniature two-bedroom home had been painted tan with green shutters framing a stained-glass window. Sean parked his Mustang along the curb, kicked his way along the leaf-strewn sidewalk, rang the doorbell and waited.

I wonder what she's going to be wearing. Hopefully not anything like what she had on at her last birthday. Sean grimaced at the memory of oversized black, orange, pink and silver bows sewn all over a dress made of a man's sweatshirt, paired with fishnet purple tights – one of her mother's 'artistic' creations. *This might not have been such a good idea.*

The door opened to reveal his date clad in a classy and touchably soft black velour knee-length dress. It contrasted with her skin and made her dark hair – done up in an elegant twist – seem to glow. Sheridan must have helped with the subtle application of makeup. Erin looked at least five years older, not to mention more confident, than he had seen her before, meeting his gaze without blushing and smiling sweetly. The sorrow in her wide brown eyes tugged at his protective instincts and he realized he did care about her. *I told Danny I did, but it was a sort of intellectual caring.* For the first time, Erin, the person, seemed real and alive in front of him.

Awareness stole his breath. "Hi," he said at last. Then he held out a corsage consisting of a single red rosebud. She stepped forward and he carefully pinned it to her dress, breathing in a waft of lilac perfume. The contrast of the vivid scarlet with the shimmering black drew his eyes to the slender curves of her figure. *She's so thin. I wonder if she forgets to eat. I've heard artists do that sometimes.*

He lifted his eyes to hers, taking in the satisfied glow of approval. "Hi, Sean. Let's go."

"Do you need me to come in and say hello to your folks or anything?" he asked, peering over her shoulder into the darkened living room.

"No, my parents aren't here." She stepped out and closed the door behind her, dropping her key into a tiny silver bag hanging from her wrist.

"Where are they?" He placed his hand on the small of her back and moved her forward. The warmth of her skin radiated through the fabric of the dress, making his fingers tingle.

"I'll tell you in the car," she said with a hint of tension in her voice.

"Okay."

They arrived at the passenger side of the Mustang and Sean opened the door for Erin. *This might not exactly be the date she wanted, but every girl deserves to feel like a princess once in a while, and I bet Erin doesn't get much of that.* Closing the door, he circled the car and slid into the driver's seat, firing the ignition before saying, "Okay, what's up?"

"My parents are splitting up," she said flatly.

Sean winced. No wonder she seems so strained. "That's too bad. Why?"

"My dad's always away at work, you know?" He nodded. "Well, Mom met someone. She's spending the weekend with *him* and Dad's gone for work again, so I'm on my own."

He reached across the console and patted her hand. "That sucks. Sorry."

"It's okay. It's not like they actually liked each other or anything."

Have I ever heard such a bleak tone from Erin? He hadn't, he realized, because she'd never let him see her real feelings. *Or maybe I just never bothered to look.* He rested his hand on top of hers. "Still. I don't care about them, but I'm sorry for you."

"Don't pity me, Sean," she pleaded. "The one thing I can't stand is for you to see me as pathetic."

Far from it. "You're not pathetic, Erin," he reassured her. "Let's say I'm sorry about your situation, okay?"

"Okay, thanks." She fell silent for a moment, considering what to say next and nibbling her knuckle. At last, she added, "I'm so glad finally to be a senior. If I can just get through this year, I'll be an adult. I'll go off to college, and I won't be at the mercy of their choices anymore."

"Where are you going?" he asked, wanting to keep the conversation positive. "Sheridan mentioned a conservatory in Texas."

"I'm not sure," she replied. "I have an appointment with their recruiter in two weeks to play an audition, but I'm also considering going to State with Sheridan. That would be nice too."

"Can you be a performance major at a state university?" he asked. *Don't musicians have to go to Julliard or something like that?*

He shifted his eyes her direction in time to see her dip her chin. "Sure. It wouldn't be as prestigious, but I would save a ton of money, and I would likely get better scholarships too. With everything that's been happening, I'm probably going to need them. Didn't you go to State, Sean, to get your business degree, before you started working with your dad's construction company? Isn't that why he made you assistant foreman, because you learned so much about handling marketing, accounting, and all those things?"

"Yeah, I did," he admitted, surprised she knew so much detail. *She and Danny must talk about me a lot.* He felt his own cheeks burning at the realization. "It's a good school. Don't sell yourself short, though. Saving money is fine, but not if you miss out on your dreams. I know you want to play your oboe professionally. You're good enough to do it, so go for it, okay?"

Another quick glance revealed a warm glow around her cheeks, not exactly a blush, but a hint of her pleasure at his compliment. "Good advice. Thanks."

* * *

They drove along in silence. Erin stared out the window at the masses of orange, gold, and vermillion trees, interspersed with the green of pine and spruce. A thrill of nervous excitement threatened to turn her belly into a knot. *I didn't really expect to go to the dance at all. Now I'm going with my crush. Amazing. Forget David Landry. He can score with Lindsey. I now have, without a doubt, the sexiest date of all.*

A motorcycle roared by, its growl interrupting her train of thought. *Noisy monster. Why do people enjoy such a rackety thing?* Sean braked abruptly as the bike swerved into their lane. His movement released a waft of spicy cologne that teased her awareness. *What would it feel like to be surrounded by those muscular arms, breathing in his scent as he tumbles you onto the mattress?* Her breathing slowed and deepened as she imagined the unknown sensation. Then, with a blink, she forced herself to refocus on reality. *Don't fool yourself. He's not here because he likes you.* Though she knew it was a favor, she appreciated it. *Escorting his sister's shy and uninteresting friend to a dance he doesn't want to go to. Sean is the definition of a true gentleman.*

He turned into the high school parking lot and guided his Mustang between two white lines near the back, where a few spaces remained. Then he escorted Erin, his hand on her back again, into the crowded and noisy gym. Paper streamers in the school's colors of maroon and white hung from the ceiling. A hand-painted cougar roared from the far wall. The noise inside the gym beat on Erin's eardrums with the force of a sledgehammer. *Why do so many girls giggle so shrilly? Do they really think their dates will find that sound appealing?* She shook her head. She could barely hear the music over the cacophony of adolescent voices.

While they waited in line to have their picture taken at a white lattice arch hung with football pennants, streamers and balloons, Erin glanced around. Just as she expected, people stared at her, and some of the girls had envious expressions on their faces.

She turned to face her date, admiring his neatly-cut mahogany-brown hair, which she found much sharper-looking than the shaggy style most of the boys were wearing. His face, tanned from working outside, made his slightly crooked front teeth seem even whiter and his dark blue eyes glow bright. His arms, chest, and shoulders bulged with muscle from long hours on the construction site, but his waist was narrow, his hips slim. In short, he was every girl's dream. *Or if not, he's certainly mine. Why does he have to be six impossible years older than me?*

At last, they reached the head of the line. A chubby photographer with a lot of gray sprinkled in his dark, bushy hair motioned them to stand in front of a mottled gray screen.

"Okay, buddy," he told Sean in a scratchy voice, "put your arms around your girl."

Erin opened her mouth to argue, to suggest they pose side by side, but Sean didn't give her the chance. He wrapped his arms around her waist and pulled her flush against his front. The noise in the room receded as Sean's warmth and wonderful scent washed over her.

"Now you, sugar, arms around his neck."

She obeyed without protest.

"Face the camera."

They turned their heads. The shutter clicked.

"Right, now go dance. Next!"

Keeping one arm around her waist, Sean escorted Erin deeper into the gym. She could feel the noise buffeting her, but the sound faded beneath the pounding of her own heart. *I'll cherish that photo forever.*

"You know," Sean said loudly, his lips close to her ear in order to be heard over the din, "I thought of a solution to your dancing dilemma."

"What's that?" she shouted back.

"Only dance the slow ones," he replied. "Those are the easiest. You just hold onto me and sway."

That sounds like a dream come true. "I think I can manage. What about the fast ones?"

"Walk around. Mingle. Get a snack or drink. It's easy." He pulled back a bit to gauge her reaction.

She smiled. "You're smart, Sean. Thanks."

His mouth curved into a beautiful answering grin that set her heart to pounding. "Shall we start right out? This is a slow song." He extended his hand.

She grasped it. "Okay."

He led her to a spot in the gym far from the congested center and stopped, turning to face her. Erin placed her hands on the back of Sean's neck. Sean looped his arms loosely around Erin's waist and demonstrated to her how to move in time to the music. While it was a different kind of movement than she was used to making, she didn't find it difficult to understand. *Remember, this isn't a date,* she told herself, *no matter how Sean's body heat sinks sinuously into me.* She could hear the soft sighing of fabric as his shirt and slacks moved with his body. She strived not to lose her sense of what she was doing. *This is not a romance. It's just a dance. It doesn't mean anything to him.* Oh, but it meant something to her. "I Swear" by All-4-One played in the background, passionate and romantic, the poetry of its lyrics wrapping around her like a cozy blanket of bliss. She hummed the melody softly to herself, committing the perfect moment to memory.

* * *

Sean could see the effect he was having on his sister's friend. *Maybe this isn't a good idea. What if her shy crush turns into a full-blown infatuation? That just isn't appropriate.* Not least of all because he wasn't as immune to her as he pretended. His off-handed charm concealed a rather alarming attraction. *Erin's pretty, really pretty, he realized. I bet beneath her timid demeanor, she has a passionate soul. Otherwise, how could she play her instrument so well? Someday, maybe, when she's finished growing up, I'll ask her out for real.* Of course, if she moved to Texas, he might never see her again. This night would only be a remembered possibility, unfulfilled, but never forgotten, to be thought of occasionally with fondness and a touch of regret.

Hmmm, it won't do to relegate the evening to memory before it's scarcely begun. Sean did want Erin to have a good time, so he hugged her a little tighter. *Surely there's no harm in that. I have to have enough self-control to dance with a pretty girl and not get too turned on, right?* It wasn't easy though. Every time Erin brushed the front of her body against his, his ability to remember why this wasn't real took a blow, especially now that she had grown more comfortable with him. As her shyness melted away minute by minute, allowing her lovely spirit to shine through, Sean found himself enchanted. *I always knew Erin was nice, but only because Sheridan has no time for mean or fake people. I never realized how truly special she is.* Try though he might, he could not conceal his growing admiration, and from the shining hope in her eyes, he could see she felt it, and liked it. *I'm in serious trouble.*

* * *

In this way, Erin and Sean passed a pleasant evening. They danced together several times, and when the songs became too fast, they wandered the periphery of the room, watching, conversing, drinking punch, and generally just enjoying themselves.

About halfway through, another fast song came on and Erin made a face. "Can you believe they're playing this at high school?" she asked Sean, waving at the offending speaker. "So dirty."

He raised one eyebrow. "I know what you mean. Makes me want to cover your virgin ears."

She laughed. "I've heard it before, you know. I don't live in a convent. It is pretty gross, though. Come on, let's get out of the way of all the dirty dancers."

They wended their way through the crowd, past a girl who was grinding her backside on a boy's crotch. Erin turned away quickly, and then pulled up short as the couple in front of them paused to kiss. Sean collided with Erin's back.

"Uncomfortable?" he asked her, indicating the scenes of decadence all around them.

She shrugged. "It's high school. There are people making out in every corner. I've seen it, but I'm not sure this is the place for it." She tried to play it cool, but Sean's body against her back, his warm breath near her ear, sent tingles racing through her body.

He hooked his arm around her waist and led her away.

After a sharp turn to the left to avoid a gaggle of teachers bearing down on the misbehaving students, she and Sean ran into Sheridan. Her friend's red face and narrowed eyes spoke volumes, as did her hissing undertone. "Jake, I can't believe you said that. Do you even know how to listen? No!"

"But, Danny," the boy whined, scrubbing the golden scruff on his jaw with the back of one hand.

"But nothing, Jake. The conversation was over before it started. You know my answer, and nothing has changed, so shut the hell up."

Erin met Sean's eyes. His tightly clenched teeth revealed his anger. As much as Erin knew Sean disliked Jake, it wouldn't take much to put him over the edge. She indicated the couple with her head, silently asking if they should intervene.

Sean didn't bother to respond to Erin's query. He waded right in, his protective big brother glare in place. "Danny, is everything all right?" He gave the handsome blond youth a hard look.

Sheridan shook her mane of golden curls as though in surprise and turned to her brother. "No, I don't want to be here anymore. I want to go home." Her voice caught.

"I'll drive you," Sean offered. "You don't mind, do you, Erin?"

Damn it, I don't want to go home yet. Do I have to let the fairy tale end already? Then she took in her friend's unhappy expression again and answered, "Of course not."

"No, I'll take her," Jake sighed wearily, running a hand through his shaggy hair.

"Danny, is that what you want?" Erin asked, glaring at her friend's boyfriend.

Sheridan looked at Erin for a long moment, and then applied the same treatment to her brother. *I wonder what she thinks she's seeing.* At last, she heaved a sigh and said, "I don't want to interrupt your evening. Jake can drive me. I'll see you Monday, okay?"

"Sure, sweetie." Erin hugged her friend and whispered, "Thanks."

"Don't sell yourself short, Erin," Sheridan breathed in her ear. "You are completely worth it." With that cryptic comment, the couple left.

"I hope she breaks up with him soon," Sean said, shooting daggers at Jake's departing back with his eyes. "I really don't like that guy."

"Me neither," Erin agreed, still wondering what her friend had been trying to tell her. "You know, I may encourage her not to wait until after the test. She needs him out of her life now. He's becoming a pest."

"What do you mean?" Sean turned to regard her. For a moment the lingering anger on his face seemed directed at her, and she recoiled.

"It's high school, Sean. He wants to sleep with her," she blurted.

Sean's jaw clenched.

Oh dear. That might have been too blunt when he's already so angry. Erin hastened to explain. "She keeps telling him no, but he's not listening. I'm a little worried about all the pressure he's putting on her." *And that's the unvarnished truth.*

"Sheridan won't succumb," he retorted, his fury giving way to annoyed amusement. "She's one of the most stubbornly upright people I've ever known."

Erin touched his arm reassuringly and he covered her fingers with his hand. She closed her eyes at the touch, trying to get a handle on herself so she could speak coherently. "Yeah, but she doesn't need it. It's disrespectful, you know?"

"Yes, it is. Erin, do you want to dance some more?"

Shifting the focus back to herself jarred Erin, and she opened her eyes as a wave of heat rolled over her. Composed of equal parts hundreds of sweaty teens, the blasting heater and her own dizzying blend of anger toward Jake and desire for Sean, it drew beads of sweat to her forehead. "Not really. Actually, it's kind of stuffy in here. Would it be all right if we step outside for a minute?"

"Okay," Sean agreed. This time, instead of a casual arm wrapped around her, he took her hand. Erin bit her lip as they wound their way through the crowd of wallflowers – Erin's usual spot at events like this – and past a table where the dance team was selling cold bottles of water at only slightly usurious rates. Skirting the line, they ducked out the door.

In the parking lot, the evergreen-scented coolness of an autumn evening quickly washed away the sweaty sensation of the crowded dance floor. The quiet whispering of the breeze through the pines surrounding the back lot of the school sounded sensual and sweet, but the wind itself contained a wintry chill. It teased its way through the thin fabric of her dress and she shivered. Sean wrapped his arm around her, lending her his warmth. She leaned on him, her head against his shoulder. His scent, which had teased her all evening, burst on her senses like a drug; compelling, addictive and impossible to resist. Lifting her head again, she met his gaze. An unreadable expression turned his eyes to blue flames.

Neither of them spoke. *Maybe we shouldn't be this close, especially in a semi-private setting,* Erin thought, willing herself to move away. Her body refused to comply. *If no one says anything, maybe it won't really be wrong.* Another gust of icy wind sent

Erin even closer into the shelter of Sean's body. His free arm angled across her back to rest on her shoulder. Her forehead warmed as Sean leaned his cheek against it. She slid her arms around his neck.

Afterward, neither one was sure who moved first, but suddenly, they found themselves kissing. It started simply enough, a feather-light brush of mouth on mouth. Harder and sweeter, the second kiss stole rational thought. For several heartbeats, Erin forgot completely that the evening was anything other than a normal date between two people who wanted to be together. Another moment passed, and Sean's mouth opened on Erin's, his tongue pressing her lips. *Is this really happening? I can't believe it. Like a dream come true. She opened to the pressure, eagerly accepting his passion, returning her own.*

The tension of so much commotion and the confrontation with Jake vaporized in Sean's arms as his mouth mated with hers, teasing arousal from her. A tingling sensation flared in her lower belly and radiated outward until Erin felt like one raw nerve ending and everywhere his body touched, hers burned. Wetness pooled, preparing her for the next step. Oh, God. If only. Again, the images of her bare, sweaty body tangled with Sean's took hold of Erin. I would never regret that opportunity. Already her skin ached for more intimate caresses.

After several long moments, Sean released Erin's mouth, and they both stood panting, looking at each other with dazed expressions.

Sean spoke first. "I'm sorry, Erin. I don't know what came over me."

Sorry? The best moment of my life and he's sorry? Stung by the painful words, she blurted, "Maybe you were entranced by my stunning beauty." Then she frowned, hearing the harsh irony in her voice. *Well, that's it. Now he definitely won't have anything else to do with you.*

"Don't put yourself down," Sean insisted, surprising her by trailing his fingers down her cheek. "You are beautiful, but it's not right for me to kiss you."

Okay, so he's still here. Still engaged in the conversation, still touching me. Desire ratcheted Erin's courage to unknown heights, allowing her to ask an unthinkable question. "Why? This goes a bit beyond trying to do your sister a favor. Am I wrong to say you kissed me because you wanted to?" Her heart hammered so hard, it hurt as she waited for his response.

A sad smile curved Sean's lips upward. "No, you're not wrong. I did want to. And I didn't come tonight as a favor to Danny; it was a favor to you."

Her stomach fluttered. *Can he really mean that?*

Sean continued. "But, Erin, you're too young. I can't be with you now, even if I really want to."

Erin considered whether it was worthwhile to ask one more pointed question. Finally, she steeled herself and said, "Do you?"

Sean sighed. "I do. I mean, you're a great girl. Anyone would be lucky to have you, but I don't want to get arrested."

"I'm eighteen, you know. My birthday was a couple of weeks ago," she reminded him.

* * *

Wait, I do know that, now that I think about it. I've been making plans to stay away from home the second week of September for as long as I can remember. It had been bad enough having to help clean up after everyone else's birthday parties but being forced to assist with one for a non-family member had been beyond the limit of his then-teenage motivation. "That's right, I remember," he told her, "but I'm not a teen, not anymore."

"I don't care." Her warm brown eyes begged him not to care either.

"I do," he answered honestly, hating the hurt that flared again in those chocolate depths. "If you're done dancing, you should really let me take you home."

Erin drooped. The corners of her mouth turning down, she mumbled, "Yes, I think that would be good. Let's get out of here before the crowd disperses and we're caught in their wake."

Erin slouched dejectedly as she shuffled to the car. She seemed lost in thought, as though struggling with some weighty and unsolvable problem. He opened the door and Erin slipped in without a word, but her eyes, when she met his gaze, spoke of deep hurt and deeper longing. *Could this be more than a crush? Not possible. What kind of man feels something deeper than mere passing attraction for his little sister's best friend? Even one as special as this. Even the attraction felt wrong. Or did it?* The sensation of her lips against his, her fragile, waif-like body in his arms had affected him profoundly, and he couldn't think of the feeling as negative.

Sean wrestled with his internal dilemma as he drove toward Erin's house. Despite the objective knowledge that kissing his sister's best friend was a really terrible idea, he couldn't regret it. *She was delicious in my arms; delicate and passionate and so very sweet. I want another kiss. I want... Erin, all of her. What's wrong with me that I can't stop myself from wanting this girl? Even though it might be legal for me to be with her, she has another year of high school to go, so it wouldn't be right...* His skin tingled. A glance revealed one dainty hand lying on the dark fabric of the seat's upholstery. It drew his touch like a magnet. He had to struggle to keep both of his on the steering wheel. *But she felt so right in my arms. I want her there again.* The thought of not holding or kissing Erin anymore caused a greater pang than he had expected. *When did this small woman become so important to me that I want to claim her for my own?* Another quick look revealed her chewing nervously on the side of her lip. She licked the spot and he wanted to groan. Willpower shattered. *No, more than want to, have to. There really isn't any other choice. Controversy be damned. Unless she says no, our evening is far from finished.*

He reached across the console and took her hand in his, raising it to his lips. "Erin..." he swallowed hard, "that was a really amazing kiss."

"Yes." Her fingers slipped over his cheek. "I loved it."

"I want more." Those stroking fingers went suddenly still.

"Me too," she said. "Are you still having a hard time with my being in high school?"

Leave it to Erin to grasp the problem immediately. "Yes, but it can't be changed for a year or so, can it?"

She shrugged off his silly quip. "Not until I graduate."

He laced his fingers through hers and set them on his knee, steering with only one hand. "Not soon enough. I want you right now. I'm pretty sure I'll still want you after you graduate, though."

"What are you saying, Sean?" The pulse under his thumb began throbbing.

"That if you want me to drop you off and leave, tell me now. Otherwise, you had better plan to see me a lot more often in the future."

Her hand tightened on his. "Really?"

"Yes."

"So, then, is this a beginning for... us?" she asked, disbelief flooding her voice.

"It is. That is to say, after tonight, there's going to be an 'us' unless you tell me otherwise." He stroked her skin soothingly with the tip of his thumb.

"Don't play with me that way, Sean. I'm nothing special," she said, her voice wavering.

He tried not to take her doubt personally. *She's so shy, it doesn't surprise me she would struggle with this.* He hastened to reassure her. "Of course, you're special. There's no reason why

I wouldn't want to be with you, and I'm not playing games, I promise. Besides, you only need to worry about yourself. You decide if you want me. I've already decided I want you."

She sucked in a noisy breath. "Are you kidding? As long as I've had a crush on you?"

"That's what I thought."

Erin sat in silence for an endless moment. At last, she said, "I can't believe this is really happening, Sean. It's like a dream."

He grinned. *She's so star-struck, as though I were some sort of celebrity and not just an apprentice builder.* Her frank admiration felt great. He wanted to enjoy it a bit longer, in private. *I can't wait to taste that sweet mouth again.* "It's no dream. You're sure your parents are gone for the whole weekend?"

"Yes."

"Good, because we're here." He grinned at her reaction as he pulled up to the curb and parked the Mustang.

Hand in hand they walked into the house. Erin led Sean to her bedroom. He pulled her into his arms for another one of those deep, drugging kisses, and eased his tongue into her mouth. She made a soft humming noise as his hand slid into her hair, releasing the pins and letting the chocolate strands fall around her back. Letting go of her mouth for a moment, Sean gazed down at her. *She's so pretty, girl next door pretty, the kind you marry.* Her warm brown eyes had gone hazy with passion and her soft, pink lips parted slightly. He took that as an invitation, sliding his tongue back inside to caress her mouth. He felt her hands loosening his shirt from his pants and slipping inside to touch his skin. Her aggressiveness startled him. *Whoa, she's moving fast.* "Erin?"

"Hmmmm?" she hummed against his lips. She seemed so relaxed now, melting in his arms.

"How far do you want to go tonight?" His thumb traced a thick line on her back.

Erin didn't even pause to think. "All the way. I want you, Sean. I want you so much." She spoke with absolute certainty, her gaze soft and trusting.

His eyes traveled down her body, taking in obvious signs of arousal. Her erect nipples pressed the front of her dress forward. From the navel down, her body aligned perfectly against his. His sex responded to the heat and nearness of hers. *Hmmmm. All the way sounds great. She's so ready. That's gonna feel good. It's been so long since I was with a girl...* Then the implications behind her words sank in with him and he blinked, nonplussed. *All the way? On our first date? Where has this Erin been hiding?* "Have you done this before?" he blurted. *Please say yes. Please say yes.*

She shook her head.

Sean sagged with disappointment. "I don't know if I can feel right about taking your virginity. It's kind of our first date," the gentleman in him forced him to say.

"You wouldn't be taking it. I'm giving it to you. Unless you don't want it?" Her confident tone turned more hesitant with each word.

There's that insecurity again. NOT want to have sex with this beautiful girl? What does she think I am, a eunuch? I'm about to bust my zipper. "I do want it. I'm just not sure why you do." He adjusted his erection uncomfortably with one hand. The move caused his hand to brush against her mound. She moaned. *So ready. Oh God. Tight, virgin heat.* His self-control took another battering.

"Because I do, that's all." She touched his face. Her tongue darted out to moisten her lip and he wanted to groan at the thought of her applying that wetness to sensitive parts of his body. "Seriously, you know how much I like you, Sean. Sometimes you just have to grab onto an opportunity or you'll regret it forever. My first time with someone so special, someone I've dreamed of so long? This is that kind of opportunity. Life is uncertain. Twenty-year marriages can end overnight. I'm here, tonight, with you, and there's nowhere else I want to be. It's magical. Can't we make it even more magical?"

He made one last stab at acting like a gentleman. "I just don't want you to regret this."

"I won't," she replied, excited, eager, and certain again.

"If it were anyone else?" he pressed.

"I wouldn't have gone to the dance at all. I would be alone now, practicing my oboe. I only want to do this with you."

Here I'm supposed to be building up her confidence, and she tosses out the greatest compliment a girl can give. "Are you sure?"

She nodded.

He could find no further reason to resist. Her offer tempted him beyond sense or decency. "Let's make a different kind of music."

Erin smiled. Reaching down, she caught the hem of her dress in both hands and pulled it over her head, shocking him with her boldness. She reached for the clasp of her bra, and his hand closed on hers.

"Slow down, baby," he urged. "We have all night. There's no need to rush."

But it seemed Erin did feel all in a rush. She slid her arms around Sean's neck and pulled his head down, this time snaking out her tongue to caress his lips and then plunging deep. He growled, pressing her to him and letting her feel how much he wanted her. She made a soft sound at the intimate contact. Then she hugged him tight, her lips clinging deliciously to his.

Sean cradled Erin in his arms. *She's so sweet.* He felt a little guilty about doing this with her, but not guilty enough to stop. He kissed her again and again, his hands wandering over her body. *She's so thin. I can feel every bone... along with her irresistible softness.* The pink of her underwear – a tiny demi-bra that lifted her small breasts, and a scrap of lace covering her mound – complemented her milky skin. He cupped one breast in his hand, pushing up gently so the soft globe spilled free. Then he leaned down and opened his mouth over the delicate, rosy nipple, sucking gently.

Erin's knees gave way and she leaned against Sean for support. He chuckled. *Like that, do you, baby? You haven't seen anything yet.* Then he worked the clasp of her bra, dropping it to the floor. Another deft movement sent her panties down to puddle around her ankles. She kicked them away. He scooped her into his arms, carrying her to the bed.

Now that the moment had almost arrived, Erin began to seem nervous. *I wonder if she will change her mind. It's all right if she does. It has to be her decision.* If she backed out, it would be no surprise. Sean waited for Erin's next move. Leaning up on one elbow, she opened the front of his pants, so he could step out of them and his underwear. He joined her nude on the bed. *She still seems so scared. Maybe I should stop. Even better, maybe I could caress her to orgasm, give her a taste of intimacy, but not take her yet. Give her time to get used to it. That would be a really good idea.*

He pulled her close for another devastating kiss, pressing his body full length against hers, and felt Erin's nerves melt away. Then he lowered his mouth to her breasts again, tasting first one hard nipple and then the other until she was panting with desire. Her back arched, offering her breasts to his stimulation. She laced her fingers into his hair, holding him close.

His hand slid down her belly, but she didn't react. *Not ticklish. Good. Makes things easier.* Then he snaked lower and she opened eagerly for him. *Wow, this girl is amazing. So eager, so bold.* He caressed the wet, silky folds and she gasped in startled pleasure.

Oh, this is very good. She's ready. He slipped one finger inside her and gently rubbed her clitoris with his thumb. Erin bowed her back, pressing herself down on his invading finger, her hips squirming. *That's it, sweet girl. Reach for it.* Her every breath emerged as a soft moan as he brought her higher and higher.

"Sean?" she whimpered, voice wavering.

"Almost there, baby. Almost there."

He pushed deep with his finger and gave her a hard rub. With a cry, she succumbed to a powerful climax, hips bucking as she tossed her head on the pillow.

Sean watched her come, glowing with satisfaction. *Erin is so responsive. This is better than I expected.* Moving back up over her body, he kissed her mouth tenderly.

"Oh Sean," she breathed, "what was that?"

"Pure pleasure, baby." He nuzzled into her cheek. *Is there anything in the world more beautiful than a well-pleasured woman?*

She collapsed, limp against the pillow. "No kidding. I never imagined anything could feel so good. Will you come inside me now?" She tugged gently on his arm, urging him closer.

"I think I should stop," he replied. "There's no need to do this tonight."

"Please? I want you to." She stared deep into his eyes, urgency twisting her lips downward.

"Are you sure, Erin?" he pressed.

"Yes. I'm sure. Take me. Please, Sean. Take me."

She sounds so... desperate. I still don't quite know why, but how can I hold out against those pretty brown eyes? "Oh, sweetheart, you don't have to beg."

What will happen if I say no? She'll feel rejected, that's what. His penis brushed against the softness of her thigh and the debate collapsed within him. *Fine. Remember how tight she is though. How do I go about deflowering her without hurting her? Relaxation. She has to relax.* He lifted her hips and gently slid a pillow underneath her, tilting her to just the right angle and positioning her thighs wide apart. "Listen, I need you to do something for me. Loosen every muscle in your body. I don't want any tension in you. Can you do that?"

"Why?" She looked up the midline of her body into his face with a puzzled expression.

"I don't want to hurt you," he explained.

"It's probably going to hurt no matter what," she pointed out.

Tiny as she is inside, there's no doubt about it. Poor Erin. "I know, but let's minimize it, okay? Relax. Especially here." He slid a finger inside her again, caressing her hymen. Erin took a slow deep breath and released it, forcing her body into complete limpness. Sean knelt between her thighs and withdrew his finger, lining himself up with her untried entrance. *She's so small. I'm not sure how well this is going to work.* One gentle thrust brought just his head into her. She squeaked, clenching her thighs around his hips.

"No, baby. Relax," he reminded her, stroking her skin with both thumbs. "If you can't relax, I have to stop. Easy, Erin."

Erin deliberately loosened her tight muscles and sweetly surrendered her virginity to Sean. He took her slowly, so slowly, but it wasn't enough. Her hymen resisted the pressure before finally giving way violently, tearing apart with force.

* * *

Erin lay still. *Don't cry, don't gasp*, she ordered herself. She could not betray to him how much that had hurt. He wouldn't like that and might stop. She breathed deeply a couple of times.

He stayed motionless, partway inside her, allowing her to adjust. "Are you okay?"

He seems so worried. She reached out one hand and caressed his cheek. "Yes. It's getting better. The pain is fading."

"Good. Can you take a little more?"

There's more? Oh God. "You can try it."

Sean nudged his way deeper. The penetration burned, and she felt ridiculously stretched, but she wouldn't complain. She had begged him to do this. She wanted it still. Inch by laborious inch he pushed forward, claiming her innocence. At last, every bit of him was buried, the tip of his sex pushing hard against her cervix.

She exhaled, trying to adjust.

"Oh wow, Erin. You feel amazing."

"Amazing," she mumbled. *Amazing I'm not crying. Damn, that hurts.* She wriggled, trying to lessen the pressure.

"Too deep?" he asked.

She nodded, biting her lip.

"Sorry." He withdrew slightly, enough to provide her some relief.

"Know what you need baby?" he asked. She drew her eyebrows together. "Another orgasm," he proclaimed. "Would you like that?"

She nodded. *Distraction would be a good idea.*

He kissed her, reaching down to caress her again. The slight touch on her swollen peak re-ignited the fire in her belly and set her squirming, but with Sean still buried to the hilt inside her, she had nowhere to go.

I'm not exactly sure this is going to work, she thought. *His finger felt good, but this is so huge and overwhelming. I feel like I'm about to split.* His stroking finger found a luscious rhythm on her clitoris. *Damn, that's good, but will an orgasm really be able to build around such an uncomfortable sensation?*

It could. Unlike the previous, gentle pleasuring, this felt wild, riding the edge of excess. Especially when he began to move, thrusting into her, gently but insistently, as his caresses continued. It seemed impossible, but as she neared her second peak, even the pain turned into pleasure and she spasmed again, violently, a cry torn from her throat.

* * *

Sean grinned at Erin's uninhibited response. She had relaxed enough to let him thrust freely, but remained wonderfully tight. Her sex fluttered rhythmically against him, and he continued to thrust until his own orgasm broke over him in shattering waves.

Chapter 3

Later, the couple still lay nude and snuggled together. Erin rested her head on Sean's shoulder, tracing spirals in the hair on his chest with one fingertip. His hand rested on her back, stroking slowly so the callouses on his work-roughened palms scratched pleasantly over her skin. *Wow. I can't believe this is really happening*, she thought. *I can't believe I just had sex, and with Sean no less.* A glow of satisfaction and pride warmed her from the inside even as the touch of his body heated her skin.

Then the pleasure of their tender afterglow shattered as the phone in the pocket of Sean's pants began to ring.

"How odd," he said, kissing her lips once and rolling away.

"What?" she asked.

He rose to his feet. "That phone is only for work. It never gets used at night. Must be some kind of emergency."

He bent down, kissed Erin softly again and rummaged through the clothes on the floor to retrieve the device.

Erin leaned on one elbow on the turquoise sheet and admired Sean's muscular physique as he moved through her bedroom. His size made her feel even smaller, in a wonderful, protected sort of way. *The way that body of his felt on top of me... inside me. It was like nothing I could have imagined.* The memory caused new heat to coil in her belly. *I wonder if we're done for the evening. I think I might want a little more.* Then she shifted and winced. *Maybe I'm more done than I realized. Ouch. Of course, if he meant what he said, if we're a couple, waiting a day or two won't matter at all.*

Sean winked at her as he lifted his slacks from the pool of scattered clothing and pulled his phone from his pocket, pressing a button. "Hello?"

Erin couldn't tell who was on the other end, but she could see that the person was doing a lot of talking, and that what Sean was being told upset him.

"She's where? ... What happened? ... Oh my God, no! ... Of course! ... I'll get there right away." He hung up and started pulling his clothes on. His sexy, playful air had vanished completely, replaced by an expression of sheer panic. "Erin, I'm really sorry, but I have to leave right now. That was my mom. There's an emergency. I swear I didn't plan to split like this, but I have to get to the hospital right away." He babbled out the words in a nearly unintelligible gush. His stunned expression alarmed her.

Erin hopped out of bed and grabbed her panties, stepping into them. Moisture pooled in the cotton liner. She couldn't help blushing as she crossed to her dresser. *Sex is messier than I realized.* "What happened? Who's in the hospital?"

"Danny."

Erin froze, drawing in a shuddering breath. "Oh no, did they wreck? Is she okay?" She yanked jeans and a sweater out of the drawer.

"No." He turned to face her, his handsome features transformed into such a mask of fury, she actually took several steps back, until her legs touched the edge of her bed. His jaw clenched so tight, she could hear his teeth grinding as he gritted out the words. "That bastard Jake Morris raped her."

Erin's clothes slipped through her fingers. "No." Clamping her hand over her mouth, she sank to a seat on the mattress, her legs no longer willing to hold her upright.

"Yes."

His words knocked the breath from her body. For several seconds, her lungs forgot to draw in air. At last, she gasped and began to chatter uncontrollably. "Oh God! I have to go with you. Please take me with you, Sean. Danny is my best friend. I have to be there too." As she babbled, she used her seated position to struggle into her jeans. The familiar task seemed complicated, as if neither her hands nor her feet knew what they were supposed to do. She fumbled with the buttons and rose unsteadily.

"Yes, okay. Let's go, though," Sean urged, holding out one hand.

Erin retrieved her sweater and pulled it over her head, then took his hand, grateful for the support as her body still fought against being upright. *Left at the doorway,* she reminded herself. Her childhood home seemed foreign as her mind replayed the devastating words over and over. *Cross the living room and into the entryway.* She scooped up her sneakers from the shoe rack by the door but didn't attempt to put them on. *That can be done in the car.* Locking the door on autopilot, she scuttled to the Mustang, slipped in, and fastened her seatbelt. Sean pulled away from the curb and tore off down the street.

As she slid on her shoes, hot tears began to roll down Erin's face. She sobbed. "This is my fault. I knew she shouldn't be alone with him. I just wanted so much to spend more time with you. I can't believe I was so selfish."

He reached over and grabbed her hand, squeezing it. "It's as much my fault. I could see leaving her with him was a bad idea," he said, his voice harsh and unsteady.

Sean drove to the hospital too fast, but thankfully not recklessly. He steered with one hand and with the other, held fast to Erin's. The knowledge that they had been enjoying a passionate evening in bed while someone they loved was assaulted hurt them both beyond their ability to bear. That they had had the opportunity to prevent it and had not taken it was even worse. Erin cried the whole way. It would be lying to suggest Sean didn't too.

Parking haphazardly across two spaces, Sean and Erin hurried into the building, up to the receptionist desk, still clinging to each other's fingers. "Where is Sheridan Murphy?" Sean asked the receptionist.

The middle-aged woman behind the plastic window gave him a hard look. "Who might you be?" she asked suspiciously.

"I'm her brother, and this is her best friend. Where is she?"

"Her brother?" The narrowed eyes gave no doubt about the woman's opinion.

"Yes."

""I swear, ma'am," Erin told her urgently, leaning forward with one palm braced on the counter, "he's not the one who did this."

Apparently, the sight of Erin, tears still sliding down her cheeks, sufficed to convince the receptionist. "Okay, she's in room 215, upstairs."

"She's been admitted?" Sean demanded, appalled.

This is not a good sign. Erin's stomach clenched, and she feared she might be sick.

"Her injuries are pretty bad," the woman explained grimly. "They want her to stay the night."

Sean's hand tightened painfully on Erin's. She flexed her fingers, reminding him to be gentle.

They left the emergency room and raced through the hospital, narrowly avoiding a collision with an elderly dialysis patient in a wheelchair, before arriving in the intensive care unit.

Outside room 215, Ellen Murphy stood in the hallway, weeping into the remains of a shredded tissue. Sean dropped Erin's hand and grabbed his mother, hugging her tight. She hid her face on his shoulder. Erin peered through the windowed door of the room. The curtain had been pulled around the bed, but periodically it lit up.

"What's going on?" Sean asked.

"The police are there. They're collecting evidence." The words had to be forced out between Ellen's broken sobs.

"Is she alone?" The disbelief in his tone reflected his expression.

That can't be right. Not when such a terrible event has taken place. Erin thought, horrified.

"Dad's with her."

Relief took the edge off a painful ache in her shoulders. That's good. She's really close to her dad.

"When can we go in?" Sean wanted to know.

"When they're done. They don't want the evidence contaminated. Sean, it's really bad. You have to be prepared."

He hesitated. Erin could see he really didn't want to know, but… "Tell me."

"She's bruised all over. It looks like he may have hit her, but she didn't say for sure. Really, she hasn't said much of anything. I think she's in shock."

"How did you know it was… rape?" *Such an ugly word, especially when talking about someone you love.* Sean mouth twisted to disgust, as though on the verge of vomiting. *And no wonder. I want to gag myself.*

"If you had seen the blood running down her thighs…" Ellen lost control, sobbed, and then visibly steeled herself to continue. "There was so much, it must have been brutal. I have no doubt what happened."

"I'm going to kill him," Sean snarled.

Erin believed it. His rage frightened her. *And as big and powerful as Sean is, it wouldn't take much. Jake might be a football player, but he'd never hold out against an enraged older brother with muscles.*

"No, Sean," Ellen replied in a hollow-sounding voice that matched the desolation on her face. She gripped her son's arm and gave it a little shake to snap him back to reality. "We're not going to take an eye for an eye. We're going to do this legally. He'll pay. She's going to press charges."

"Do you understand what that means, Mom? There's going to be a trial. Danny will have to relive the whole thing, again and again, before he can be punished." Sean shook his head. His inhalation sounded far from steady.

"I know." Ellen began to cry even harder.

Erin walked over to Mrs. Murphy and placed her hand on the older woman's arm. Ellen lifted her head, startled. "Oh, Erin. I'm so glad you're here."

"Of course. Where else would I be?"

Of one accord, Sean and Ellen opened their arms and drew Erin in, as though she were a member of the family. They remained like that, holding each other, until the police officer – a kind-looking older woman – exited the room.

She regarded them for a long moment before saying, "You can go in now. I'm finished. I'm so sorry." Erin could see she meant it. No matter how long one worked in law enforcement, some sights still retained the power to appall.

They entered the room on weak legs. The curtain around the bed stood open now, revealing a tableau of devastation. Sheridan's shock had finally worn off and she cuddled in her father's arms, shaking with sobs. He rubbed her back, but his own eyes burned red. Tears shone on his weathered cheeks. His salt and pepper hair stood on end, as though he'd been raking his fingers through it.

Hearing the footsteps on the tile floor, Sheridan lifted her head. A swollen bruise, deeply cut in the center, reshaped the planes of her face. Sean made a strangled sound and stopped in his tracks. Erin flung herself at the bed, scrambling up beside her friend and throwing her arms around her. "Oh God, Danny," she wept.

Sheridan turned and hugged her. "Erin." Her voice sounded weak and harsh from so much crying. The girls clung to each other in misery. Now that the ice had been broken, Sean and his mother approached the bed, hugging Sheridan.

"Danny, I..." Sean broke off but squeezed his sister tight. She squeaked.

"Easy," her father warned. "She has bruises..." he indicated her middle.

Sean sank onto the edge of the bed near Sheridan's feet, his legs no longer able to hold him. Erin bit her lip. *Bruises on her belly too? Oh God.* "Danny..." Her voice stopped, and Erin was glad because she had no idea what to say. In fact, no one knew what to say, so they mostly took turns holding Sheridan and crying.

After a couple of hours, a nurse came in.

"Folks," she said in a soft, sympathetic voice, "we've gotten word from the doctor that Sheridan will be spending the night here."

"Spending the night?" Sheridan asked in a voice Erin couldn't even recognize. "How do they figure I'll sleep?"

The nurse smiled, but it was a sad, tired smile. "The doctor suspected you might have trouble. He prescribed you a sedative." She shook a clear plastic cup inside which a bright blue capsule rattled. Sheridan nodded, accepting the medication eagerly and washing it down with a swig of water from an identical cup.

"And now," the nurse continued, smoothing back a strand of graying black hair that had escaped her ponytail, "there are too many people in this room. Visiting hours ended ages ago."

"I'm not leaving my daughter alone after what she's been through," Mrs. Murphy hissed.

"Of course not, ma'am," the nurse replied. "The armchair pulls out into a bed. You're more than welcome to stay."

"Daddy," Sheridan said to her father, tugging on his arm, "please stay. I need you both," she begged, and Erin noticed something pointed in her voice and expression.

"Well," the nurse said, "we normally try to stick to only one overnight guest, but under the circumstances, I think I can just borrow an extra sleeper chair. That's it, though."

Erin nodded. "Thank you for letting me stay this long."

Sean took his sister's hand. "I'll always be here for you, Danny, no matter what."

Sheridan wrapped her hand around her brother's arm and hauled him down, crushing him. She whispered something in his ear that Erin couldn't hear, something that made him nod.

"Come on, Erin," Sean suggested when Sheridan released him. "I'd better get you home."

Before leaving, Erin gave her friend a fierce hug and whispered, "I love you, Danny. I'll come back tomorrow."

Sheridan didn't speak, but her arms tightened around her friend. Then Sean took Erin's hand and led her away.

Tears kept streaming over her cheeks as they traversed white tile corridors of the silent hospital until they stumbled through the sliding door into the October chill. Outside, by the Mustang, Sean pulled her close.

"Oh, Sean," she whimpered, "what are we going to do?"

"I don't know. Poor Danny! I can't believe it." They huddled together, trying to block out the cold October wind, and the horrible memories of what they had just seen.

She squeezed him tight, her front warm against his body. The night wind cut right through the back of her sweater, slashing at her skin. She shuddered in cold and revulsion.

"Let's get you into the car, baby," Sean suggested. "It can't be more than forty degrees out here."

He handed her in and shut out the wind behind her.

As they drove, a mean, selfish thought occurred to Erin. *I wonder if this means the delicious beginning Sean and I shared is over, if this really will be a single night instead of a relationship after all. I don't want that, but that's no way to be thinking when your friend lies wounded and violated in the hospital.* She tried to ignore the desperate longing for Sean, but she couldn't. Finally, the words burst from her. "Are you still going to be with me?"

"What do you mean?" Clearly lost in dark, sad thoughts about his sister, Sean struggled to understand the question.

"I mean, we sort of said we were going to be a couple. Is that still the case? I know how terrible it sounds to ask this right now, but I have to know. Are we through?" She clutched her hands together in her lap, twisting her fingers. *Please don't hate me for asking, Sean. I care so much for you.*

"No, baby. We're not through," he assured her with sweet intensity. "I don't know how we're going to do this without upsetting people, but I would never have taken your virginity if I didn't intend to stand by you. Don't think for a minute that I'm doing this out of duty either. I still want you as much as ever. This is really hard, this situation with Danny, and..." His voice broke and he swallowed a couple of times. "We're going to need all the support we can get. You're part of it too. So, for tonight, we're going to stay close, and after, well, we can see how this develops. Do you think it would be possible to keep our relationship... private, at least for a while? I hate being sneaky, but I don't really see any other way."

"You're right, and that's fine. I wasn't planning to broadcast it anyway, especially not under these circumstances."

They had arrived at the house by that time and trailed back inside. Erin's mouth tasted terrible, so she hurried into the hallway bathroom to brush her teeth. Sean followed, and she found him an unused toothbrush in the cabinet. While he brushed, she washed the last of the makeup off her lips and eyes before leading Sean back into the bedroom and pulling him to her again. They kissed endlessly, their burgeoning passion for each other exacerbated by their terrible grief.

He lowered her to the bed and they cuddled up, their hands running over each other's bodies.

"I'm a bit worried about this," Sean said as their caressing began to take a more intimate turn.

"What? Why?" Erin tried to burrow even closer to Sean, tugging at the waistband of his slacks.

"Aren't you sore?" He arrested her busy fingers with one big, calloused hand.

"A little," she admitted, "but it doesn't matter. I need you, Sean. I need you as close to me as possible."

He nodded, seeming suggest he needed her just as badly. Their caresses continued, and when the moment came, he eased inside her so gently and slowly, she only felt the slightest twinge. The second time was just as sweet as the first, especially as Erin now knew Sean intended to be with her. Falling asleep in his arms was one of the sweetest things she had ever experienced. *If only it didn't have to be coupled with such tragedy.*

* * *

Late the next morning, Erin called the Murphy house as Sean still slept in her bed. It made her feel weird, talking to people she knew in some ways better than her own family while keeping a secret that affected them all.

Roger Murphy answered the phone.

"Hello, Mr. Murphy, this is Erin. I'm just calling to see if you guys are home. I'm not going to ask if you're okay. Do you think it would be all right if I came over later?"

"Yes, Erin, please come over," Roger said. He sounded strained. "Sheridan is sleeping now, but I think maybe this afternoon, say around one? It would be good for her to have you here."

It would be good for me too. I can't leave her to face this without me. No friend would do that.

"I'll be there at one. Hang in there, Mr. Murphy."

The voice on the phone sounded weary but appreciative. "You too. Goodbye."

Warm arms wrapped around Erin from behind and she snuggled against Sean. He leaned down and kissed her cheek. "What's the word?"

"They're home. I'm going over there this afternoon. I think it would be good for us to drive separately. No one would take kindly to finding out we spent the night together."

"Right. I'm glad though. It would have been terrible to be alone." He hugged her a little tighter.

"I know. I feel a little guilty about doing something so wonderful when poor Danny is…" She sniffled.

"I know, but it's understandable. When you're hurting, you want to cling to people who care about you. Danny needed Mom and Dad. We're lucky to have each other so we didn't burden them with our pain, in addition to what they're already dealing with."

"Is she going to be okay?" The words fought her, emerging as a strangled whisper.

"I hope so. She's strong, but no one should have to live through that." Sean's Adam's apple bobbed as he swallowed hard.

"It's so unfair," Erin wailed, abandoning her attempt to maintain composure. "She always tries to do the right thing. Danny is the kind of girl who should have been a virgin on her wedding night."

"Yeah." Sean visibly struggled to come up with any words to help, but clearly couldn't think of anything to say, and remained silent.

Beckoning Erin, he walked down the hall to the bathroom and turned on the shower.

Erin blinked as he drew off the sweatpants and tee shirt she'd pulled on to sleep. He led her into the steaming water.

I've never showered with someone before, except in the icky locker room, which of course involved nothing like this. The water hit her tense body and her muscles relaxed, especially the ones inside her, where Sean's lovemaking had left her sore. She sighed in relief.

"Tense, baby?" he asked, squirting shampoo into his hand and gathering up her long, dark hair. His fingers slid against her scalp, eliciting tingles that radiated down her spine. "You're going to hurt yourself if you don't relax."

"How can I stay tense with you touching me like that?" she mumbled.

He chuckled, though it lacked conviction. "I aim to please, ma'am. Here, stand in the water." She backed up to rinse and the warmth spreading down her back reduced her to the consistency of Play-Doh. Sean wasn't finished with her though. Grabbing a bottle of body wash, he soaped his fingers and ran them over her body, teasing hidden pockets of tension away and arousing the erogenous zones he'd discovered the previous night. Erin grabbed the bottle from him and returned the favor.

When they were both clean – not to mention terribly aroused – Erin led her boyfriend back to her room for one more taste of deep, sweet loving. It struck her, before her orgasm obliterated thought, how deep a connection she felt. *Sex means more than Sean easing in and out of me. It feels like he's entering my heart, filling it as surely as he fills my body.* Emotion that eclipsed physical pleasure welled up and overflowed. She drew him down for a kiss, and for that moment, trouble faded in the wake of joy.

* * *

"Do you really have to leave?" Erin asked as she walked Sean to the door. "I don't want to be alone."

"I don't either, baby," he replied, wearily giving her a little squeeze. "But I'll see you at the house later, okay?"

She kissed his cheek. Unsatisfied, he swept her into a passionate embrace. "Sweet girl," he said, "I'm so glad you're mine."

Then Sean kissed Erin long and lingeringly before getting into his Mustang and driving away. Another half hour remained before Erin could leave, so she put together her oboe and spent the time practicing her music for the audition she would play for the recruiter from Texas. She'd had all the notes well in hand long since, of course, but was experimenting with different stylistic elements, trying to find just the right mood. Oboe naturally lends itself to sounding melancholy, which suited her mood perfectly. Today, the piece rolled off her fingers with a passionate and mournful keening, her instrument weeping with her grief. *Strange, I chose a piece that so perfectly expresses my emotions.* It had never sounded better, but by the time she played the last cadence, her tears completely obscured the music stand.

She managed to pull herself together long enough to clean her instrument and put it away and make the short drive to her friend's house safely, but she didn't stop crying altogether. It would be a long time before the Murphy family and their friend really began to recover from the trauma.

Chapter 4

Sheridan took a week off from school trying to come to grips with what had happened. Erin, however, returned on Monday. Winding her way through a herd of freshmen milling around the cafeteria, she ducked past the hallway monitor and crept to the counselor's office.

Ignoring the empty secretary's desk, she crept down the hallway, shoes swishing along a faded carpet that had once had a pattern of tiny blue and gray squares, now almost indistinguishable. The school's central heating system clicked on, and with a roar, blasted hot air from vents in the ceiling, immediately warming her chilly skin until she broke out in a sweat. She slipped into the familiar, glass-fronted cubicle of an office.

Mrs. Carroll, the counselor who handled last names beginning with the letters H-O, tugged off her jacket and blazer and opened the window a crack. A waft of fresh, outdoor air lightened the sultry atmosphere.

"Good morning," Erin said in a soft voice.

"Erin, what are you doing here?" Mrs. Carroll demanded in friendly exasperation.

"I need to change my schedule," Erin replied.

Mrs. Carrol frowned. "Why? It's a bit late in the semester, hon. You're going to run into problems if you take on something new."

Erin shook her head. "It won't be a problem. I want to drop A.P. chemistry and take regular instead."

The older woman's face twisted further in confusion. She lifted a sheaf of papers and fanned herself with them. "What will that accomplish? Are you struggling? There are A.P. tutors, you know."

Erin compressed her lips. "I have an A in that class so far. Did you hear about Sheridan?"

Mrs. Carroll lowered her gaze. "I had hoped it was just a rumor."

"No. I was there... right after. I know what happened." Her eyes burned in a way that had nothing to do with a horrible waft of exhaust that had filtered in the window, having been belched out of the rear end of a late-arriving jalopy. The car backfired and then settled in with a groan. "Anyway, I don't want Sheridan to have any more classes without me than is absolutely necessary. I know she's got all those English electives and I have music, but if I take regular chemistry with her, we'll have all our core classes together. That's important. It will also make it easier for me to get her homework to her until she can come back." Erin blurted her plan out fast, hoping to avoid interruption, and it worked. Mrs. Carroll stared, her mouth slightly open, the breeze disarranging her carefully placed curls. She scrunched the tea-colored strands back into place carelessly, causing them to stand on end.

"You have it all figured out, don't you, Erin? You're quite a friend. But what about you? What about your AP credit?"

"I really don't like chemistry that much," Erin replied. "It would be nice to get college credit for it, but wouldn't that mean I'd have to take some other, harder science?"

Mrs. Carroll nodded. "All right then." She settled on her chair and fired up the computer.

"Will Mr. Jones be available? I don't think this is going to go well." *There's no doubt Danny's going to need someone to talk to, and as he's the social worker, it's kind of his job.*

Mrs. Carroll bit her lip. "I hate that this happened. Mr. Jones will be prepared for her to come in. In fact, I'll suggest he allow her to use the conference room if she needs to... get away from everyone. You're welcome to come with her."

Erin smiled, but sadly. "That's a good idea. I'll let her know."

* * *

"Danny?" Erin called, knocking on the door of her best friend's bedroom. "Danny, can you help, please? My hands are full."

Sheridan opened the door. Erin winced at the sight of the still-livid bruise on her cheek. The cut stood out bright red in the center of it.

"That was his class ring," Sheridan said in a flat voice.

"I'm sorry. I didn't mean to stare." Mortified, Erin could feel her face burning, but her hands were so full of books she couldn't do anything about it.

"I'd better get used to people staring. Come on in. What do you have there?"

She sounds like a zombie. A sob tried to climb its way out of Erin's throat, but she swallowed it down again. *Be strong. You don't get to be the sensitive one anymore.* "I have your homework. Chemistry, A.P. English, poetry, and trig. Lucky you." Her attempt at cheer sounded false, even to her own ears.

"Joy," Sheridan sighed. "Well, at least it's normal. I had almost forgotten what normal was like."

"What did you do today?" Erin asked, setting the stack on Sheridan's bed.

"Counseling," Sheridan replied. "It sucks. Have you ever pulled out an ingrown toenail or popped a really deep zit?"

"Yes," Erin nodded cautiously, wondering where this was going.

"Counseling is like that. It hurts like hell while you're doing it, and it hurts like hell when you're done, but at least it relieves some pressure." All this Sheridan delivered without the slightest change in expression or intonation.

That monster. Every day that went by, Erin came to realize more how a single act could have repercussions that rippled on and on forever.

"I'm not looking forward to what comes next," Sheridan said, sinking to the floor where she sat, arms wrapped around her knees.

"What's that?" Erin asked, joining her and unconsciously mimicking her pose.

"Tomorrow, instead of the counselor, we're consulting with a lawyer whose house Dad fixed a few years back. He can help me… with the trial."

"So, you're definitely pressing charges then?" Erin asked. "Good."

"Yes," Sheridan replied. "Of course. If there's anything good left in the world, it's that he's behind bars and can't come near me."

"You'll win too," Erin said. "I'll testify if it will help. No one should ever have to see him or be afraid of him again."

Sheridan inhaled a gasping breath and blew it out. "Enough of that. What's up with chemistry?"

* * *

Midnight had come and gone by the time Erin made her way home. The living room light, which she distinctly remembered turning off before she left that morning, spilled yellow light onto the night-dark grass.

Cautiously she opened the door. Her mother, Valerie, sat on the sofa, playing with a cell phone. "Oh, there you are," she said, glancing at her daughter for a second before lowering her eyes back to the screen. "Where were you?"

"Do I suddenly have a curfew I don't know about?" Erin drawled. "I was taking Danny her homework, and I stayed to help her."

"Until 12:37 at night? Really?" This time, Valerie made no attempt at eye contact.

"Yes."

"Was she sick or something?"

Wow. I never thought to call her. Erin rubbed her eyes. Her bed down the hall seemed to call to her, and she could still smell Sean's cologne on the sheets. "She's not sick. Something terrible happened."

"What's that?"

Can you pretend to care, Mother? Can you look up or at least use a tone of voice that shows you're paying attention? "Danny's boyfriend sexually assaulted her. He beat the crap out of her too."

"Hmmmm." Clearly, her mother had already stopped listening.

"Good night, Mom." Shaking her head, Erin left for the bedroom. Once again, she chafed at being unable simply to walk away from her family and take care of herself. *Too bad my symphony job only pays enough for gas and car insurance. It's not enough to live on. For the time being, I guess I'm stuck.*

* * *

By the time Friday rolled around, routine had resumed, yet to Sean, it all seemed fake, like a pretense of reality since the innocence of everyday life had been shattered forever. He drove his Mustang into its usual space outside his apartment and headed in. Every day, it seemed autumn's grip tightened on the lakeside town. He could practically smell Old Man Winter's breath in the air. Climbing up the cement stairs that led to his second-floor flat, his stomach growled. *Cook mac and cheese or order pizza? I can't go to Mom and Dad's. It's too oppressive there.*

He opened the door and let himself in. The phone was ringing as he entered his living room, and he raced to grab it, his less than polished work boots making muddy prints on the linoleum. "Hello?"

"Hi, Sean," came the unsteady voice on the other end. "Are you doing anything this evening?"

"I don't have plans beyond a shower," he replied, trying for humor. "What about you?"

"I'm making dinner."

His stomach growled. *Food. Wish I had some. I think that leftover pizza is a bit too old to eat.* "Is your mom there?"

"No," Erin replied. "She's spending the weekend with *him.*" No need to ask who. Erin never referred to her mother's lover by his name, though she'd mentioned him more than once during their habitual phone conversations.

"So, you're on your own again?" Sean guessed.

"Yeah. Wanna come over?"

Hot damn. An invitation. Food and Erin. Perfect. "Of course," he replied. "And, um, should I bring my stuff? Do you want me to stay over?"

"Yes, please," she replied, her voice eager.

"I'll be there in half an hour."

* * *

When Sean arrived, he found Erin in the kitchen, toasting ham and cheese sandwiches under the broiler, while a pot of soup bubbled on the stove. He kissed her cheek and she turned, sliding her arms around his neck for a tight hug. He could see she had been crying again. Her eyes were red and puffy, and a faint trace of mascara ran down her face.

"What's wrong, baby?"

She sniffled. "Danny's going back to school on Monday. I wish she didn't have to. Everyone knows what happened. Jake's stupid friends blabbed. They're making it sound like her fault. It's horrible. I don't know how she's going to handle it."

Sean shook his head, aching at the thought of what his sister would be facing. "It's so unfair. I would have thought, in a new millennium, that people would stop blaming rape on the victims."

"I guess whoever's less popular will take the blame. That's how high school works. I hate it!" Her voice sounded fierce but unsteady, and she leaned her head against his shoulder. "I hate it so much."

His arms tightened around her. "I know. Just try to stick it out and finish as best you can. Don't let this destroy your dreams. You have to finish well, Erin."

"I know that. It just really sucks."

"It does." He squeezed her comfortingly and then noticed a tell-tale aroma. Grabbing a red and gold oven mitt from its hook above the stove, he rescued the sandwiches from under the broiler, moments before they could blacken.

"Sorry," Erin said, scrubbing at her eyes.

"Hey, they're fine. No worries." He set the hot baking sheet on a trivet on the countertop next to the stove. Opening the mahogany cabinets, he searched until he found a little cutting board in the shape of a pig. He pulled a knife from the block and sliced pickles and tomatoes for the sandwiches while Erin stirred the soup and poured it into mugs.

Sean watched her while she worked, feeling pleasantly surprised at how well everything was turning out. *Erin takes our relationship seriously without the cloying clinginess younger girls sometimes torture their boyfriends with.* For his part, he hoped, as time passed, to find a balance between sex and conversation so she would know she was desired both for her beauty and her soul. That was the truth. The more time he spent with Erin, the more she drew him in. He couldn't imagine ever wanting it to end. He hoped they could find a way to maintain their relationship after graduation while she pursued her dreams.

For now, however, they would enjoy each moment together, starting with this simple meal.

Chapter 5

Erin firmly put thoughts of Sean out of her mind until later and concentrated on taking notes over *Macbeth*. She glanced beside her at her friend. Sheridan looked pale and strained but tried hard to pay attention. The horrible bruise on her face had faded to a sickening yellow, although the cut remained livid.

"Remember, guys," Mr. Hernandez nagged with a good-natured grin, "essays are due on Tuesday. Late work will not be accepted, and do try to move beyond identifying theme, tone and mood. You need to make an argument and defend it."

"Yes, sir," they chorused with varying degrees of enthusiasm.

"Remember the Toulmin model and your Aristotle. And remember, I have five A.P. classes worth of essays to read. Don't be boring."

The class laughed. The bell rang, and they began packing up their notebooks and binders. Then the girls rose, turned left at the doorway and headed down the hall to government.

"After English, government is such a letdown," Erin complained, trying to act normal. "Talk about boring. Most days the only thing I remember is the sun shining on Mr. Milligan's bald spot."

"I still hope to pass the A.P. exam," Sheridan replied. "At least I could get out of PoliSci in college. Take some other humanities elective."

"If I know you, you'll take more English classes," Erin teased. "Good luck. I'm not even going to attempt the exam. I'll be lucky to pass the class."

"A *B* isn't failing, you goof," Sheridan teased back, a ghost of her former smile creasing her lips as they passed the commons, a meeting of the corridors where the cafeteria and offices resided.

"Bitch," a feminine voice hissed at them, just out of range of several vice principals and teachers monitoring the hallway and directing traffic.

Erin glared at Lindsey Jones. Her smooth ponytail swished as she focused on Erin, returning the glower, red lips pouting. A bit too much cleavage peeked out of her dress.

Stupid slut. "Shut up."

Sheridan turned from Erin to Lindsey, puzzled. "What?"

"It's nothing, Danny. Ignore her," Erin urged, tugging Sheridan's arm to keep her friend moving down the hallway.

Sheridan planted her heels and turned to address Lindsey directly. "What did I do?"

"You put Jake in jail," the girl sneered, as though talking to an idiot. "Now there's no way our football team can make the playoffs. He's going to miss his senior year because of you." Sheridan squinted her eyes in silent confusion, so Lindsey continued. "It's your fault, you know. If you weren't such a prude, this wouldn't have happened." She accompanied her words with a snotty toss of her perfect hair.

Erin pushed herself between them, forcing Lindsey to look at her. "Shut up!" she snarled. "It's her choice, stupid. Don't you know anything? If the woman doesn't want to, the conversation's over." She thought a moment and added, "Plus it's none of your business. Come on, Danny. Lindsey's just a slut. She's never thought once about saying no and can't possibly understand." Erin took her friend's arm and led her away towards the government classroom. Once they moved out of the congested central hub, the student traffic flowed more smoothly.

"Does everyone know?" Sheridan asked in a tiny, wavering voice.

"Pretty much," Erin replied, wishing she could lie. "I'm sorry."

"How many are against me?" She bit her quivering lip.

Erin gave Sheridan's arm a little squeeze. "Hard to say. Jake's really popular, you know? But I'm here. I've got your back, sweetie."

"Thanks." Sheridan seemed more shaken than ever. As though everything that had happened weren't bad enough, to discover her classmates had turned on her was the final straw. Erin had known it would be.

By lunchtime, Sheridan's fragile composure hung in tatters. Erin walked her to the counselor's office where Sheridan spent her free period in tears. Erin stayed with her, rubbing her back and trying to support her friend.

The day passed every bit as horribly as Erin had expected. Several people made ugly comments to Sheridan. Despite her well-earned reputation for shyness, Erin fiercely defended her friend, but that hardly slowed the flow of abuse. At last, the final bell rang, releasing them from their newly-shared chemistry class. Sheridan washed out a test tube while Erin packed up the pipettes. "Do you need me to go home with you today?" she asked.

"You have rehearsal," Sheridan replied firmly. "I'll be fine. Mom is there."

Oh, right. That will help. "But the parking lot. At least you have to let me help me walk you to the car."

Sheridan rolled her shoulders, which Erin took for assent. The two of them walked down the hall to the locker they shared and pulled out a pair of letterman jackets – Erin's for band and Sheridan's for UIL. Then they made their way into the cold, autumn afternoon.

Erin fixed a fierce scowl on her face, daring anyone to make a comment, and though ugly whispers filtered their way, no one attempted an outright confrontation. She sighed with relief, allowing her expression to relax when they arrived at the Murphys' spare station wagon. "You sure you're all right?"

"Get to rehearsal," Sheridan ordered. "I can drive home, you silly goose. I'm not broken."

Erin frowned at the waver in her friend's voice but nodded. *She is broken, but she doesn't want to be. I hope I can help her heal.* She waited until Sheridan shut the driver door and fired the ignition before scooting back into the building.

She arrived at the band hall a couple of minutes late. Mr. Abrams didn't say a word. *He must be aware of the situation.* Erin sank into her chair, exhausted, and poured the last fragile remnants of her stamina towards her music. When the rehearsal finally ended, she hurried home to call Sean.

"You sound terrible, baby," he told her bluntly.

"I'm not bothering you, am I?" She rolled onto her back on the bed and laid her free arm over her aching eyes.

"Of course not. How did it go?"

"It's worse than I imagined. I don't know how I'm going to cope, let alone Danny. I *hate* being a teenager, Sean." She struggled to control herself, tears warring with her pride. *Stop whining, you twit. No one likes a whiner.*

"You don't have the temperament for it," Sean said in an understanding voice. "You'll feel better when you're done with high school. I think you must have been born an adult."

"That's what my mom always said. She says I'm older than her," Erin commented, trying to be lighthearted. Her gloomy tone undermined her attempt completely.

"That could well be," Sean said seriously. "Is she there now?"

"Yes. I wish she weren't. I would love for you to hold me." Her voice broke again. *Come on, damn it. Get a grip.*

"I would if I could," he said, sounding concerned. "Can you practice? Would that help?"

"I have no emotions left to give, not even to my oboe. I'm all wrung out."

"Poor Erin. This is too much for you, isn't it?"

She closed her eyes, struggling for control again. "I'm not the one going through it. I'm just trying to help. It's what any friend would do."

"Not any friend. Only a really special one."

Sean's kind words touched Erin deeply, and her feelings came spilling out of her unbidden. "I love you, Sean. You should know that. You don't have to say anything back, but I do love you."

"I know you do, Erin," he replied tenderly. "You're an amazing girl, and that means a lot to me."

"I think I'm going to try and sleep for a while. Maybe the rest of the night."

"Dream about me," he urged.

"I always do."

Erin skipped dinner, went to bed and cried herself to sleep. Her mother never noticed anything was wrong.

Chapter 6

The next day, at work, Sean decided to ask his dad for advice. He didn't want to give away too much, but he felt a little out of his depth with this serious, passionate relationship. His feelings for Erin had become powerful at a speed he had never anticipated. *It's nice, but a little daunting.*

"Dad, can I ask you something?" he said as the two of them unloaded hardwood flooring from the back of a royal blue Murphy Construction and Renovation pickup. Sean followed his father through the gaping doorway of the 125-year-old Victorian painted lady they were renovating. Cold autumn air whistled around them as they traversed the yard, but working so hard, the men scarcely felt it. They handed the wood to the guys inside, who were repairing the water-damaged floor, and headed back out to the truck.

"Sure, Sean, what's on your mind?"

"Do you think it's wrong for me to be dating someone… younger?"

Roger looked at him, his eyebrow quirked. "You're not very old yourself. How much younger?"

"Eighteen," he replied.

"Are you sure she's actually eighteen and not lying to you?"

Sean met his gaze without flinching. "Yes. There's no question about that."

"Well then," Roger said in his slow, thoughtful voice, rubbing his hands together to warm them, "it kind of depends on the girl. A lot of eighteen-year-olds are immature and silly, and don't really make good girlfriends for an adult. I think it's possible there may be exceptions to that."

"Oh yes," Sean assured his father. "She's much more mature than her age would suggest."

"I imagine. Otherwise, I doubt you would be interested. Are you already dating?"

"Yes."

"Care to elaborate?" his father suggested.

"Not really."

Roger gave his son another questioning look, but Sean refused to comment further.

Roger sighed. "Fine. Just be careful with her. Be sure you plan to take your time and let this move slowly. Sometimes these young girls think they're ready for more than they are. Don't let her give up her life in favor of a romance."

That's the last thing I want. "Of course not."

They gathered up another armful of boards and headed in again.

Chapter 7

Finally, the day for Erin's conservatory audition arrived. Clutching her hall pass in one hand, her oboe case in the other, Erin left government class and exited the main building, crossing a small courtyard that separated it from the arts complex. She pulled open one of the big double doors into the music hallway and passed the choir room, silent for the teacher's planning period; the orchestra room, where the freshman strings made unpleasant scratchy noises on their instruments; and the band hall, where trumpets blared loud enough to rattle the ceiling tiles while tympani pounded in the background. *Well, they're certainly enthusiastic. After the football team's win last weekend, I'm not surprised.* At the back of the building, past the bathrooms, she entered the indicated practice room and found the recruiter, Dr. Louise Chen, waiting. Inside the tiny, whitewashed box of a room, barely large enough to hold two plastic chairs and a music stand, Erin regarded the delicate woman whose face had been shaped by years blowing into a double reed. *That's what I'll look like someday.*

Erin extended her hand, and the two shook. "Erin James?" Dr. Chen asked, somehow sounding like both China and Texas.

"That's right," Erin replied.

"Take a seat, please," Dr. Chen said. "Why don't you put your instrument together while we talk?"

Erin seated herself in the chair and set the case on her lap, opening the clasps to reveal the parts of her beloved instrument, each nestled in its spot like pieces of a child's puzzle. She grabbed a double reed and stuck it in the corner of her mouth to moisten it before taking hold of the bell and fitting the lower joint into it.

"We have four possible majors available for musicians," Dr. Chen informed her. "Performance, pedagogy, theory/composition and independent studies. Do you have any idea which direction you'd be interested in?"

"Performance," Erin replied around a mouthful of double reed, sticking the upper joint into the lower joint.

The recruiter smiled at her decisive answer. "Excellent. For performance majors, while you still have theory requirements, as well as music history, of course, we also arrange for summer-long internships at various professional music venues."

"How cool is that," Erin said with a grin. "Sounds great." For a moment, the image of Sean floated up before her eyes. *Going to Texas would mean not seeing him the entire year. The summer internships would take away my last chance to visit.* Firmly she pushed the thought away. *Focus, Erin.*

"And starting their senior year, we assist all our soon-to-be graduates to find positions with the smaller, rural symphony orchestras. With a few private lessons, it's enough to live on while you gain experience. Most of our performance majors are playing in major symphonies worldwide within ten years."

Erin's eyes widened. "That's quite a track record. No wonder admissions are so exclusive."

Dr. Chen nodded. "Moving to Texas and working on your art for four years straight is demanding, and our professors expect the best. Some students don't make it through the whole course of study and end up either switching to a pedagogy major or going home. We try to minimize that by carefully screening our applicants."

"Good idea," Erin said. "I like what I'm hearing."

"And we also have senior performance majors who act as mentors to the freshmen, which really seems to help retention rates. If you are selected, you'll be paired with an upperclassman. When you become a senior, you'll be paired with a freshman of your own. We also use the cohort system. Our woodwind majors take all their courses together, so they can support each other."

Wow, Erin thought, *they don't fool around. Sounds intense.*

All right, Erin," Dr. Chen said, "do you have a piece prepared?"

"I do," Erin replied.

"You may begin when you're ready."

So much was happening in Erin's life that she didn't have any extra energy to devote to feeling scared, so her hands remained steady as she removed the reed from her mouth and fitted into the opening on the top of her instrument. *I'll just do my best. Whether I get in or not, either way is an answer.*

She experienced the faintest flutter as she raised the oboe to her lips, but as the first notes of her piece washed over her, she ceased to exist. All was notes, tempo, crescendo and diminuendo, and emotion, until conscious thought became not only unnecessary but impossible. Every choice, done without reflection, was the only one possible for that moment. The terrible grief she felt for her friend's continued suffering wound itself into her playing. The oboe raged and wept.

As the final notes faded away, Erin returned to awareness and glanced at the recruiter. The older woman looked absolutely stunned. Dr. Chen sat in silence for what seemed like a long time. Erin didn't mind. She had to reassemble her own composure.

Finally, Dr. Chen said, "That was very good." She swallowed hard, drew a deep breath, and continued. "It will take some time for us to process the applications, but we will contact you one way or the other around Christmas. Thank you."

Erin nodded, shook hands with the woman again, and left the room. *I did my best, and it* was *very good. The rest is out of my hands.*

* * *

A couple of weeks later, Erin crept into her least favorite classroom and took her seat in the corner closest to the teacher's desk, trying to become invisible. *God, this is embarrassing every single day. Why didn't I take health years ago? Here I am, a senior, stuck with the giggling freshmen.*

Whispers emanated from the back of the room.

"Did you go to J.D.'s party?" one immature female voice asked.

"You were there, dumbass. We talked," another hissed back.

"I did? I don't remember. I was drunk off my ass," the first girl giggled.

"You sure were. Completely shit-faced and hanging off some college guy. Did you score?"

"I don't remember."

Erin rolled her eyes. *Was I ever that young?* She supposed she must have been, but even at fifteen, she had been more interested in band than beer.

"Listen, kids," Mrs. Heath told them earnestly, cutting off the whispers with a narrow-eyed glare, "it's really not necessary for you to have sex in high school. I have never heard of anyone who regretted waiting. Your mental and physical health will be much better overall if you do." She paused for breath. Erin fought the urge to roll her eyes. "Remember, I'm not encouraging any of you to go this route. However, I am aware some of you will ignore my advice. If you feel you must be intimate with someone, please be monogamous, and please use protection. Free condoms are available in the nurse's office, and can they also be purchased cheaply from any convenience or grocery store. Aside from the risk of getting pregnant, there are several sexually transmitted diseases circulating, yes, even in this school. Some are permanent, and others are deadly. Protect yourselves with abstinence if you can, but please protect yourselves somehow."

Erin could have recited this speech by heart. She had heard it at assemblies for years. *Even Mom has been giving me the condom talk lately. I guess even someone that obtuse must have noticed I'm not talking to Danny half the evening. Or maybe it's the late nights.* She had never had a curfew, but she used to bring herself home much earlier on weekends. Erin smirked, remembering her own previous weekend. No beer, but she had certainly scored.

Well, Sean and I are monogamous, so at least we've got that covered. It occurred to her, however, that their actual condom use had been rather hit or miss. At Sean's apartment, where the little box resided, they used them most of the time. But at Erin's house, often they didn't. Overwhelmed with passion, they didn't take time to consider the consequences.

Suddenly, the mention of pregnancy struck Erin. *It never occurred to me before, but we have done it unprotected at least a half-dozen times.* For the first time, she thought about what that might mean for her. *We've been quite careless, really, in the... oh Lord, in the five weeks since we got together.* Five? Shouldn't her period have come... three weeks ago? *Yes, three weeks. This is not good.*

Only by concentrating on her breathing, slowly pulling air into her lungs and just as slowly releasing it, was Erin able to get through class. The second the bell rang, she bolted out the door, down the hall, collecting Sheridan and all but running her to the counselor's office, where she sank into one of the stained and threadbare chairs at the huge conference table. They spent time in there so frequently, no one noticed.

"What's wrong, Erin?" Sheridan asked, startled by her friend's urgency.

"Oh God, Danny, are you feeling all right today? I have a problem," Erin babbled in a nearly incoherent gush.

Sheridan's eyebrows drew down with concern. "Yes, I'm feeling fine. I think I might be a little better, actually. What's your problem?"

"Are you sure?" Erin pressed. "I don't want to add to what you're dealing with."

"You know, it's kind of tiresome how everyone treats me like I'm about to break," Sheridan replied in gentle exasperation. "Please, Erin, spill it. I'm looking forward to thinking about problems other than my own for a change."

Erin attempted to answer but choked. Her voice fought her attempt to use it, and she forced the words out quickly. "I think I might be pregnant."

Sheridan gave her a puzzled look. "Erin, you have to have sex to get pregnant."

"I know," she wailed. *Dear God, no. Not this. Anything but this.*

Sheridan's mouth dropped open. "What? When? Who?"

The truth, a long-standing habit between the girls, nearly fell out of Erin unbidden. *No, don't say. She can't know. No one can know.* "I can't tell you. Oh God, I'm scared."

"Erin, you have to tell me," Sheridan insisted.

Erin shook her head violently. "You'll be mad. I can't. What do I do?"

"First, you breathe and calm down." Sheridan wrapped her arms around Erin, soothing her with a hug. "Panicking won't help. Okay, do you have rehearsal today?"

Erin forced her racing brain to focus on the simple question. "No." She rested her forehead on Sheridan's shoulder.

"Good. Try to get through the rest of the day. After school, we'll go to the store and get you a test. Then at least you'll know. You've been late before," she reminded her.

"Yes, but that was different," Erin mumbled against her friend's shoulder. "There was nothing to worry about then. Besides, I've never been three weeks late."

"Okay, hang in there. Try to stay calm. We'll take care of this today." Sheridan squeezed her tight.

* * *

After school, Sheridan drove them to the grocery store, where by a strange coincidence, two-packs of home pregnancy tests were on clearance, marked cheaper than the singles.

Nerves set Erin's slender frame shaking by the time they arrived at her house. "Mom?" she called as she opened the door. Silence.

Good, Sheridan thought. *The last thing Erin needs to deal with is her mother, which is such a shame. I know if it was me, I'd be leaning on my mom for support. She'd be disappointed, but I know she'd be there for me anyway.* She couldn't imagine what flaky Valerie James would do under these circumstances. *Something lame and pointless, no doubt.*

Sheridan led her friend to the hallway bathroom. "Do you know what to do?" she asked from the doorway.

"Kinda," Erin replied.

Sheridan frowned. "Close the door."

As Erin complied, she removed the instructions from the box and scanned them. "Okay, slow five count."

A few seconds later she heard the toilet flush, and then the water running. Erin opened the door. Her normally pale face had taken on a ghostly hue, and her panic-stricken eyes had gone so wide, she resembled an owl.

Sheridan stepped in and put her arm around Erin's shoulders. They watched grimly as the little window slowly developed a dark blue line. Erin closed her eyes as Sheridan hugged her.

"Let's get rid of this," Sheridan said at last. "Staring at it longer won't change anything." She wrapped it up in the toilet paper and tossed it in the trash, then led Erin out of the room, down the hall and urged her to a seat on her bed.

Erin sank limply onto the mattress, lying on her side, her face in her hands, breathing slowly. Sheridan rubbed her back in soothing circles.

"I didn't realize you were seeing anyone," Sheridan said, her voice coolly neutral. "It's not David Landry, is it?" *And I sure hope not, because he's a nasty manwhore. Still, Erin is so... so shy. She might be susceptible to any attention.*

Erin made a strange sound that might have been a gag and peeked at Sheridan between her fingers. "No."

Thank God. "Well then, I can't imagine what you have been up to, girl. If it's that clear, this can't have been too recent."

"Five weeks," Erin said flatly.

The thought produced a swoop of discomfort in Sheridan's belly, and she frowned as she asked, "Around the time of... homecoming?"

"Yes. It could have been that night." Erin pressed her hand over her mouth, head shaking from side to side as though to unsay words that revealed far too much.

"That night?" Sheridan furrowed her forehead, confused. "I don't understand. You went with Sean. And you were with me... later. I don't see how you could have been... busy in between. Did you ditch Sean? Go with someone else? No, that doesn't make sense. You were with him at the hospital... OH! MY! GOD!"

The suspicious wetness in the corners of Erin's eyes spilled over and her inhalation turned to a shaky sob.

"Erin, this might sound stupid, but... are you sleeping with my brother?"

Erin didn't answer.

Sheridan picked up the phone and dialed Sean's number. *I'm getting to the bottom of this right now.* "Big brother, I'm at Erin's house. You need to get here right now. She needs you." *Let's see what you have to say to that, mister.*

"Is she all right?" His voice sounded far more concerned than it should have when discussing his sister's friend, someone he casually cared for but was not particularly involved with.

Busted, buddy. Oh, you're in for it, Sean Murphy. "No, she's not. Come now."

She hung up and lay down beside her friend, wrapping her arms around her.

Erin's fragile grip on partial control exploded in a flood of guilt. "I'm so sorry, Danny," she sobbed. "I swear, if I had known, I wouldn't have let you go with him. I can't stand it. I should have stayed with you. I knew he was no good. It's my fault."

Where did that come from? "Don't be stupid, Erin. It's his fault, not yours. Don't waste another moment feeling guilty about it."

Erin whimpered. "I can't help it. I was doing... *that*, having a wonderful time and all the while..."

Enough already "You didn't know," she interrupted, cutting off the unwanted words. "I can't believe it though. You and Sean. I knew you two belonged together, but I didn't think you would move so fast. What about saving your virginity?"

Erin choked, took several deep breaths and managed to speak clearly. "That was your deal, not mine. It wasn't a big priority for me. Not when I was with Sean. I never did it before because I didn't care about anyone else, but I love him. Why do you say we belong together?"

"Just a feeling I have," Sheridan explained. "I know you love him; you have for a while. That's why I set you two up; I thought you would be good for him. I didn't think he would be...like that though. Did he hurt you?"

Erin's lips turned upward, but her dark eyes remained sad. "No, Danny. It's really nice when you're with the right person and you want it so much. I hope someday you know that."

"That day is not close." Sheridan broke eye contact. *Even the thought of sex terrifies me. I can't imagine choosing it on purpose.*

"Of course not." Erin returned her friend's hug, giving and taking comfort from the same embrace. They lapsed into silence, Erin's eyes sliding closed. Her breathing deepened. *She seems to be falling asleep, which is probably a good thing.* Sheridan stepped out of the room to call her parents and let them know where she was.

* * *

About half an hour later, Sean arrived. Using the key Erin had given him, he let himself in rather than knocking and headed straight to her bedroom. She lay on her bed asleep, her pretty face streaked with tears, her hair disheveled. Sheridan sat beside the bed on the desk chair, keeping watch over her friend.

He looked down at the sleeping girl with such a powerful expression on his face that he would have completely given himself away to his sister even if she hadn't known already. *My beautiful baby. The woman I never dreamed would come to mean so much to me.*

Sheridan left the bedside and beckoned him out of the room, softly shutting the door.

"What's wrong with her?" he asked. *She looked so... destroyed. It must be huge.*

"She's pregnant, Sean. You made my best friend pregnant."

It took several seconds for the words to sink in. *Pregnant? Erin? How can Erin be pregnant?* "Oh shit, really?"

"Yes, really. Why were you sleeping with her?" Sheridan asked harshly, her eyes filled with accusations against which there was no argument. "There are tons of women out there. Why Erin?"

"Hey, you were the one who set us up." His defensive answer could not conceal the guilt that welled up in him.

"Yes, but not so that you could seduce her," Sheridan protested. "She was a virgin."

"I know." He closed his eyes. *It made so much sense at the time.* Now he felt like a bastard. "It's not like I was just trying to score or anything. You know me better than that."

Her pursed lips called his assertion into serious doubt. "But, Sean, don't you realize how susceptible girls are when their parents don't love them enough? They're getting divorced too. She's so vulnerable. She would have done whatever you wanted. Did you really have to go all the way?"

"I didn't take advantage, Danny," he vowed. "I tried to stop twice. She begged me."

Sheridan made a disbelieving face.

"I'm serious. She wanted it so bad, and she's so pretty and sweet. There's only so much a man can take. Besides, everyone gives it up sooner or later. The lucky ones get to do it with someone who cares about them."

Sheridan flinched.

"Oh God, Danny. I'm sorry. I didn't think." He hugged his sister in apology. "Anyway, that doesn't count. Someday, you'll meet someone wonderful, who will love you, and it will be just as good for you as it is for us." *You're making excuses, his conscience snarled. How stupid.* As though he were a naughty child caught with a cookie in each hand and chocolate smeared over his face. *It wasn't like that, and I need to stop being defensive and tell the truth.* "As for this situation, she's not alone. I know how special she is. I want to keep her forever." He took a deep breath. "I love her."

"Does she know that?" Sheridan demanded, still eyeing him suspiciously.

"She wasn't ready to hear it. I'm working on it." *And that's the only reason I haven't said anything. I don't want to make my declaration, knowing she'll argue with me and reject my words. It's not because she doesn't want them, but because she has no confidence in herself.*

"Well you need to work faster, Sean," Sheridan insisted, not giving an inch. "She's really going to need you now."

Sheridan's right. Erin's security is more important than my pride. "I'm not going anywhere," he told his sister.

"Good. You had better go and tell her that."

He nodded and returned to the bedroom. Kneeling beside the bed, he stroked Erin's cheek until she opened her eyes. She smiled sadly, her eyes wistful. He kissed her forehead.

"I'm sorry." His regret bled into his soft tone.

"Me too." She sat up slowly, as though her body ached.

"I'm here, no matter what," he assured her.

"I know." But the flatness of her voice held no assurance.

He drew her into his arms. She laid her cheek on his shoulder. "I love you, Erin," he breathed into her ear.

Her head shot up and she stared at him with wide, haunted eyes. "What? Why?"

Such disbelief. It stung him, just as he had known it would. He trailed one thumb along her cheek, smoothing away a tear. "Because you're Erin. That's reason enough."

As the seconds passed, he felt the tension drain out of her until she lay limp in his arms. He stroked her back.

"What are we going to do?" she whispered, and the fear in her voice made his heart clench.

"I don't know, baby, but we'll work it out together." He kissed her cheek tenderly, wanting to show her the love she didn't know how to believe in.

Chapter 8

A couple of days later, the Friday of the week before Thanksgiving, Erin made her way into her family's bungalow near the University. Fatigue and worry dragged every step until she felt as though she were trying to wade through molasses.

"Erin, is that you?" her mother called from the living room.

"Yeah, I'm home," she answered in a tired, listless voice, not caring how bad she sounded. *Or how bad I look, dark circles under the eyes, hair all messy from the wind. Ugh. I even managed to spill food on my jeans. All I want is a hot shower and a nap.* She trudged into the living room. Valerie sat on the brown leather sofa, her blond highlighted hair pulled back into a clip, plucking her eyebrows.

"What did you need, Mom?"

Valerie glanced up for a moment, and then returned her gaze back on her little mirror. "I needed to tell you that we're moving. As part of the divorce settlement, the house is going to be sold and your dad and I will split the money."

"Where are we going to live? I know of some apartments downtown." *Sean lives there. That would be nice.*

"No. Bill lives in Motley. We're moving in with him," she told her daughter off-handedly, her focus on her reflection.

Erin stared at her mother in disbelief. *This can't be happening.* "Motley? Are you joking? That's hours away. I can't live in Motley." Her belly churned, and she swallowed hard against a hint of nausea.

"Why not?" Valerie asked, raising her eyebrows, and then taking advantage of the movement to catch a stray hair. "I know it's not ideal, moving your senior year, but what difference does it really make? You're leaving to go to college in the fall anyway. Your time here is so short."

"But, Mom, that's a super small town," Erin protested. "Do they even have a symphonic band there? All-State tryouts are coming up. I can't miss that."

"Erin, you've already made All-State twice." Valerie pulled out a snippet of hair, winced, and rubbed her orbital bone.

So many arguments rose up that they blanked Erin's mind and left her stammering. "But... no... Uh... I mean, that doesn't matter." *Who wouldn't want to attempt All-State again? And scholarships. And... senior year. And Sean...* But Valerie had never had much interest in Erin's dating habits, she knew, or in her oboe either. Her mouth continued talking without her awareness. "Besides, I have to be here for Danny. She's having a really hard time right now."

"She has a family. She doesn't need you." In an attempt to cut off the argument, Erin's mother tossed out the most painful, cruel thing she could have ever said to her daughter flippantly, as though it didn't matter in the slightest.

Erin blanched. "Yes, she does!" she insisted, her voice growing increasingly shrill at pace with her growing panic. "I need her too. My life is here. My boyfriend is here. All my opportunities are here. I don't even know Bill. Why would I want to live with him? Can't you just wait to sell the house until I graduate, please?"

"Settle down." At last, Valerie set her toiletries aside and met her daughter's eyes. "No, the sale can't wait. We're moving over Thanksgiving break."

"I won't go with you," Erin insisted, shaking her head from side to side rapidly. The movement did nothing to quell her rising nausea. "I'm eighteen. I don't need to live with my mother anymore."

"How will you support yourself, Erin? You don't earn much playing in the symphony." Valerie's calm, reasonable tone annoyed her daughter further.

"I'll figure something out," Erin snapped. "Don't worry about me. You never have anyway. I'll take care of it myself."

"Don't be like that. Please just consider it." Valerie rose and laid her hand on Erin's arm.

"I won't. My God, you're selfish. I'm not going anywhere." Erin jerked away from her mother and fled the house. She didn't slam the door, although the part of her that really was still a teenager wanted to.

Hopping into her car, she drove over to Sheridan's needing her friend's advice. *I can't leave,* she recited to herself as she drove. *Band. All-State. Scholarships. Danny... and Sean. Especially Sean. I need him more than I need the mother who never wanted me.* Pressure in her lungs made her aware that she'd been holding her breath. She released air in a slow sigh that helped quell her roiling belly.

Time to face the facts, she told herself. You're pregnant. You're also a senior in high school. Yes, it's embarrassing, but at least you'll be able to graduate before... before the baby is born. Baby. For the first time since this crisis began, she pictured in her mind what the blue line on a stupid white stick actually told her. *I might have a boy. A little boy with dark hair and Sean's beautiful blue eyes. And he will be mine to keep forever.* She didn't know what all the ramifications would be, but she suddenly felt certain she would never regret having Sean's baby. She placed her hand on her flat belly and let the slow joy spread over her. *It can't be changed. There's nothing left to do but celebrate it.*

At the Murphy home, Erin rang the doorbell and waited anxiously on the step. Today, agitated as she felt about the prospect of moving away, the perfectly symmetrical windows of the second floor glared down at her with malicious intent, and the four fluted white columns on the porch seemed like bars on a jail cell, closing her in. Time stretched out endlessly before the door opened. Mr. Murphy, his expression grumpy, glared down at her. She suddenly realized how he towered over her, much taller than her own father. With his salt and pepper hair and rugged, sun-browned face, his heavy forehead and dark eyebrows, when Roger Murphy glowered, he looked nothing short of dangerous.

She drew back with a sharp intake of breath. She had always gotten along well with the Murphy parents. *What did I do?*

Then he recognized her, and his expression lightened. "Oh, it's you, Erin. Come in. Sorry to keep you waiting. Someone has been playing with the doorbell, ringing and running away. I didn't know if anyone was here."

"Oh, okay. Sorry. Is Danny here?" She willed her heart to slow its nervous pounding. *He wasn't angry with you. Calm down. Breathe.*

"Yes, she's in her room. Come on." He indicated the interior with one hand, and she stepped past him over the threshold and into the cozy warmth of the Murphy family's formal living room. The interior of the house provided all the welcome the exterior had lacked, as though being in this place somehow changed everything.

Erin climbed the stairs, her legs unsteady. *I really hope Sheridan can help me think through this mess, so I can find a way to stay. Moving to stupid Motley just isn't an option.*

Sheridan had a pile of homework spread all over the floor. She lay on her belly on a shaggy lavender area rug, struggling through a page of balancing chemical equations. Her history book and a copy of *A Midsummer Night's Dream* lay nearby. *Looks like she's got a big night. Of course, she might just be reading the Shakespeare for fun, too.* "Danny?"

Sheridan lifted her head and a wide, glowing smile spread across her face. "Hi, Erin. I didn't know you were coming over. How are you feeling?"

"I'm feeling fine," she lied. "I can see you're busy, but I need some advice."

"Erin, I'm never too busy for you, sweetie," she said, turning over and rising to a sitting position. "What's up?"

"Mom's moving," Erin blurted, sinking to sit cross-legged on the rug beside her friend. She tugged at the lush pile with her fingers.

Sheridan took the news in stride, not showing surprise. "Where?"

"To Motley, to live with *him*. She wants me to go with her." Unkind thoughts crowded Erin's mind, but she pushed them away. *Being angry with Mom is not important and will only distract me from finding a solution.*

The pronouncement garnered a reaction. The corners of Sheridan's eyes tightened. She sat up taller. "When?"

"Next week."

Sheridan's jaw sagged, and then her lip sneaked between her teeth, where she worried it nervously. "You can't move now! What about... everything?"

So much everything, I don't even know where to start. "I know. I don't want to go, but what am I going to do? I can't afford an apartment on my salary from the symphony, and I don't want to get a better paying job. I don't have time to ring up groceries or wait tables. I have so much practicing and homework to do..." Erin gushed out, blushing but unable to stop babbling.

"And you're pregnant," Sheridan added softly, "so the last thing you need is this kind of stress."

"Right. Can you help me think? I'm all in a panic." Erin pressed both hands to her belly as though to shield the tiny life inside from her raging emotions.

Sheridan considered, and then her consternation dissolved into another smile. "Actually, the solution is easy. Come with me."

Sheridan led Erin back through the house to the family room, where her parents watched the news on a set of matching tan recliners.

"Mom, Dad?" Sheridan said to get their attention.

"Yes, darling?" Mrs. Murphy replied, pressing the mute button on the remote. Both parents turned to face the girls.

"I need to ask a favor of you," Sheridan said, speaking slowly and with confidence. "Erin's mom is moving and wants to take her away. I can't have that. I need Erin too much, and besides, she has a ton of stuff going on here that she has to do in order to get ready for college. She can't afford to live alone, so I thought, can she just stay with us until the fall? With Sean and Jason both moved out, there's plenty of room, and it would be really nice to have her around all the time." Unlike Erin's hysterical gush, Sheridan used the calm, rational tone one would expect from an attorney addressing the court.

"Hmmm," Mrs. Murphy hummed, considering. "I don't mind having Erin here. That would be fine. But, dear, would your mother agree?"

"I'm eighteen," Erin replied stiffly. "It's not her decision."

"I see. There's some tension between you, isn't there?" Mrs. Murphy reached out, grasped Erin's hand, and patted it.

"Not tension exactly," Erin said cautiously, not wanting to sound disrespectful, "I just don't think much of her choices these days."

"I hate to say this, but I agree with you." Ellen released Erin's hand and turned to face her husband.

"Roger, what do you think about Erin moving in with us?"

"I don't see it as a problem," he replied. Erin found it interesting to note that when he relaxed, Roger Murphy's craggy face only brought to mind safety and protection, no threat at all. *My nerves must have been my own fault. Hormones maybe.* He continued speaking. "Would you like that, Erin? Sheridan has done most of the talking."

"I would. You're both so kind." Erin struggled not to break down. *Will they still be so welcoming when they find out about Sean and me... and the baby? It's not a secret that can be kept for long, but I need a little longer. I'm still coming to terms with it myself. I'm not ready to share. Not yet.*

"All right then, why don't you pack up and move in right away?" Mrs. Murphy suggested, tucking a strand of curly silver and gold hair behind her ear and smiling so her hazel eyes crinkled in the corners.

Erin smiled in relief. "Wonderful. I'll do that. Bless you both."

As the girls walked away, Sheridan grinned hugely. *I've missed that smile these last few weeks, but she's smiled more in the last half hour than she has in the previous month.*

"I'm so excited," Sheridan gushed, her reasonable demeanor dissolving into adolescent enthusiasm. "I can't wait for you to get here. Where do you want to sleep? I bet Sean's old room would be appealing."

"You have no idea," Erin replied. "But I don't know if I would dare. Isn't there a guest room?"

"It's too small for more than a few nights," Sheridan reminded her as they passed the tiny door. *Oh, that's right. I remember that place from hide and seek. It's like a big closet with a bed in it.* Sheridan continued, "Besides, I think he would like knowing you're there."

What a lovely thought. "You might be right. Okay, I'm going back to my ... my mother's house to start packing up. Finish your homework. I'll see you tomorrow, okay?"

"Sure, sweetie. I'm so glad you're not leaving. I don't know what I would do without you." Sheridan threw her arms around Erin and hugged her.

* * *

It only took Erin a short time to box up all her possessions. As she tucked the two boxes of books and sheet music, two trash bags of clothes, and her precious oboe case into the trunk of her car, her mother approached. "Erin, please, reconsider," Valerie urged.

"The words are right," Erin observed, calm now that the crisis had been resolved, "but the tone suggests the opposite. Don't lie, Mother. You're glad I'm staying. Now you and Bill can enjoy your time together and not worry about me."

She glanced and saw the relief flash in Valerie's eyes. *You never did want me, did you? Why did you even bring me into the world?* Every thought these days led back to her own pregnancy, and this thought more than most. *I promise, little one, no matter what, you will always be wanted.* More focused on her own issues than her mother's continued piping, Erin returned to her room.

Valerie trailed behind. "What are you going to do?"

"Move in with the Murphys," Erin replied. "They do need me, and they want me there."

"Don't be a nuisance to them, Erin," Valerie pleaded.

That captured her attention. *What does she think I am? A two-year-old prone to temper tantrums?* "I'm not a nuisance, Mother, unless you just don't want me around. I'm also not an infant, though I doubt you've ever grasped that."

A quick glance at her bedroom revealed nothing else she cared to keep, so she grabbed her purse and pushed past her mother.

"Erin..."

Whatever Valerie planned to say, Erin didn't stay to hear. Hopping into her car, she drove to Sean's apartment, climbed the stairs and let herself in. She smiled to see her boyfriend slouching on the second-hand gray couch he had rescued from the curb, his attention fixed on a car auction.

She slipped into the room and joined him.

"Guess what, Sean?" she said, cuddling up against him.

"What, baby?" he asked, cradling her face in his hand.

"I'm moving in with your parents," she replied, covering his fingers with hers.

Her words arrested his stroking fingers. "With my parents? Why?" he asked.

"My mom's leaving, but I can't move away now," she explained.

"Of course not." He kissed her forehead. "You could move in with me, you know."

Her cheeks heated. *But wouldn't it be nice to be with Sean all the time?* "Don't you think that might look kind of bad?"

He half frowned. "Erin, at this point looking bad is the least of our concerns."

She released a lungful of air and answered lamely, "You're right. But still."

"Have you thought about what you want to do?" Something about the way he phrased the question suggested he meant more than this immediate relocation.

She considered. "I haven't come to any conclusions. I think on Monday, after school, I'll stop by the local university, and, you know, check out their music program."

Sean lowered his eyebrows. "Lakes? You never wanted to go there."

"I know," she replied, twisting her lips, "but everything is different now. Since I'm having a baby this summer, I can't very well take off to Texas or even to State in the fall. I have to stay here." She guided their joined hands to her belly.

"I hate this," Sean said, his mouth sinking downward until grooves bracketed it. "My carelessness is having such a terrible impact on your dreams."

"I was just as careless as you," she reminded him. "Dreams can be modified, Sean. Besides, staying close to you doesn't sound so bad to me." She snuggled closer, and he squeezed her gently.

"We'll need to get married, you know. I'm Catholic. I can't let you have my baby when we're not married." His hand dropped hers and caressed the flatness of her belly.

She gave him a crooked smile. "I know. I'm kind of Catholic too, remember? Does the idea of marriage bother you?"

"Only to the extent that it limits your options. Marriage is what I wanted from you, but not like this. I meant someday, when you were ready." Sean sighed. "Poor Erin. Being with me hasn't been that good for you has it?"

"Are you kidding? I wouldn't want to be anywhere else. I love you, Sean." She threw her arms around his neck.

"I love you too. And I hate that you're so stressed." He studied her face, and then a hint of a smile spread across his face. "You know something? You look like a girl who needs to be made love to."

"Yes, please," Erin begged, rubbing her body against his.

Sean kissed her deeply and led her to the bedroom where he proceeded to erase the memory of every stressful event she had endured in the last several weeks.

Chapter 9

In the end, the move proved quick and rather painless. By Saturday afternoon, Erin finished unpacking her clothing, books and sheet music in Sean's old room. She set up her music stand and a small chair in the corner between the bed and the window and regarded the effect. *Nice. Homey. I wonder if this is the same bedding Sean used before he moved out. Bet he did. It matches the rest of the décor.* She shivered with pleasure. *Sean slept under these covers.* She carefully lifted her pictures from the box of music, setting them next to his on the dresser. *I like how that looks, like the two of us live here together. Once we're married, I'll hang these in the hallway of the apartment.* Her heart fluttered at the thought of being, not just Sean's girlfriend, but his wife, his publicly-acknowledged woman. Shaking off the distracting thought, she continued her unpacking, placing her clothes in the empty dresser before heading downstairs to seek out Mrs. Murphy.

She found Ellen chopping vegetables in the kitchen at the butcher block counter, preparing to make stew. Erin pulled out another cutting board from the island's lower cabinet. *Some conversations are best done under the cover of carrots and onions.* "Mrs. Murphy, I wanted to thank you again for letting me stay with you. It means so much to me," Erin began, her eyes on the knife.

"You're very welcome, dear," Ellen replied. "After all you've done for us, it was the least we could do."

The compliment made Erin glow. "I wanted to ask you something. You see, I've never really had... rules before. I don't want to upset anyone. Could you please tell me what the expectations are?"

Ellen set the knife down and turned to face Erin. "How sweet of you to ask. Yes, there are rules for anyone who lives with us, and even though you're eighteen, we will still expect you to abide by them. I hope they don't seem too strict to you. First, you will have a curfew, of course. Sheridan has to be in by ten on school nights and midnight on weekends. I would appreciate it if you would do the same. There will be no staying out all night. Do you have a boyfriend, dear?"

Oh boy. "Yes."

"Well, he's welcome to visit," Ellen continued. Erin could see that, though she never lifted her head from attending carefully to her food, she also had her focus on their conversation. *So, it can be done. Interesting.* "but you will need to stay in the public parts of the house with the door open at all times. There won't be any goings-on here. All right?"

How to address this without lying? Choose your words carefully, girl. "You don't need to worry. He's shy and I don't think it's likely he will want to visit."

"Well then," Ellen continued, returning to her chopping as she spoke, "we need to know where you are at all times. If you have to stay late after school or if you have an appointment, please write it on the calendar, along with a number where we can reach you."

"I have a cell phone," Erin offered. "It's off during school, but the rest of the time, I keep it with me. I'm easy to find. I'll write the number down on the calendar, all right?"

Ellen grinned. "Good. I know this probably doesn't apply, but it needs to be said anyway. There is to be no smoking and no drug use here. If you want a drink now and again, such as during family dinner or a cookout, the limit is one. You may not drink away from the house, where you are unsupervised, as long as you are underage."

"That's fair." *It's also not going to be an issue.*

"Last, we attend Mass every Sunday and have dinner together after. If you are going to be part of this family, we will expect you to do both."

"No problem. I can live with those rules." *What a dream come true; to be part of this family. I would have agreed to a lot more.*

"Good. I think this will work out fine." She paused, a little grin creasing her lips, then added, "Erin, would you be willing to... play for us now and again? You do such a nice job, and I really like listening to it."

"Of course. I would love to." Erin tipped the carrots into the pot and went over to the calendar to mark out her schedule of after school rehearsals, college interviews, and a note labeled 'doctor appointment', which she placed on Monday. She didn't really have an appointment per se, but it was time to get a handle on the reality of her situation.

* * *

On Monday after school, Erin drove to The University of the Lakes, the small public institution that served their community. She parked outside the music department and hurried across the parking lot to get out of a bone-chilling drizzle that had appeared out of nowhere earlier in the day and lingered depressingly over the town. She headed down a covered outdoor walkway with a pebble-studded concrete floor and ceiling, riddled with pigeons and the mess of their presence, even this late in the fall. The chilly birds made unhappy cooing noises as she passed them. Wrinkling her nose at the birdy aroma, she hurried to a small hallway of offices and knocked on the open doorway of room 212.

Dr. Abrams, who played in the symphony with Erin, sat at his desk, melting the glue on the loosened pad of a clarinet key with a cigarette lighter. The department's wounded instrument lay on his desk, awaiting the operation. The flame flicked out as the professor looked up. "Well, well, well, Erin James," Dr. Abrams said in a booming voice that more than matched the tuba he played. "What can I do for you today?"

"Hi, Dr. Abrams," she said softly, "I was wondering if you can tell me more about your music program here."

"Here?" He dropped the lighter onto his desk and wiped his forehead, though the room felt cold to Erin. "I've never heard that you wanted to go here. Didn't you get into that conservatory?"

"I haven't heard, yet," she replied, "but it's awfully far away."

"Homebody, are you? What about State?" he suggested. "That's only a few hours' drive away."

She inhaled deeply and then blew the air out between her lips as she considered her words. A strand of damp hair danced in the breeze she created. "I'm not sure I'm able to go anywhere. What about the program here? Do you have a double reed performance major?"

Despite his bluff appearance, the professor clearly had a streak of intuition. He gave Erin a puzzled, concerned look. "We don't have any performance majors. Only music education."

That's what I was afraid of. "And that would qualify me to do what? Teach high school band?"

"Actually, most people have to start with middle school," he clarified.

Yikes. That takes a special sort. "I don't think I really want to be a school teacher," Erin admitted. "I would like to have some private students someday, but not a whole band program. Mostly I just want to play. Isn't there any way to do it here?"

He pondered. "I suppose… you could major in independent studies in music. That might work, but I have to tell you, we're not well set up for it. Our woodwind lady isn't a double reed expert. She's more into clarinet and sax." Seconds passed as he contemplated some more. "Listen, Erin. It would be really nice to have you here, but I don't think it's in your best interests."

"I understand that, but I may not have any other option," she admitted. Nerves made her want to bite her nails, so she rubbed her hands together to warm them and keep them occupied. "Okay, thanks, Dr. Abrams. I need to think about this and let you know."

"All right, Erin. Good luck." His expression again urged her to reconsider.

She walked quickly back to her car, shaking her head. *What a mess I've made of my life.* A little frisson of nervous nausea hit her, and she gagged once, swallowed hard, and turned the key in the ignition. It sputtered in protest of the inclement weather before agreeing to start, and she carefully pulled out of the parking space and drove to the family medical clinic for her checkup.

* * *

It was a good thing I planned to take care of my business early in the week. Erin realized as she walked into the house and found Sheridan and her mother sitting in the formal living room, deep in conversation. Her arm stung where the technician had drawn a blood sample, and the words of advice she'd been given ringing in her ears. *No alcohol. Limit caffeine. Get enough sleep. Do plenty of low-impact exercise. Try to minimize stress. Eat healthy and avoid unpasteurized cheese.* The rest faded into an incomprehensible buzzing and she pushed it aside.

"So, I'm hoping to start the make-ahead items tomorrow, after school," Ellen reminded her daughter. "Do you have anything big coming up, or can I count on your help?"

Sheridan considered. "I'll try. Nothing major is happening at the moment." A huge yawn interrupted her comment. "I'm awfully tired though," she admitted. "Too many exams, I suppose."

"I, um...." Erin began, but two sets of eyes turned her direction reduced her to stammers. *What are you going to do, dummy?*

Offer to help? You don't know how to cook. "I, um, I don't know much about making food. My family didn't celebrate Thanksgiving..." she swallowed. *Stop stammering, you idiot.* "I, um, if you wanted me to help out, I would, but you'd have to tell me what to do."

Ellen's lips immediately curved into a welcoming smile. She patted the couch beside her. "Of course, my dear," she replied. "I'd love to have another set of hands. Cooking is fun, and I'd be happy to show you."

Erin beamed. "Thank you. I'd like that."

* * *

Wednesday, after school, Erin dumped her backpack in her bedroom and meandered down to the kitchen. Interesting noises had drawn her attention the moment she walked in the door, and she wanted to see what was happening today. Yesterday had been pie filling and homemade cranberry sauce, which could be made ahead and left to chill in the refrigerator. Today, it appeared, it would be dinner rolls. As Erin peeked shyly from the doorway, Ellen poured the oozing lump of yeast dough from the mixing bowl onto the heavily floured butcher block counter. It slurped as it released from the metal, and then fell with a moist plop.

Erin took a step closer, fascinated. She had never before seen bread that didn't come in a plastic package.

Catching the movement in her peripheral vision, Ellen lifted her head. "Erin. Hello, love. Come here." Erin approached cautiously. "Have you ever kneaded bread before?"

"No," Erin admitted. "How do you do it?"

"Like this. Look." She folded the dough in half and pressed with the heel of her hand, stretching it across the counter. Then she turned the mass a quarter turn and repeated the process. After several revolutions, Ellen lifted the dough, spread more flour underneath, and flipped the lump over. "Would you like to try it?"

"Oh, but what if I mess it up?" Erin protested.

"You can't," Ellen reassured her. "All you do is fold and press and turn. It's simple, and the more you work on it, the better it gets, and the more relaxed you feel."

Erin nodded. *I could use some relaxation.* As Ellen had said, the process proved to be simple. After only a few tries, Erin got the hang of it. Letting her mind wander, she pummeled and stretched the dough while Ellen turned to another bowl of flour.

"What are you working on?" Erin asked.

"Pie crusts," Ellen replied. "They're a little more complicated than bread, and nearly the opposite to make. If you overwork a pie crust, it will turn tough, so you have to blend in the butter gently, without melting it." She demonstrated, using a funny little tool with a handle and five tiny, blunt blades, thin as wires, which wrapped around in a semicircle. With this, she cut the fat into the flour. "Then you add just a little bit of ice cold water... but not the ice... like this." She scooped carefully with a tablespoon, dripped the water onto the flour and butter, and stirred gently with a fork. "And then gather it up, wrap it, and chill it. Tomorrow we can fill it with the apple and pumpkin pie fillings we made last night and bake them, at 350 degrees until they're golden brown."

"Where did you learn to do all this, Mrs. Murphy?" Erin asked, flipping the bread dough over yet again.

"From my mother," the older woman replied as she patted the crust into two circles and wrapped them in plastic wrap.

"And you taught it to Danny?" Erin guessed. *No wonder I like the Murphys. They do things together, and it's one way they show they care.*

"Yes, of course. It's our legacy," Ellen agreed, "but today she wasn't up to it. I think she's a little under the weather." Ellen placed the dough rounds into the fridge and returned to Erin, showing her how to divide the dough into balls to create cloverleaf rolls.

"You might be right. She did seem awfully quiet in English today. Normally she answers *all* the questions." Erin grinned as she created three equal-sized balls and dropped them into the muffin tin. "I'm glad you're teaching me to do this. It's... fun." Actually, Erin found it powerfully moving to be included in a Murphy tradition that had been passed from mother to daughter for untold generations. It made her feel, in some small way, like part of the family.

* * *

Late that evening, Erin woke with a start. A strange sound, a kind of low moaning, dragged her up from deep slumber. Light from the bathroom spilled into the hallway with an eye-piercing glare. Pulling on her slippers, Erin went to investigate.

Sheridan sat on the bathroom floor, hugging her knees and keening softly. The stench of vomit made Erin want to gag too.

"Danny are you all right?" she asked after several convulsive swallows.

"Noooo!" her friend wailed.

Erin swept a sweaty blond curl from her friend's forehead. "What's wrong, sweetie? Are you sick?"

"I've been sick for days. I can't shake it. I can't hide it anymore." Sheridan's breath came so fast, Erin feared she was near hyperventilation.

"Why are you trying to hide it?" she demanded. "If you're sick, tell your parents. Have them take you to the doctor?"

"No. It's not that. Look." Sheridan held out a small object. Erin stared, aghast at the second pregnancy test, the one she'd tossed into her toiletries when she moved, and then had completely forgotten in a bathroom drawer. It showed a blue line even darker than Erin's had been.

"Oh God, Danny, won't this ever end? Please tell me you went to bed with someone," Erin begged, desperate but knowing the answer before she voiced the question. *As if she would.*

"Of course not. No. It's HIS!" Sheridan's words rose in pitch until she was nearly screaming.

"Oh shit." Erin dropped to her haunches and drew her friend into her arms.

"Why would God do this to me? It's not fair!" Sheridan wailed.

"You're right, it's not," Erin agreed. *Oh, please, not this. Anything but this.* "Can I do anything?"

"Get me some water, please," Sheridan whimpered.

"Okay. I'll be right back," she promised, squeezing her friend's shoulder before she padded down the stairs and along the hallway towards the kitchen. Midway there, she changed her mind and turned down the hall that led to Sheridan's parents' bedroom. "Roger, Ellen, please wake up," she urged softly, knocking on the open door.

"What is it, Erin?" Ellen asked, sitting up, instantly alert.

"It's Danny. She's bad. She needs you."

"What's wrong?" Roger asked in a slurred, sleepy voice.

"She's upstairs in the bathroom. Please come."

Alarmed, they hurried to their daughter. Erin didn't want to intrude, so she continued to the kitchen and slowly poured a glass of water. By the time she made it back up, she could see the truth had been revealed. In the hallway outside the bathroom, the three sat on the floor, Ellen holding her daughter and rocking while Roger had a hand on each woman's shoulder. Erin set the water on the floor beside them and returned to her room. Even though the clock beside the bed read 12:47am, she called Sean.

"Hello? Baby is that you?" he asked, his voice thick with sleep and sexy.

I love talking to him when he first wakes up. "Yeah." The word emerged as a choked whimper.

"What's up?"

"I feel sad and I wanted to hear your voice. I'm sorry I woke you." *I can't tell him this over the phone. It'll have to wait until morning.*

"It's okay, baby. I feel a little sad too. Here's this big empty bed and you're not in it." He yawned audibly.

Oh man, that sounds great. "I love you."

"I love you too. Go back to sleep, okay?" Sean urged.

"Okay, good night."

* * *

Sean arrived around ten the next morning. Erin met him outside and smuggled him quickly into his old room before anyone could see them. She wrapped her arms around his neck and he held her gently.

"Something's up, Erin. What's going on?"

"Kiss me."

He pressed his lips to hers. She clung to him, drawing strength from the warmth of his arms around her. Finally, she ended the embrace and from the cradle of his arms said sadly, "Danny's pregnant. That asshole knocked her up."

Sean reacted as though he'd been hit. His body rocked backwards from the shock. "Oh my God. Do Mom and Dad know?"

"Yes," she admitted, and then sniffled. "She found out last night. She got really sick, and that's how she realized."

Sean struggled visibly with his composure, his throat convulsing. Finally, he gritted out, "This just isn't right. Why does she have to suffer so much?"

"I don't understand it. This, I get." She gestured towards her belly. "We did this to ourselves, but why Danny?"

"I don't know. Damn it. I just don't know." He hugged Erin tight, his breathing harsh and ragged.

"I have to get back to the food in a moment," she said. "I don't want anything to burn, but, please can you kiss me one more time?"

"Food? What do you mean?" Sean stared at her, blinking, one eyebrow lifted in confusion.

"No one felt like cooking, so I'm doing my best. Your mom showed me a whole bunch of things, and all the recipes are sitting on the counter. It'll probably be terrible."

Sean's confusion warmed to a sad smile. "You're really the most amazing girl. I would love to put a big, sparkly diamond on your finger right now and show everyone."

"You could any time you want. I hate pretending."

"Do you want to tell them about us now?" Sean suggested. "We can. It's not going to be a secret much longer anyway."

"Yes," Erin agreed, "but not today. Today has been hard enough."

"You're right. Come here, baby." He kissed her hard. In some indefinable way, his lips on hers seemed to invigorate her flagging strength. Even in the face of unimaginable trauma, a glow of hope flared to life in Erin's heart. She clung to him another endless moment, drawing as much strength as she could from the impossible gift of Sean's love, then slipped reluctantly out of his arms and returned to the kitchen.

* * *

Later that evening the family gathered in the living room and she played for them, hoping to distract them and earning herself a measure of solace as well. She managed to lose herself in her music and forget the overwhelming problems they all faced. After the impromptu concert, Erin put her oboe away.

"Family conference in the den," Roger informed her.

"Don't worry, I'll stay out of the way," she promised, and then glanced his direction to see his head tilted in confusion.

"Sheridan specifically requested you be part of it," he informed her. "And besides, it's a family conference. I'm pretty sure you're family."

Erin's eyes stung. She couldn't make herself work through the implications, so she deliberately blanked her mind, ran her oboe back up to her room, and entered the den, perching on the fireplace hearth. From there, she had a perfect view across the room to Sean, sprawled beside his sister against the arm of the sofa. The urge to go to him and snuggle up almost broke Erin's resistance, but she restrained herself.

"Mom, Dad, I hope you're not planning to cancel your shopping day tomorrow," Sheridan told her parents firmly. "Nothing is different from this time yesterday; I just understand more. I know how much you both look forward to this. I want you to do it."

"That's sweet, dear, but I hate to leave you," Mrs. Murphy replied, clearly building herself up to admitting she wasn't going anywhere.

"I won't do anything drastic, I swear," Sheridan assured her mother. "I need time to process this, and I want to think without anyone hovering over me. I don't know why this had to happen, but there's no point dwelling on the past. The thing to do is move forward, but I have to decide what moving forward means."

"Danny," Erin said softly, "I know how you feel about... abortion, but no one would blame you under these circumstances."

Sheridan's face contorted, and Erin knew her friend's soul was hurting, twisted as it was with unanswerable questions. "I know, but I always said people should think about adoption too. I want to do what's right, and I need time to think. *Alone!*"

Erin accepted Sheridan's comments with a dip of the chin. "Okay. You know, I don't have anywhere to go tomorrow. I'll stay here if you want. I promise I won't bother you, but at least if you... need someone, I'll be in the house."

"That would make me feel a lot better, Erin," Ellen told her.

"I'll come over too," Sean offered. "In fact, I'm staying the night. I can't hang out in my apartment and watch football while my family goes through hard times. I'll crash in Jason's room."

He gave Erin a quick glance. *I know what he's telling me. He's worried about his sister, but he's also worried about my ability to handle everything. I'll definitely need his support.*

"Ellen, we should go," Roger told his wife. "It's fifteen minutes away, not in another country."

"But what if there's an emergency..." Ellen started, fretful mother mode fully activated.

"I'm not a baby," Sheridan insisted. "I'm still seventeen and old enough to stay home for the morning while my parents shop. I promise not to throw any last-minute parties." Her tone held enough bite to turn her joke into something darker. No one laughed.

"I'll lend you my cell phone," Erin volunteered, digging the device out of her pocket and crossing the room to offer it to them.

"You see," Roger said, accepting the phone. "If there's an emergency, Sean or Erin can call. We won't be out of touch for a moment. Sheridan is almost an adult, and she has to make this decision for herself. Stop hovering."

Sheridan sniffled a broken sob.

Enough talk. Erin turned and shuffled across the polished wooden floor, plunking onto the sofa between Sheridan and Sean. She drew her friend into a hug. Sheridan squeezed her so tight that, for a moment, she couldn't breathe. "Tell me what you need, and I'll do it for you," she whispered in her friend's ear.

"Just be here," Sheridan said. "I don't know what I need except that I need you."

"Always."

* * *

That night, Erin struggled to relax. It wasn't the sorrow over Sheridan's crisis pregnancy that interrupted her sleep. It was the knowledge that Sean, her beautiful perfect Sean, lay on the other side of the wall. Her body screamed at her to go to him.

It had been a while since they had been alone together, and she really wanted to make love... now!

She tried to restrain herself, knowing Sheridan's parents didn't want her having sex in their house. She didn't want to abuse their hospitality, but she felt like she was on fire.

Bedsprings squeaked on the other side of the wall. A door opened, and Erin's breath caught. *Maybe he's going to the bathroom. Don't assume anything.*

The handle on the bedroom door turned, and Sean's muscular frame filled the opening, clad only in a pair of black shorts. He closed the door, moving on silent feet across the carpet, and climbed into the bed beside her, taking her in his arms.

"I love you, Erin," he breathed against her ear, "and I need you right now. How quiet can you be?"

"As quiet as I need to be, to have you with me," she whispered in response.

His mouth came down on hers in an endless, tender kiss while his fingers busily opened the buttons of her pajama top. Never releasing her mouth, he slid the garment from her shoulders and pressed her against him so her small breasts rubbed on his chest. Her hands slid inside the waistband of his shorts, lowering them so she could touch the silky skin of his lower back, and so his erection could press enticingly against her belly. She sighed with pleasure. *Sex with Sean is one of the greatest joys in my life.*

He ended the kiss and she protested softly, trying to cling to him. In the darkness, she saw the flash of his teeth as he grinned at her eagerness. He grasped her pajama bottoms and she lifted her hips, so he could pull them from her. Then she lay back on the bed, nude and spread out before him, her dark hair spilling over the pillows.

* * *

Sean gazed down at his beloved. *Her beauty is so arousing.* Then more details registered, and he frowned. *She should be getting rounder. She's almost three months pregnant after all, but instead, she's thinner than ever.* He could see each rib, even in the darkness of the room, and her hip bones stood out in sharp relief. *The strain of her own problems and my family's must be too much for her to bear. I'll have to help her get back in balance, starting tomorrow. It's not good for her or the baby to be so malnourished.* But nothing could be done about it tonight, and the desire had grown volcanic between them.

He quickly shucked his shorts and knelt between her thighs, leaning over her to caress and fondle her nipples. Erin's breath caught. As always, she responded eagerly to his gentle touches. He leaned forward to kiss and suckle first one straining peak and then the other before kissing his way down her belly, lower until his mouth pressed against her intimate flesh. He parted those lips with his tongue and began to tease her clitoris.

* * *

Erin had to concentrate hard on her breathing, keeping it silent as Sean went down on her. It was one of the most intense sensations she had ever experienced, and it just kept building higher, especially when he slid two fingers inside her. A soft sound escaped, and she brought her hand to her mouth, biting her knuckle in an attempt not to scream as she neared orgasm. One more firm lick sent her over the edge. She panted but held in her cry as pleasure rocked her. Before the spasms died away, Sean's fingers withdrew, and he quickly replaced them with his sex. Drenched and ready for him, her body relaxed, allowing him easy entry. He plunged deep, fast, sealing his mouth over hers to prevent her making a sound.

Even though they had made love so often over the last couple of months, Sean remained a little too big for Erin, and normally entered her slowly, but tonight there was no time. *He needs me*, she realized, and he took what he needed, hard and fast, driving recklessly into her.

If it hadn't been for his mouth on hers, Erin would have awakened the whole house. Sean's powerful thrusting hurt a little at first, but as she adjusted, it began to feel amazing. She had never been so full before, not just in her body, stretched to its limit, but in her heart. She had never been well-loved until Sean, and she adored him beyond any limits. She had no doubt that despite his talk of marriage, their relationship would end someday. She simply wasn't interesting enough to keep him forever, but she would have him now, tonight. And in the future, she would have his child, a little piece of him that was hers forever, and it was enough.

The flames of Erin's desire increased, burning her up, bringing her to another hard, wild climax that bowed her body. Her back arched, pressing Sean even deeper inside her and he growled softly against her lips as he let go, allowing his own pleasure to reach its peak.

It took many minutes for them to calm down from a loving so intense. Finally, the pounding of their hearts quieted, and their breathing returned to normal.

"Did I hurt you?" Sean whispered in Erin's ear.

"No. It was amazing," she replied under her breath. "Do you have to leave right away?"

"I would love to hold you all night," he breathed, his expression filled with tenderness, "but that really isn't the way I want to tell them about us."

"I know."

"I'll stay until you're sleeping, okay, baby?"

Perfect. "That would be great."

They cuddled together. At last, Erin relaxed enough to let sleep claim her.

* * *

On the far side of the wall, Sheridan also lay awake. She had heard every soft sound and knew exactly what it meant. Despite her own convictions, she didn't begrudge her brother and best friend their pleasure. *It sounded... interesting: wild, sweet, and comforting. I don't know if I will ever heal enough to want to sleep with a man, but Sean and Erin give me hope that someday I might.*

Chapter 10

♪

Erin woke late the next morning and discovered to her surprise that she lay nude under the covers. *Guess I forgot that part, but it was so warm and comfortable in his arms, skin to skin.* She grinned and then quickly pulled her pajamas back on and headed to the bathroom. She felt a little uncomfortable this morning, with a twinge in her belly. *That was some really wild loving last night.* Her grin turned to a smirk. *It isn't bad having sex so powerful you can still feel it the next day. I really need to pee, though, which is nothing new these days.* She also felt strangely wet. *Of course, it's not surprising. It must just be Sean's semen running down my thigh.* She lowered her pants and glanced down. A red streak had already trickled halfway to her knee.

She sat down quickly on the toilet, not wanting to get blood on the floor. "Sean!" she called.

There was a knock on the door. "Erin, are you all right?" Sheridan asked, knocking on the door.

"Get Sean, please, Danny," Erin begged.

"Okay."

A moment later Sean appeared outside the door. "Erin, what's going on?"

"I'm bleeding," she moaned, hunching over, clutching her cramping belly.

He entered the room, and his expression turned to dismay as he saw the blood she had already passed into the toilet. "What's happening?"

Erin sucked in several deep breaths, trying not to panic. "I don't know. I need to call the clinic emergency line. Please get me my purse and the cordless phone."

He returned within moments and Erin quickly fished out a business card, so she could dial the call center. She explained her situation and was transferred to the labor and delivery desk at the hospital.

"Hello? What can I do for you?" a calm, soothing female voice spoke into the phone.

"I'm about ten weeks pregnant. This morning I started bleeding." She could hear the frantic note in her own tone.

"How bad is it?" the voice asked.

Think, Erin. Try to stay rational. "Like a heavy period." A sharp pain gripped her, and she moaned. Sean placed his hand on the back of her neck.

"Do you have cramping too?"

"Yes. It hurts pretty bad." Erin rubbed her belly in slow circles.

"Okay, it sounds like you're having a miscarriage," the woman said.

Miscarriage? Erin's attempt not to panic collapsed. Her breath came in wild pants and her fists clenched. "Oh, God. What do I do?"

The voice didn't lose one iota of calm. "There's nothing to do, really. Just wait it out. It shouldn't take long. I know it's scary, but this isn't an emergency. There's no reason for you to come to the hospital for it. Are you alone?"

"No." She gripped Sean's free hand in hers and squeezed hard. "My boyfriend is here, and a friend also."

"That's good. Okay, basically, just go with it unless you start bleeding really heavily, like more than one maxi pad's worth every half hour, or if you feel faint. Then have someone drive you over here quick… but that probably won't happen."

A horrible thought occurred to Erin. "Did I cause this? We had sex last night."

"No, you didn't," the anonymous voice reassured her. "Sex during pregnancy is safe. This was going to happen anyway."

"Are you sure?" *Oh God, please don't let me have hurt my baby!*

"Yes. Listen, once it's over, you need to bring in… whatever you deliver to the clinic. We need to examine it and make sure nothing was left behind, because that can cause infection."

"Okay." Erin sucked in air, waiting for the next comment, but the phone went dead. *That's it? That's all the support I get? Oh, God.*

She lifted her eyes and saw Sean hovering over her, his face contorted with worry. "What is it, baby?"

Erin sniffled. "I'm miscarrying. There's nothing they can do. They said just to wait it out here."

"Really?" He looked as appalled as she felt, his mouth turning down and eyebrows drawing together.

"Yeah. I can't believe it." Erin whimpered in distress. Whirling thoughts transformed into tight shoulders and jaw, and the ache in her belly ratcheted up to a new level.

Sean moved to lay his hands on Erin's shoulders. Sheridan stood nearby trying to support her friend with her presence.

Erin breathed slowly through increasing pressure that twisted her belly, and all the while a constant prayer, like a litany, repeated in her mind. *God, please, don't take my baby. Please don't take him.* And yet the pains continued, drawing her closer minute by minute to the inevitable conclusion.

About an hour later, she felt a popping sensation and a gush of fluid, followed by a strong pressure. She pushed and something large lodged itself inside her vagina. She pushed again and delivered into her hands a mass of bloody tissue about the size of an apple. She regarded the gruesome object, revolted, before curiosity compelled her to turn it over. A sharp cry of disbelief forced its way out of her as the movement revealed a tiny, mostly formed human about the size of Sean's thumb. It had a head and body, eyes, and arms and legs with hands and feet. She could recognize the beginnings of fingers and toes. It lay limp and completely still.

Erin bit her lip at the sight of her baby. *You're so perfect. Why do you have to be dead?* A tear slid down her cheek as she realized, finally, what she'd been privileged to hold, and what she'd lost.

"Is that what I have inside me too?" Sheridan breathed. "Okay, I know what I have to do now." She fled to her room and shut the door.

Sean had been silent up to this point. His face showed the devastation she felt. "Did I do this? I was so rough with you last night."

"No, Sean, you didn't. I asked, and the nurse said it was going to happen anyway. Us having sex right before was a coincidence. We need to take… this… to the hospital to be sure it's intact, okay?" She indicated what she held; the loss of all their dreams fit in the palm of her hand.

He gulped and met her eyes. "How are you going to go anywhere? You're still bleeding."

"I know. Can you please get me some clothes?"

He did, and she reluctantly handed him the baby, with its unpleasant mass of placenta, so she could clean up and dress. *Thank goodness there are maxi pads under the sink.* She grabbed the overnight size and hoped for the best.

Sean stared at his dead child as Erin pulled on her jeans and sweater. She could see how he struggled to take it in. *We both made peace with this pregnancy, with what it would mean for us. Look at him grieving. He wanted this little one as much as I did.* The sight of Sean's devastation clenched Erin's heart tighter. *What are we going to do now?*

* * *

At the clinic, a kind nurse practitioner examined.

"This amount of bleeding is normal," she said, "and the fetus and placenta are intact. No tissue left behind."

Erin accepted the information with a dull nod.

"Do you have any idea why...?" Sean started, and then lapsed back into silence.

"These things happen, hon, and we usually don't know why. Something about this pregnancy went wrong, probably in the division of cells. Chances are, down the road, you'll be able to conceive and carry a child again with no complications."

I don't want another child. I want this one. Tears stalked Erin, but she fought them down. *Soon I'll have to let go, but not yet. Not here.* "What's next?"

"You'll need to come back in a week for a blood test," the nurse practitioner informed her. "And another the week after that. If in that time your hormones normalize – which they almost certainly will – you'll be just fine. I don't suspect you'll have any problems."

Her upbeat tone made Erin want to hit her. *Don't you know I'll never be fine again? That I'll never return to what I thought was normal?*

"You know," the nurse told the young couple gently, "this is probably for the best, especially for you, Erin. You're too young to deal with a pregnancy. Please be more careful in the future. You're not ready to be a parent."

But I was ready, she fought down the agonized cry. *I was ready, willing, even excited.* She felt shattered, broken pieces of Erin poised to fall all over the floor. "Can I get on the pill?" she asked, climbing carefully down from the examining table and seating herself on a chair. *I don't want this to happen ever again.* Sean took her hand.

"You can't yet," the nurse explained. "If everything is fine after your second blood test in two weeks, then you can. I don't suppose I have to tell you not to have sex again before the bleeding stops?"

"Of course not," Sean said. "I wouldn't even ask it of her."

The checkup concluded, Sean and Erin returned to his Mustang and he bundled her in. The cold of late November clawed her flesh through her sweater. The air smelled of impending snow, of winter bearing down on them like a white-fleshed monster. Sean drove in silence, a silence Erin felt no inclination to break. Back at the house, she exited the car without a word and without waiting for Sean to help her. As they climbed up the stairs, Sheridan poked her head out of her room, and then quickly withdrew it, shutting the door again.

"It still hurts," she said, her hand flat on her belly. "I want to lie down."

"Of course." Sean tucked her into his bed and lay beside her, holding her. It didn't take much time for her to break down and she cried quiet, endless tears in Sean's arms. He made no move to shush her, to cut off the flow of her misery. He remained still, silent and strong, like a rock that anchored her in place while her world shattered all around her.

Finally, the storm passed. Erin sniffled. "My God, this must be the worst senior year in the history of high school."

"I know," Sean agreed. "The nurse was right though. This really is for the best. You can go to college where you want now." He stroked his fingers over her arm as he spoke, but his words, well-intended though they might have been, provoked rather than comforted.

She rolled over and glared. "I don't care about that. I want my baby back."

She instantly regretted her harsh tone as agony flashed in his eyes, but he continued trying to reason with her. "Later, when you're finished with your degree. If you still want a baby then, I promise to give you one, okay?"

She didn't answer. *That's a long time from now.*

* * *

By midafternoon, Erin decided to stop feeling sorry for herself. *There's still a lot going on, and I need to act normal. Besides, the Murphys will probably be home soon and I really don't want them to find me in bed with Sean. They've been through enough.* She dreaded their return because it meant he wouldn't be able to hold her. The thought brought fresh tears to her eyes.

She showered, and then constructed a sandwich out of the leftover turkey. Eating it made her feel marginally better.

Roger and Ellen returned to the house about an hour after that, quickly carrying bags into their bedroom to hide them. At that point Sheridan emerged, her eyes red, but her face composed.

"Can you all come into the living room please," she asked solemnly. They trailed after her like lost ducklings. *Or at least, that's how I feel,* Erin thought as she perched in the armchair.

"I know what I need to do," Sheridan announced, leaning her back against the wall beside the sofa, "and I hope to have everyone's support. I'm going to have this baby, but I'm not going to keep it. This is no situation for a child to grow up in. I'm going to find a family to adopt my baby. It's the right thing to do."

"Are you sure that's what you want, Danny?" Erin asked.

Sheridan gave her a long, speaking look. She fell silent.

"Of course, dear. I agree that's probably best," Ellen said, "and we do support you."

Roger nodded.

Chapter 11

"F sharp, not natural, dummy," Erin muttered to herself, setting her oboe on her lap and making an ostentatious circle on her music with a dull pencil. "You'll sound like the big, smart musician if you can't even handle a simple accidental."

She lifted the instrument to her mouth and played the offending phrase correctly five times, to offset the mistake and re-establish a memory of doing it right. *The Murphys are incredibly patient with the sounds of oboe music coming from the upstairs bedroom by the hour. My own parents would have been howling by now. Guess they're busy with Sheridan... she said she was meeting with some prospective adoptive parents. She sure has thrown her heart and all her brains into finding that baby the perfect family.* Erin tried to imagine such a thing and failed. *It's completely different,* she reminded herself. *And it makes a lot of sense to do it this way. She's stronger than I ever knew.*

Shaking her head, Erin packed up the oboe. A fine trembling had begun in the tips of her fingers, but she ignored it. *Oboe. Check. Music. Check. Lunch. Check. Note for the Murphys...* Gathering up her supplies, she made her way down to the kitchen, found the ever-present notepad beside the phone, and wrote, *Dear Ellen, I have the All-State Audition today, so I'll be gone this afternoon, and I have a date as well. I'll see you at curfew. Erin.*

Satisfied that she'd handled everything correctly, she retrieved her lunch from the refrigerator, made visual confirmation of all her pieces again, and made her way out to her car, opening the trunk. *The music is hard, but I've got it. I actually feel pretty confident about it.* Her trembling had increased, calling her statement into question, but she ignored it. *Stage fright is a facet of my life forever. Might as well get used to it. Especially with that very interesting bit of mail I got yesterday. I can't wait to tell Sean.*

She circled the car and opened the driver door. *I'm feeling pretty good overall, actually. No more bleeding, my hormones are normal, and I'm on the pill.* She grinned to herself. *Even if I blow the audition, this still has the makings of an excellent night.*

She cranked the key in the ignition and the grumpy beast sputtered and protested. "Come on, don't be a jerk," Erin pleaded, trying again. The ignition fired, and she drove off to the high school to catch the bus to the audition site.

* * *

That afternoon found Sean puttering around, tidying up his apartment while he waited for Erin. *She's supposed to arrive soon. Can't be too much of a slob for her.* He tossed beer cans from the sturdy, serviceable coffee table into the trash, added an empty pizza box, and swept the chilly white tile floor. *I wonder how she's healing.* A soft sound alerted him to Erin's key turning in the lock of his apartment door, and she entered, her lovely face glowing. She looked happier than he had seen her since homecoming night, when they were in bed together.

He gathered her into his arms. "Hey, beautiful baby," he said, pressing a soft kiss on her upturned mouth, "how did the audition go?"

"It went fine," she said, her tone coolly neutral.

I wonder what that means. "Did you get in?"

She lingered a moment, savoring the anticipation. "Yes. I made first chair!"

She explained this to me once. The lower the chair number, the better. He blinked, not surprised, but overjoyed. *My gorgeous girl has just been voted the best high school oboe player in the entire state. Wow.* "Congratulations, Erin. You deserve it."

A broad smile spread across her face. "There's more, too. Can we sit down for a minute?"

"Sure." They walked hand in hand to the sofa and sat. Erin leaned on Sean's chest and he cuddled her close, toying with the ends of her hair and enjoying her shivers. Her warmth turned him on and he cursed their forced celibacy for the thousandth time. "So, what's up?"

"I got some interesting mail yesterday," she explained, grasping his free hand and tracing the lines on his palm with her fingertip. "First, I got a letter from that school in Texas. I was accepted! It's a really big deal, you know."

Her words stopped him dead, his hand falling away from her back to rest beside him on the sofa. "So, you're going then?" The thought felt like a knife in his gut.

"Hold on, I'm not finished!" Erin laced her fingers through his. "I did a little research and found out something I hadn't realized. That conservatory is crazy expensive. They offered me a scholarship, but a pretty small one. Everyone there is that good. To attend would cost me thirty thousand dollars... a year. I could buy a small house for the cost of those four years of tuition. Sean, there's no way I want to go into that kind of debt."

Sean lowered his eyebrows. *Wow, that is expensive. Who can afford schools like that?*

Erin continued speaking. "Classical musicians don't get paid *that* well. I would be making payments until I die. I'm honored to be accepted, but I'm not going to Texas. That's where the other letter I got comes in. I was accepted to State months ago, but they just informed me they're giving me a free ride. Think about it, Sean. College I don't have to pay a cent for. They're covering tuition, housing, even books, just so long as I pursue a double reed performance major there and keep my grades up.

There's no way I can turn that down. I'm going to State." She beamed.

He relaxed, relieved she would be staying close. "That's great, baby. I'm glad your answer was so clear. I wanted you to go to Texas because it would be good for you, but I'm not sorry you'll be nearby." Conflicting thoughts crowded his mind and one burst out before he had time to reflect on it. "Erin, do you still want us to... stay together while you're in college?"

Her mouth dropped open at the unexpected question. "Yes, don't you?"

"Of course."

A tornado of emotions twisted her face to one expression and then another. Her eyes widened to huge, haunted chocolate pools and a frown pulled her plump lips downward. "Why are you asking this? I thought we were forever."

She sounds... desperate, terrified. Damn, what was I thinking asking a question like that? "That was my intention, my desire," he insisted, trying to reassure her.

"Was?"

Wrong again. Damn it, Murphy, think. Speak more carefully. "Is, Erin. Calm down." He hastened to explain, stroking her fingers to try to soothe her. "It is my intention. I just had to be sure you still... wanted this, now that there isn't going to be a baby, and you're going away to school, and all."

Erin sat up and turned, meeting his eyes with the same intensity he saw there when she played her oboe. "Sean, I love you. I plan to spend as much time with you as possible, even though I won't be living here anymore. Once I finish that degree, I'm coming right back here to you, if you'll still have me."

"What will you do here?" he asked, probing to understand her thoughts.

"Play in the symphony and teach oboe and maybe bassoon lessons," she replied without reflection.

She's thought about this before, he realized. *A lot, by the sound of it.* "What about your career?" he asked, still digging. *Dad said not to let her give up her dreams. I don't want her to do that.*

"That is my career. That's what I want."

That can't be right. She just placed first in the state, and she wants to teach oboe lessons here in Nowhereville? "I pictured you in some high-powered program, maybe in New York or L.A., traveling, making recordings, all that stuff."

Erin wrinkled her nose. "No, I never needed to be famous. I just want to play my instrument... and be with you, of course. That sounds like a perfect life to me."

Sean didn't argue with her that such small dreams were a waste of her considerable talent. *She's the best, a truly high caliber musician. I love her too much to hold her back forever. She needs to live her dreams in a big way, and I will not stand in the way. She doesn't realize she needs it yet, but she'll understand later, when her accomplishments start piling up. When that time comes, I'll have to try hard to let her go graciously. It's what she needs to do, and I love her too much to keep her in this small town with so few opportunities. I've been blessed to have known Erin, loved and held her, for this short time. And for now, I'll make the most of every moment. Eventually, she'll leave, and I won't try to make her stay.*

The thought hurt, tore at his insides as badly as the miscarriage had, and a small, selfish part of him clung to the idea she'd refuse. *Maybe I can keep her after all.* He trailed his fingers over her cheek. She covered his hand with hers. Heat flared. *Enough talk. You should be kissing your girl, congratulating her success, not asking hard, heavy questions. We don't have so many days left until she leaves. I hope she'll heal soon.* He did want to put the mark of his love on her heart, body and memory so she would always remember him fondly.

* * *

I wonder what Sean is thinking so hard. He looks almost grim. In order to erase the little frown from his face, she scrambled into his lap and kissed him for all she was worth.

"Easy, Erin," he told her, smiling, but the sadness in his eyes turned the grin to a grimace. "You can have all you want. You don't have to fight for it."

"I want more. Can we please go to bed?" One hand slipped down his torso to scratch enticingly on the muscles of his lower belly.

"Are you sure?"

"Yes. Everything is fine, I'm not bleeding, my hormones are normal and I'm on the pill. I'm totally ready for a good time. Would you like to show me one?" She rubbed up against him with a sexy little shimmy.

"Oh, baby, would I!"

He scooped her into his arms and carried her to his bed, where he proceeded to make love to her for so long, she was nearly late getting home.

* * *

For a year that had begun so badly, the second half went much better, at least for Erin. The All-State concert was a rousing success, and even featured a small oboe solo for the first chair player. Sean went to hear her, which really warmed her heart. Warmed the rest of her too, later, when he showed her how much he had enjoyed listening to her play.

The rest of the time she studied, did homework, played her instrument at the high school and the symphony and spent every possible moment with her boyfriend. They started being seen out in public, no longer caring if people knew. Too much had gone on between them to worry if the odd person looked askance. They didn't tell Sean's parents though. The time never seemed right, not when the difficult situation with their daughter just kept lingering on and on.

Sheridan eventually settled on a family she wanted to adopt her baby; a lovely couple in their mid-thirties named Christine and William Potter. Erin hoped Sheridan would be able to recover from all the trauma eventually, though she knew it wouldn't be soon. At least knowing the baby would be safe and well cared for should help... a little.

Erin returned home quite late one Friday just before spring break. She'd had rehearsal after school, and then a date with Sean, and so naturally, she felt quite relaxed and content, a hint of a smile lingering around her mouth. The clock in the Mustang, after she'd received her final goodbye kiss, had read 11:52, so she locked the front door and hurried to the family room to let the Murphys know she had returned on time. She knocked and entered to see Mrs. Murphy sitting on the sofa with her arms around her daughter. Sheridan had her face buried in her mother's shoulder, her whole body shaking.

Erin ran right to them and embraced them both, her happy mood dissolving into concern. "What's wrong?" she asked.

Sheridan couldn't speak, so Mrs. Murphy answered, her voice bleak. "We got some bad news from the attorney. In order for the adoption to be legal, both birth parents have to sign a termination of parental rights. They sent the paperwork to Jake, but..."

"He's refusing to sign?" Erin guessed. Sheridan nodded against her mother's shoulder. "But why? Does he want the baby?"

"No. Not at all," Ellen replied with a pained sigh. "His attorney says he won't sign unless the charges against him are dropped. Since he's known to be the father of the child, if he doesn't sign, the adoption won't be legal."

"Hell with him," Erin said bluntly. "There has to be some way to terminate his rights without his signature. He's a criminal. Surely under these circumstances..."

"No." Sheridan sobbed the word rather than spoke it. "What if he's acquitted? He could cause trouble for her and the Potters.

He could take her away at any time." She placed her hand to the side of her swollen belly.

"Oh, sweetie, I'm so sorry. It's just terrible. What are you going to do?" She rubbed her hand up and down on Sheridan's back.

"This is so hard, damn it," Sheridan mumbled, her words almost indistinguishable.

Ellen made a face at the curse but didn't protest.

"If it were me," Erin said fiercely, "I would tell him to go to hell. Take your chances. You have a strong case. You can win. He belongs in prison for what he did."

"I know, and what if he does this to someone else..." Sheridan choked, then took a deep breath. "But how can I risk my daughter this way? She didn't ask for this. She needs to have the best future. That won't be with Jake or living under the threat of him taking her. She needs to live in peace with the Potters."

"You're not seriously considering dropping the charges? My God, Danny."

"It's done," Ellen said grimly. "The charges were dropped this afternoon. It's over."

"Oh no!" Erin cried, squeezing the other women again. *It's just so unfair. Can nothing, not even one thing, ever go right for poor Sheridan?*

* * *

The first week of June, robed in blue polyester gowns, nearly buried in cords for academic honors and the National Honor Society stoles, Erin and Sheridan crossed the stage that had been erected in the football stadium and received their diplomas. The Murphy parents and their son cheered loudly for both girls. The James parents were conspicuously absent at the graduation of their only child.

Later, after the ceremony, the girls put their arms around each other and posed, cheek to cheek, smiling hugely, so Roger Murphy could take their picture.

"High school is over," Erin sighed with relief. *Life can finally begin. Thank God.*

Sheridan nodded. "I can't wait to get out of this town. One summer and we're off to bigger and better things."

The Murphy parents' grins froze in grimaces. *Oops. This must be hard for them. Still, I'm ready for adult life to start. I hope they can adjust to an empty nest.*

"So, what's going on this evening?" Ellen asked, changing the subject. "I assume there's some kind of celebration."

"The high school is hosting an overnight party at the country club," Erin explained. "I plan on going." She swallowed hard, eyes skating away as the lie cut into her insides. "Call my cell if there's an emergency."

"Not me," Sheridan said firmly. "I'm going home. My feet hurt, and the thought of playing silly party games with these gawking goons doesn't excite me." When her parents turned their backs, she pursed her lips at Erin.

She won't go because I'm not going, Erin thought with another twinge of guilt. Then her friend began pushing her fist into her back. "Sore?" Erin asked.

Sheridan nodded. "Everything hurts. I think I just want to go to bed. Mom, Dad, can we get out of here?"

"Of course," Roger agreed. "See you in the morning, Erin."

Erin waved goodbye. As soon as the MC&R pickup disappeared around the corner, she drove to Sean's apartment. Instead of partying, she spent her graduation night in bed, but not alone, of course. Sean made love to her again and again until she felt quite certain she would never be able to get up. In between, they cuddled close. The time for heavy conversations was over. All the plans had been made, and the couple, knowing they faced years of separation, clung frantically to the few waning moments they had left to be together. It had taken the whole school year, but Erin finally believed Sean actually loved her, almost as much, perhaps, as she loved him. She had never expected this and savored it. The best part of the evening was actually not the sex at all, even though it had been tremendously pleasurable, as always. The best part was when Sean pulled Erin close to his chest and they both went to sleep, spending the entire night together for the first time since the very beginning of their relationship. *If I can sleep beside this man for the rest of my life, I'll never want anything more.*

* * *

Sheridan spent her evening alone in her bed, touching her belly and wishing things were different. She had long since stopped being angry about this pregnancy and now wanted to memorize every sensation of her daughter moving inside her body.

"Little girl," she said tenderly, "I'm not sorry you're here." A foot pressed against her hand, and she smiled sadly. "I know you may never understand this, but I'm not giving you up because I don't want you. You are wanted. You are loved. They told me I could help name you, and we agreed that you will be called Desirée, because there's never been a baby more wanted than you. I wish I could keep you, I really do. It's going to kill me to hand you to the Potters." Her voice broke. "I have to do it, you know. It's what's best for you. Christine will be your mommy, and William will be your daddy, and you'll have a wonderful life. I can't give you that life by myself." Her voice broke again and this time a tear slid down her cheek. "There are hard things here, little Desirée, things I hope you never know, about how you came to be. They don't matter, but I don't want them to hurt you. I don't want anything to hurt you. So, I have to let you go. I have to because I love you."

A tiny limb pressed against her palm in what seemed like a response. Sheridan touched that foot, and the other, and felt the life inside her, and wept long into the night.

* * *

At the end of June, just after her eighteenth birthday, Sheridan went into labor and delivered a healthy baby girl. Both Ellen and Christine supported her during the delivery. She returned home from the hospital the next day, completely devastated.

Erin met her inside the door and took her arm. She looked pale and shaky. "This is worse than the rape," she said bleakly. Instead of attempting the stairs, she opened the door to the tiny guest room and sank onto the bed. She lay unmoving, staring at a wall, her breathing ragged while one tear chased another down her cheek to disappear into the pillow.

Erin had no idea how to help her friend. *The loss of my pregnancy was excruciating, but this is just as bad.* Eventually, she did what Sheridan had done for her when she was upset. She lay beside her on the bed and held her by the hour, while Sheridan cried and cried until she fell asleep. Ellen sat beside the bed on a chair, holding her daughter's hand and stroking her hair. Eventually, Erin dozed a little too, exhausted by her friend's misery.

Later, when Erin woke, she found Ellen had gone. Sheridan lay staring at the wall, finally all cried out. "I can't do it, Erin," she said, her voice disturbingly blank.

"Can't do what, sweetie?" Erin asked, rolling her shoulders to try to work out a crick in her neck.

"Can't go to college. I don't see any way that I can handle it. I'm just devastated. How would I even begin to concentrate on classes?" Sheridan sighed, her breath catching a half-dozen times on a single exhalation.

Uh oh. This isn't good. "I'll help you. I'll be there. Remember, we're going to be roommates? I'll be with you every day. You'll get through."

Slowly Sheridan turned her head to the left and then to the right. "It's too much. I won't even ask it of you. You have so much to live for, and I feel like my life is over."

Erin felt panic creeping in. *I can't let Sheridan talk this way.* "That's a lie, Danny. Your life is just starting. Eventually, somehow, you'll heal from this, and be better than ever, stronger. Don't give up, okay? And I'll help you. I'll take care of you. I want to. It's fine." She grasped Sheridan's arm. "We'll be fine. Danny, listen to me. You can't stay here. You have to get away from this town and its terrible memories and make a fresh start somewhere else." *You're babbling, slow down!*

"Is that what you're going to do?" Sheridan asked, and even her voice seemed to hurt. The girl winced every time she enunciated a letter.

"You know it's different for me," Erin replied, taking Sheridan's shoulder in her hand and willing her friend to understand. "I have to do this, so I can be whole, but I don't intend to stay gone forever. The only person who ever loved me is here. Once I finish school, I'm coming back to stay, but by then you'll be better. You'll be ready to stand on your own. And until then, you have me to help you, I swear. Be strong, Danny. You can do this. You have to."

Sheridan considered her friend's words in silence. At last, she said, "I don't know how I'm going to manage it, but I'll try. And you're wrong, Erin. Sean loves you, but he's not the only one who does. *I* love you. I would never have gotten through this miserable, shitty year without you."

The words drew sobs up from Erin's throat. She hid her swimming eyes in her friend's golden curls. The prospect of what lay ahead frightened her, and she would have to do it largely alone, without Sean to hold her and lend her his strength. *I've never been a strong person, and now I have to give everything I have, every day, without support. Please, God, let me be up to the challenge.*

* * *

Sheridan rubbed her friend's back. She knew what a terrible thing she was asking, far too much for anyone to expect. That Erin was willing to do it made her love this girl even more. *Could there ever have been a better friend? Someday, I'll find some way to express my gratitude to Erin. I'll have to think about what will make my friend truly happy.*

Chapter 12

Independence Day dawned bright and warm, a perfect day for outdoor activities, which was what the Murphys had planned. They started at noon with a cookout, grilling steaks and chicken, to be served with corn on the cob, potato salad, and cherry pie. After lunch, the elder Murphys, Erin, and Sheridan jumped into the MC&R pickup and drove to the municipal park for an afternoon and evening spent celebrating the holiday.

* * *

Jason Murphy, Sheridan's middle brother arrived to meet them. A journalism major, Jason had a fancy camera hanging around his neck for recording the festivities.

"Hiya, everyone," he said, tugging a strand of dark, gelled hair out of his eyes. Then he turned to Erin. She recoiled, making him want to tease her even more. *Such an easy target.*

"Good Lord, Erin," he drawled, staring at her, "you'd better cover your legs. The glare will shatter my camera lens."

Erin blushed.

"Shut up, Jase," Sean said, as he approached the family. "Leave Erin alone."

Jason glowered at his brother. Sean had never joined in teasing his sister and her friend, but he had never defended them before either. On the other hand, Sean's profession had shaped his body into an intimidating physique, bulky and strong. Slender, artistic Jason wouldn't stand a chance if his brother got really angry, so he turned away from Erin to Sheridan, planning to pester her instead. She sat on the blanket, looking despondent, her expression far away. Only two weeks after the delivery, her body remained distorted, bloated and miserable. He decided not to make fun of her but wandered off in search of candid shots of the crowd.

* * *

Erin sighed with relief. *Jason is such a hard man to know. He's always been a little mean, but since this situation with Danny, he's become much worse; angry, aggressive, and cruel. How strange.*

But he no longer hovered over them, and the family set up folding chairs for Mr. and Mrs. Murphy before sprawling on the blanket to watch the air show. As always, she felt a pang being close to Sean and not able to touch him. Erin ached to come clean with his parents about their relationship. *It's past time, and there's really no reason to keep it secret anymore.* Sean, however, seemed unwilling to take that step, and she deferred to his judgment.

A set of Vietnam-era bombers roared over the crowd. A pyrotechnics team on the ground set off a number of small explosions, mimicking machine gun fire as the two planes zoomed past each other with delicate precision, banking sharply before turning upside down overhead and returning to skim the ground again amid another volley of pseudo explosions. The crowd applauded and cheered, the noise drowned out by the roar of the heavy engine.

Erin glanced at Ellen and Roger, to see their gaze focused skyward. She changed positions, sprawling nonchalantly on her side, her head propped on one arm. The other she extended to where Sean sat and ran her fingers down his leg. He must have been looking at her, not at the planes, since he didn't jump at the touch. His fingertips brushed hers. He also shifted, sidling back a bit, and towards her. It still wasn't obvious they were trying to be close, but it did allow him to press his hand against her back.

The warmth of his fingers sank into her, soothing her nervous energy. His body blocked the view from his parents.

The bombers roared away, only to be replaced by a one-quarter scale remote control aircraft that zipped and hovered and skimmed inches above the ground before climbing into the sky and returning, tail down, nose up, held perfectly still. At last, it executed a feather-light landing and was packed away in preparation for a set of seven little jets that flew in formation, and then a solo aerobatic artist in a blue airplane. Act after act entertained the crowd while Sean sat close to his girlfriend, touching her, but not in a way that acknowledged their relationship.

At last, the air emptied, and the smoke dissipated. Sean pulled back from Erin as his parents retrieved the picnic basket from the car, and they ate sandwiches and carrots and drank sodas. Then Erin left the group and headed over to the bandstand where the symphony orchestra sat preparing to entertain the crowd, as the sun began to set, with patriotic and military tunes. As she played, Erin recounted in her mind how the afternoon had gone. *It's starting to bother me a lot that Ellen and Roger are in the dark about my relationship with Sean. It almost seems as though he's ashamed of me. He never acts that way, except where his parents are concerned. Okay, so maybe I'm on the young side, but so what? I'm legally an adult, no longer in high school. Is it really so bad that I'm his girlfriend? I love him. That has to count for something, doesn't it? And he loves me. I know he does.*

She was so deep in thought she missed the cut off and her oboe blared a half-beat too long. The conductor gave her a dirty look and she forced her mind back to the concert. *This is no time for ruminations.* Concentrating on the music, she managed to finish with no further errors, and then packed up her instrument and put it away under the back seat of Sean's Mustang, before returning to the blanket.

"Sure, you won't stay for the fireworks?" Sean asked his parents.

Ellen shook her head. "All that noise. You must have noticed by now I never bother with this part."

"I must be getting old," Roger added, "but the traffic gets to me more every year. Since your mother wants to leave now, I'll take her. You don't mind running the girls home, do you?"

Sean shrugged. "It's no problem."

Oh, goody, Erin thought. *Now we don't have to pretend anymore.*

Erin bid the departing parents goodbye with hugs and watched them wend their slow way to the parking lot. At last, the pickup disappeared, and Sean scooped Erin into a passionate embrace, his mouth coming down hard on hers for a devastating kiss. She kissed him back eagerly, twining her arms around his neck. *How I adore you. I could stay cradled forever in these arms and be happy.*

"Guys, stop," Sheridan said urgently. They released each other to see Jason approaching the blanket, a scowl on his face.

"What?" Sean asked his brother belligerently.

Jason shrugged and drawled, "Nothing. Hell of a show, that's all. You know, there are kids here."

"Shut up."

"Defensive much?" Jason shook his head and moved a messy strand of dark hair out of his eyes. "I never thought you'd be the sort to rob the cradle, Sean."

"Leave them alone, Jason," Sheridan told her brother in an exhausted voice.

"Humph. Why should I?" Jason demanded. His handsome face twisted into its habitual sarcastic smirk. "I don't get ammunition like that every day. How cliché, bro. The little sister's best friend? Seriously? Couldn't you do any better than that? Is she good, at least?"

"Jason, if you don't shut your mouth right now, I swear I will shut it for you," Sean gritted out through clenched teeth, deliberately wrapping his arms around Erin and pulling her close to him. She laid her cheek on his chest.

"Jason," Sheridan said, intensity radiating from every pore of her body, "I'm not kidding. Leave them alone. With all the shit that's been going on in this family, at least let *someone* be happy."

"Whatever. I'm outta here. See you around." He sauntered off.

Night had almost fallen by that time, and the three young people stretched out on the blanket again. This time, Erin pressed close to Sean, her head pillowed on his shoulder, his arm around her holding her tight. Erin's body relaxed at the contact. *That's better. The best antidote to Jason – to any problem – is Sean's arms around me.*

* * *

I could hold her forever. I think that would be just perfect. He turned his head and traced her features with his eyes. *She's so beautiful. I love her so much. If only she could stay here, be with me, not go away.* He would miss her every day until she returned. *What would I give to keep her from leaving?* He knew if he asked her right now to marry him, she would agree. She would go away to college engaged and plan her whole future around that fact.

The thought appealed so much, the words almost burst from his mouth, but he stopped himself. *This is selfish. What will happen when some amazing opportunity presents itself, and she refuses it, tied as she is to me? She has such talent, such skill. What use will those things be here? Teaching music lessons? Playing in the little community symphony. It would be a criminal waste. It's what she says she wants, but honestly, she's too young to know what she really needs.* Life would change, her circumstances would change, and it wouldn't be fair for her to make permanent decisions when barely more than a child. *No, her feelings today are not to be taken seriously. Someday she'll want more. I know it, and I can't hold her back.*

The revelation stunned him. He had always imagined love would be different. He pictured the progress of a relationship would be simple: meeting a girl, falling in love, getting married. Yes, there would be problems to face, adjustments. But he had never, not for one instant, envisioned anything like this. He had never realized loving someone could be so brutally painful, that it meant giving up your own happiness for the sake of that other person. He had to choose. He could keep Erin and steal her future, or he could let her go so she could live. The excruciating thought made his eyes burn, his breath catch.

Hearing the soft sound, Erin turned to him.

"No matter what, baby," he told her, his voice intense, "no matter what happens, always know you're loved. I will love you forever."

* * *

Erin saw the conflicted, haunted expression and knew what it meant; saw the goodbye in his eyes. It hit her like a hammer blow. Desperate, she leaned forward, capturing his lips in a kiss that pleaded for some other outcome, but there was none. As the first volley of fireworks exploded in red, white, and blue sparks, their dreams of forever slowly died.

* * *

Labor Day weekend drew to a close. Saturday evening, the day before the girls planned to leave for the university and get settled, in preparation of classes starting Tuesday, Erin sought out Mrs. Murphy. She had something important she needed to tell her host and substitute mother. As usual, she found Ellen in the kitchen, this time baking cookies.

"Hi," Erin said, pulling out a cooling rack from the cabinet and setting it up for the double chocolate monsters Ellen had just pulled out of the oven.

"Hello, Erin. Thank you." She set the cookie tray on the stove to cool and slid another pan into the waiting heat.

"You're welcome. I needed to ask you something. You know I'm leaving in the morning?" Though Erin's tone remained neutral, her heart pounded so fast she feared she might throw up.

"Of course."

"Do you and your husband plan to drive Danny, or would you like me to give her a ride?" *Okay, so I'm stalling. So what?*

"No, we'll drive her. You can certainly come with us if you would like." She began to scoop the warm cookies onto the cooling rack with a bright purple spatula.

"No thanks. I want to have my car with me. You don't know how long I saved up to pay for that Buick and I want to keep it."

Ellen smiled. "Oh, that's fine. We'll see you up there then."

Erin sighed. *Okay, get to the point, girl.* "Sure. Listen. There's something I have to do. You're not going to like it, but it's absolutely necessary."

"What's that dear?" Ellen set down her spatula and turned to face Erin.

Erin swallowed hard and tried to ignore the burning in her cheeks. "I'm not coming home tonight. I'm staying with my boyfriend. I don't know when I'm going to see him again, and I can't pass up the chance to spend the night with him one last time."

Ellen's face twisted in disapproval. "You're right, I don't like that. Are you sure that's a good idea? Are you... giving up your virginity to this boy?"

"No," Erin replied bluntly. "I did that a long time ago."

Ellen's expression contorted into disapproving concern. "Oh, Erin, I really wish sometimes you were my daughter, so I could have had some influence on you."

"Believe me, you have. I would have loved to have you for a mother. Your children are so lucky." *And you have no idea how I hate disappointing you.*

"Don't do this, Erin," Ellen pleaded.

"I'm very sorry." Erin turned and walked out the door.

Part II

Chapter 13

November 2005

"Sheridan, you know that boy in our political science class, the one with the crazy hair? I think he wants to ask you out."

"What – Eric?" Sheridan rolled over on the purple lilac comforter covering her dorm bed and made a face "No thanks. I'm not much interested in a boy who wears leather and chains."

"Come on, step outside your comfort zone," Erin urged, only half teasing her friend. "You never know. Maybe he's this closet poet who will write you sonnets and make your heart melt."

Sheridan laughed. "Nice try, Erin. Sorry, but you know these boys don't do anything for me. Too young. We both like an older man, don't we?"

An image of Sean as she'd last seen him floated up in Erin's mind. She pushed it away. "Yeah, sure. I hope you're not still talking about Dr. Burke though. I really don't know what you see in that guy. He sure isn't hot." The image of her lost love disappeared as a vision of Sheridan's scraggly-haired, big nosed crush appeared in her mind's eye. She shook her head to dispel the image.

"Who cares? I think we're soul mates." Sheridan sighed at the thought of her favorite professor.

"Has he ever expressed even the slightest interest in you, apart from being your teacher?" Erin demanded, irritated by her friend's mooning.

Sheridan thought for a moment. "I'm not really sure. He's pretty subtle. Sometimes I think he likes me, but it's just hard to tell."

"Sheridan, everyone likes you," Erin reminded her. "It's impossible not to. That doesn't mean he's suddenly going to propose."

"I know," Sheridan replied, her cheerful expression drooping. Then she brightened and continued her gush. "But here. Let me show you something, and you tell me what you think." She opened her backpack and pulled a messy binder out onto her dorm room bed. Flipping open the battered cover, she withdrew a sheaf of papers.

"What's this?" Erin asked, rising from her music-note-spangled bedspread and taking the two steps across the white tile floor to her friend. Grasping the stack, she began leafing through several sheets with short lines centered on the page.

"Some stuff he gave me in that poetry class I'm taking," Sheridan explained, grabbing back the papers and shuffling them until she found one. She pointed. "Here. Read it. Am I imagining he likes me?"

Erin took the papers and scanned them. They consisted of some pretty passionate anonymous love poems clearly written for a girl who closely resembled Sheridan. "Sunshine woman? Glorious smile? These do sound like you, but if they were from class… that doesn't really mean much, does it?"

"Maybe not, but he didn't give them to everyone, only me. The others were reading Robert Browning." Sheridan raised her eyebrows, as though willing Erin to connect the dots.

"What?" Erin's dark eyes widened.

"Yeah, he said I had already read those poems last semester in Brit Lit, and he wanted to give me something harder." Sheridan couldn't suppress a hint of a smirk.

Erin scanned the lines more closely. "Danny, these aren't hard."

"I know." Sheridan's signature smile seemed on the verge of bursting into full blossom, "but please don't call me Danny anymore, remember?"

"Yeah, sorry. Old habit." Erin shrugged an off-handed apology. "You may be right that he likes you, but that still doesn't mean he's going to ask you out."

"Someday he will. I'll make sure of it." Sheridan's buoyancy faded, and a hint of tension creased the corners of her eyes. "Besides, I'm not ready yet."

"It's been four years," Erin reminded her gently.

"I know. I'm much better. I just don't know if I'm ready for that yet. It's still scary." Sheridan quickly deflected the conversation away from herself. "Besides, it's not like you're dating either, and I know there are guys that would love to ask you out."

Actually, I did go out with a boy last year, twice, a friend from the music department, Erin recalled. *On the second date, I even let him kiss me.* She shuddered at the memory. While the embrace itself had not been poorly executed, it had left her so unmoved she had immediately let him know there was no future for them and he should forget about her. *Now he's practically engaged to a nice girl. I'm happy for them, and I've never felt a hint of regret or jealousy over that decision.* "Yeah, right," she snapped, an edge creeping into her voice. *I know where this is headed. Please, don't talk about Sean anymore. It kills me to remember.*

Sheridan regarded her, a considering look on her face.

Just. Don't. Do it. Erin urged silently.

"You know, if you're really over my brother..."

Damn it. I knew this was coming. Erin plunged in, tearing her heart to bloody shreds in hopes of making herself understood at last. "It's different for me, you know. I already met the love of my life, dated him, slept with him, everything. I wish it could have lasted, but I'm thankful to have been with him for a while. After that, no one else seems appealing. I would no sooner try to replace Sean than I would my oboe."

"Then call him," Sheridan insisted, not dissuaded by her friend's anger. "We're going to graduate next semester. You're about to launch yourself into your adult life. If you're ready to settle down, get married, all that, why not call up your one true love and ask him to be part of it with you?"

Marriage with Sean was my lifelong dream. Sobs tried to claw their way out of her throat, but she swallowed them down. "He doesn't want me anymore, you know that. It's over, Sheridan. I haven't talked to your brother in three years." Her sorrow translated itself into a harshness of tone that had Sheridan eyeing her.

"I know," Sheridan said, her expression mirroring her friend's sadness. "I wish you would. He's not over you, any more than you're over him. He doesn't date either. I know he misses you and would take you back in a second if you just told him you were still interested."

"If that's the case, then why did he stop calling me? It was really deliberate. I don't want to call him only to have him tell me right out that he doesn't love me anymore." Her tone grew harder with every word. *I do not want to talk about this.*

Sheridan pressed on, determined. "That would never happen. He loves you as much as he ever did. The reason he stopped calling is that he was trying to be noble, not hold you back." Sheridan wrapped her arm around Erin's shoulder and squeezed.

Erin made a face. *What is she talking about? He stopped calling me because I was too young and boring to keep his attention.* "That's stupid. He didn't hold me back, he held me together. I would never have gotten through high school without him."

"I know. And I wish you had that kind of support now."

"I don't need it. I'm fine," she said stubbornly, but inside she couldn't stop a little voice from wailing at the thought of the support he used to give her. *Hugs and kisses. Conversation. A listening ear and a strong shoulder Sweet, sweet sex. Everything I needed, he provided. I miss him more than words can say.*

"You're not. You need support and love as much as anyone else. You're not a cold person, Erin."

Erin snapped, "Can you please drop it, Sheridan? I don't like talking about Sean. It still hurts how easily he got over what we had." She had nearly reached the limit, but still, Sheridan pressed.

"He didn't get over it at all. God, you two are stubborn. If you would just talk to each other –"

"It's never going to happen!" She slashed the air with her hand. "The one thing I can't stand is to be pathetic, begging him to take me back. There's just no way."

* * *

Sheridan shook her head at Erin's nonsense. *I feel so much better now, and I want to give my friend that token of gratitude I've been thinking about all these years. The only thing Erin ever really wanted was Sean. I'm furious over the way those two let each other go, each thinking they were doing the other a favor. They still belong together as much as they ever did, and I'll see them back as a couple if it's the last thing I do.* Wisely, she changed the subject. *This isn't over, but it has to be done delicately.* "I got a new letter from Christine. Do you want to see it?"

Erin sagged with relief. *Oops, maybe I pushed a bit too hard.* "Sheridan, why do you torture yourself this way? You know those letters always make you cry."

"I know, but it's helpful for me to know how well she's doing. It reminds me that I made the right decision. It's not like I can ever forget." *And now you know what Erin was feeling, loving someone you can't have back, and missing them until you want to die of it.*

"You're the lucky one, you know," Erin said, anger rolling over her features.

"Why?" Sheridan blinked at Erin's unexpected return to lividness. *What's going on, hon?*

"Because your baby is still alive."

"Oh sweetie, does it still bother you that much?" *As if you don't know exactly how much it hurts not to have your baby in your arms, Sheridan. Man, you put your foot in it this time.*

Erin's voice caught. "What do you think? For that brief couple of months, I thought I would be able to keep a little piece of Sean with me forever, and then it was gone, and he was gone, and I'm alone. I lost the only child I'll ever have."

She walked out of the dorm room, tears streaming down her cheeks, and let the door slam behind her.

Wow, Sheridan thought. *I had no idea Erin was still grieving her miscarriage, although given how much she still loves Sean, it's no surprise.* She hated seeing her friend so sad, but how to help? *Hmmmm.* An idea, like divine inspiration, clobbered her.

She grabbed her cell phone and dialed her brother's number.

Chapter 14

Two days later, the second to the last day of class before Thanksgiving break, Sheridan met Sean in the parking lot of the English building.

Sean climbed out of his car – the same neon blue Mustang he had bought years ago – and gave his sister a hug. Time had been good to Sean. At twenty-six, he no longer appeared so young. There was a new hardness to his face, the bones standing out more clearly. His skin had become faintly weathered from so many hours in the sun, and there was just the slightest indication of what would eventually become lines around his eyes. It suited him. *He looks like a man in his prime, the kind who makes girls weak-kneed and fluttery. He's an absolute titan of masculine beauty, and I'm about to unleash him, full force, on her susceptible friend.* She hid a smirk. *I hope Erin will be completely overwhelmed. I know Sean will be. He'll never know what hit him.*

"Hey, baby sister. How are you doing? You look happy," he commented.

"Oh, I am," she replied, beaming. "I'm so happy, you can't even imagine it. Life went on after all. Who knew?"

"I'm glad. I've been worried about you for quite a while. It's good to know you're thriving." He released her from the embrace and held her at arm's length, gazing into her face as though searching for answers. Behind him, a brown scrap of leaf let loose from a tree and floated past on a chilly late autumn wind.

"It's the environment here. I just love it. I wish I could stay in college forever," she replied fervently.

Sean chuckled, but Sheridan found it interesting to note that his normally radiant, crooked-toothed smile seemed somehow dimmed. *All is not right in my big brother's world. I knew it.* "I never felt that way. I just wanted to hurry up and finish my degree, so I could go build stuff."

"Well, we're not exactly the same, are we? I could stay forever. And now that I'm teaching a class, it's even better, even if I do have so much grading I couldn't make it home for Thanksgiving."

"Busy girl," her brother chuckled. "I'm not sorry for a bit of a break. We've been booking it trying to finish up the exteriors of not one, but three houses before the snow flies. I'm glad to get away from work."

He doesn't suspect a thing. Excellent. Sheridan hid a smirk. "Hey, Sean, would you walk with me a bit? I have some stuff to do in the English department before I can take you out to dinner." She tugged on his arm.

"Sure, no problem." He moved with her easily, not resisting, though continuing to pour out abuse on her favorite place on earth. "Man, I used to hate this building. Reading Shakespeare really didn't do anything for me."

"Ha," Sheridan scoffed. "Everyone likes Shakespeare. It's full of sex."

"Come on, sis, don't talk like that," he bantered back. "I want to imagine you're still innocent."

"I'm no less innocent than I was the day I arrived here, for your information," she teased, sticking her nose in the air.

He laughed. "Well that's good to know. I pictured you cutting a swath through the male population, you and your roommate."

Since he brought up the subject... "Come on, silly, you should know us both better than that," she told him as she escorted him through the door and down the hallway to the teaching assistants' office. *I can hardly stand being in there, it's so close to Dr. Burke's office.* She shivered *Sometimes I swear I can feel his presence through the walls.* "Erin and I have been studying, and not men either, by the way. She's no more moved on than you have. She hasn't been on a single date since you took her out on Christmas break of our freshman year." She broke eye contact as she stated the lie, pretending to scrutinize a notice for a student offering tutoring services. The sign needed a heavy proofread. *Surely those pointless, innocent movie nights didn't count.*

* * *

Sean remembered that last meeting. After months of separation, his 'date' with Erin had been spent entirely in bed. He hadn't seen her since. When he realized how much she was still clinging to him, and he to her, he had purposely begun limiting contact. *She deserves better than to be the wife of a small-town builder, and I still intend to see that she not waste her opportunities.*

It had hurt like hell. Now, years later, the ache remained raw. *I miss Erin every day, but I will not be the cause of her missing out on life.* Shaking his head, Sean forced his thoughts back to the conversation. "I don't want to talk about Erin."

"Come on, Sean," Sheridan urged, sidestepping a knot of faculty hanging notices in a glass-fronted case. "There's so much unsaid between you. At least you should talk to her. Explain why you cut her off. You broke her heart, you know."

"Danny, you know why I had to let her go. She would be wasted back home," he reminded her.

"No, she wouldn't." Sheridan insisted. "She would be wasted out there, in the world, alone. That's how she's going to live, Sean. Alone. No one to love her. Is that really what you want for her?"

"Of course not. She needs to let go of me and find someone who can give her everything she deserves." He pictured some scruffy musician kissing *his* woman and his stomach clenched. *She's not yours anymore, remember?*

"And what exactly would that be?" *Is that a sneer in Sheridan's voice? She certainly sounds like she's talking to a simpleton.*

"Well, for one thing, the recognition that she's an amazing musician." *I can match you for sarcasm, missy. I taught you how to do it. You're on thin ice, Sheridan Murphy.*

"She can be an amazing musician back home, too. In fact, think of the accolades someone of her caliber would get for playing there. She's better now than she ever was before."

Oh Lord, better? Sean blinked hard. *How much better can she get? And why is Sheridan insisting a professional musician would be better off stuck in a small town with a builder for a husband and probably a pile of kids to distract her from her art? They must be crazy.* "It's too small a venue."

Sheridan stopped outside an open door with a combination lock comprised of silver buttons instead of a keyhole. The door stood open, rendering the lock irrelevant. Inside the room, a row of computers sat shoulder to shoulder on a long table. A student with an Asian cast to his features typed at one.

Sheridan leaned against the dark wood of the door frame and glared at her brother, dismissing all his beliefs with an angry glare. "For whom? It's what she wants. It's all she's ever wanted. You were her dream, Sean. She didn't dream about being a great musician, because she already is one. People dream about what they don't have. She dreamed of you, of being part of a loving family. She doesn't care about fame. She only cares about having a home with people who love her and getting to play her oboe. I suspect she would also like a baby. She can have all those things with you. Without you, even if she became the most famous oboe player in the world – and let's face it Sean, how famous do oboe players really get? – she would have no one. That instrument can't love her back, and she won't let anyone else get close. Think about it."

Sheridan's pointed words struck Sean like a sledgehammer. They chipped away at the defenses he had erected to keep himself from scooping Erin out of her dorm room, carrying her off to the nearest priest and marrying her. Every blow unleashed a wave of agony he could scarcely stand. Finally pushed beyond his limit, Sean lost his temper. "That's enough, Sheridan!" he shouted. "Leave me alone about her. It's over. Do you think it was easy for me to let her go? You of all people should understand about walking away from someone you love for their own good. It had to be done, and I hate it every day, okay? Just let it go."

"What is going on here?" A tall man with long black hair, a large beaky nose, and a ragged gray suit stalked out of a nearby office and approached them. He turned from Sean to his sister and back, clearly startled. "Sheridan?"

"Dr. Burke," Sheridan said, stricken. Sean's attack had undermined her composure, and her lip quivered, her eyes filled with tears.

The professor walked over to her and slipped his arm around her shoulders, leading her towards his office. "Come on, let's go." He turned and gave Sean a hard look, his black eyes glittering dangerously. Sean walked away.

* * *

Back in his office, Dr. Michael Burke, still holding Sheridan with one arm, peered into her face with an intense, unreadable expression. "Are you all right?" he asked at last.

"Yes." She made herself smile. "I'm sorry if we disturbed you. I was having a little disagreement with my brother."

"Your brother?" Dr. Burke seemed surprised, almost relieved. "I thought he was your boyfriend."

"No, I don't have a boyfriend."

"Hmmm." He released her and stepped away, but only a small step. She could still smell his aftershave. "Well, I'm glad I found you. I wanted to ask you something. You're just about finished with your Bachelor of Arts. Do you have any plans for the future? I hate to say it, but a B.A. in English isn't exactly a career path in and of itself. What do you want to do with it, Sheridan?"

"I don't really know. I wish I could just stay here forever." She twirled a golden strand around her finger, deliberately flirting.

The message seemed to be received well enough, if the intensity in his dark eyes provided any indication. "You could."

"How?"

"Get a Master of Arts in English," he replied. "Then you could teach here."

"A master's? Do you think I would be able?" She stared at him with wide eyes.

"Of course." *Is that a hint of a smile on his serious face?* "You're only the smartest student we've ever had. I would suggest a doctoral program, but we don't have one. You would have to leave to pursue that."

The compliment warmed her all over, and something in his expression made her dare to hope he didn't want her to leave. "I don't want to go. Can I teach at a university with a master's?"

"Yes, especially if you don't mind teaching freshman classes, like the ones you assisted with this last year."

"That was fun. I actually love teaching freshman composition," she told him. *And that's the truth. Teaching writing is fun.*

One thick, dark eyebrow shot towards his hairline. "You may be the only person who does. Most professors see it as a chore."

"Do you think I should?" she asked, lowering her eyes to the floor, and then looking up through her lashes.

He blinked and swallowed before answering. "I think, Sheridan, that it would be a good idea for you to consider it. In fact, I hoped you would. I have the application here if you want to fill it out, and, of course, I would write you a recommendation, not that you would need it. Are you interested?"

"That depends. Would you keep on helping me, being my mentor?" She touched his sleeve.

"Of course."

"Then, yes. I think that would be the perfect solution, except... how would I pay for it? The money my parents set aside for me to go to college is spent." She smiled ruefully.

His hint of a grin disappeared. "I've been thinking about that. You assisted with that one class this semester, and you did a good job, too. If you were to get a teaching assistant position, you could work for your tuition, and there's a small stipend too. And if you're concerned about housing, well, when I was in grad school, I was a resident assistant. You would have to stay in the dorm, but it would be paid for and you would get a room to yourself."

"You thought of everything, Dr. Burke. Thank you. This is exactly what I want. I hope I can do it." Flirtatiousness melted into sincere enthusiasm.

"You will. You're always successful, Sheridan."

Her breath caught. "Thank you."

"By the way," his tone suddenly became casual, too casual, "if you're teaching here, you're going to be more my colleague than my student. I would like it very much if you would call me Michael."

Sheridan's eyes widened. Then a grin that put the late autumn sunshine to absolute shame broke over her face. He met her grin with a look of intense longing.

"Michael." She tested the word as though it were a delicious confection. Impulsively, she hugged her professor. *I want him so badly sometimes I fear I might burst. If only he knew...* but alas, she had been rather free with her hugs, especially with him, and for all he knew, it might only be a friendly gesture. *I have to do more.* She leaned forward and pressed her lips to his cheek. Then, embarrassed, she scooped up the applications from his desk and fled.

Chapter 15

𝄞

Sean stormed through the English department, furious his sister had tricked him into driving three hours just, so she could try and manipulate him. *How dare she interfere?*

He was so intent on his angry thoughts, he almost crashed into a small figure running the other direction down the hallway. He stopped just in time to avoid a collision and looked down at the person he had nearly run over.

Oh, dear Lord. It's Erin. She froze, her gaze running up the length of him to his face, recognition dawning on her beautiful features. Her soft pink lips parted slightly in surprise. *God, she looks wonderful.* She had put on some weight. Not a huge amount, maybe seven pounds, but oh, they were strategic. Her tiny breasts had filled out, as had her hips. She now had a womanly curve to her slender frame. She had cut her hair too. Instead of hanging long down her back, it ended just above her shoulders, with little swinging layers at the ends and a sweep of long bangs that crossed her forehead diagonally to tuck behind her ear. The cut suited her, made her seem more grown up. In fact, she seemed all grown up, sexy, and even more heart-stoppingly beautiful than ever before.

As he watched, her mouth soundlessly formed his name.

* * *

Got to get the key to that damned self-locking dorm room door before Danny gets tangled up talking to Dr. Burke again and I have to spend hours stuck in the hallway with my oboe inside, especially with juries coming up. I need to pract... oof! Big hands clamped down on her arms, arresting her headlong dash. Her eyes traveled up the length of a tall and muscular frame. Then she met his eyes, and the university faded.

Despite trying so hard to put memories of Sean behind her, never once had she forgotten how she loved him. She had forgotten, however, just how gorgeous he was. She stared, so frozen with shock that she forgot to breathe for several seconds. Then the weight of their shared history crashed over her like a flood. *This is my first love, my only love. I gave him my virginity. We conceived, and lost, and grieved a child together. He's the only person who ever cared what happened to me. And then he abandoned me without explanation.* She had expected it, but that hadn't made it easier to take. And now here he stood, in front of her, close enough to touch.

Suddenly, she no longer cared about being pathetic. If he knew how she'd pined for him, so be it. She couldn't bear to go another moment without touching him.

Erin launched herself at Sean, throwing her arms around his neck and pulling him down so she could kiss him. She didn't care if the other students milling around them saw; she wanted them to see, wanted everyone to see that she, Erin James, loved Sean Murphy with every fiber of her being.

* * *

After a startled second, Sean wrapped his arms around Erin's slender waist and began to kiss her back. He had almost forgotten how bold she could be. He had also forgotten how sweet Erin's mouth was, clinging tenderly to his. *Nothing has ever been sweeter, at least not anything I know about.* These were certainly not the actions of a woman who had moved on. *Sheridan's right. We need to talk.*

Gently he disengaged his mouth from Erin's, still keeping his arms around her so she would know it wasn't a rejection. She tried to hang onto the kiss, sucking softly at his lips.

"Easy, Erin," he said. *How many times have I said that to her, trying to slow her down when she was clawing with passion?* The familiar words broke through and she released him reluctantly.

"Sorry," she said, "I just... I can't believe you're here. Sean, I've missed you so much."

"I've missed you too, baby," he told her, his voice gruff.

"Then why, Sean? Why did you stop calling me? I thought we were forever. That's what you said." Her grief over his actions burned no less powerfully for all the years in between.

Sean winced. *Did I really hurt her as badly as that?* "Walk with me, Erin. Let's talk, okay?"

"Yes, let's." She took his hand in hers. Lacing their fingers together the way they used to do, they left the building.

* * *

Outside, the chilly autumn air set Erin shivering. She remembered suddenly that their relationship had begun the same way, with a shiver. Sean released her hand and wrapped his arm around her shoulders instead. She snuggled into his warmth.

A bench sat in the courtyard, in a patch of feeble sunlight, and they claimed it, ignoring the piles of cigarette butts on the ground around their feet.

"Okay, Murphy, spill it. What the hell were you hoping to accomplish by making me fall madly in love with you and then dropping me like a rock? Was I just an easy lay after all?" She tried to sound playful but knew it lacked conviction.

Sean frowned. "Of course not. Don't cheapen what we had like that. I loved you and you know it." He sighed. "I'm sorry, Erin. I know I hurt you. I didn't want to, but I didn't see another way. I didn't want to get in the way of you pursuing your dreams."

She snorted. "Sean, you were my dream; you and our life together. The symphony, the music lessons, the family..."

"It's too small," he interrupted. "You could achieve whatever you want."

She laughed, and it sounded bitter and ironic in her own ears. "Funny, isn't it, how people say that when it's so clearly not true? Did you ever stop to ask what I wanted? I never asked to be famous, to be in some high-powered orchestra and deal with all the internal politics and backbiting. That was your goal for me, but did you listen to my goals? No. I just wanted to play my instrument, make music, be part of a group and make people happy. And I wanted to come home to you every night. I told you that, but you didn't listen. You were so sure you knew me better than I knew myself. What I wanted was to get my degree and come home. I certainly didn't achieve that."

"You almost have your degree. A few more months will do it," he reminded her, his expression pleading for… something.

What are you trying to tell me, Sean? Is this the conversation you were trying not to have? Is this your way of letting me down easy, or do you truly not understand?

"I have no home to go to." She let that sink in, wondering if he would finally get it.

He regarded her in silence, as though trying to read a story in the planes of her face. "Home is wherever you decide it will be."

She laid her head on her palm in dismay. "Home isn't a place, Sean. It's people. The people I want to be close to don't live out there somewhere." She pantomimed a wide circle with one hand and then returned her eyes to his, laying that hand on his knee. He immediately grasped her fingers again.

He shook his head, not in rejection of her words, but as though still not quite believing them. She focused her gaze on his eyes, telling him in no uncertain terms that he would not be able to wiggle out of her intended meaning. Sean's eyes widened, and then his eyebrows drew together. "Erin, if what you're saying is true, why didn't you insist I talk to you? You just let it go, didn't ask any questions, didn't protest. I thought you were done with me; glad I stopped meddling in your life."

Erin shook her head. "I didn't want to bother you. I guess I figured you were done with me, that you were sick of your silly adolescent girlfriend and wanted to move on, find someone else, someone not such a baby, not so... I don't know... boring."

His handsome face twisted into lines of utter disbelief. "How could you think that? You're not boring. You're amazing. Didn't I keep telling you that?"

Erin rolled her eyes. "You know what they say, Sean, about actions and words." Her shoulders slumped and the ugly feeling she'd always had about herself spilled from her lips like poison. "No one has ever really wanted me. I was glad you did for a while. I didn't expect it to last. I dared to let myself hope, but then you did what I had expected. You got over me." She broke eye contact, watching a leaf fragment slowly creep along the pavement, pushed by the autumn wind. *That's me. Every force pushes me where I don't want to go, and no matter how I fight it, I'm powerless to resist the pressure.*

"I never did. I thought you were over me." Sean sounded irritated, and he grasped her chin, forcing her to meet his eyes. The expression there – tender passion mingled with disbelief and a good bit of repressed longing – took her breath away. She licked her lips nervously, not able to believe what she saw, any more than he'd been able to believe her. *Oh, my love, what have we done to each other?* Silent, wordless emotion passed between them until at last, Sean burst out, "This is ridiculous. You know, both of us have been doing a fair bit of assuming. I think it might be a good idea for us to stop second-guessing each other and just say what we feel."

Erin swallowed, the words welling up, clamoring to be said, but the fear choked them down again. "That's hard."

"It is, but isn't it time to be honest?"

"Yes." Neither of them spoke for another long moment as they pondered how to proceed. *You know what you want, Erin. If you don't at least ask for it, you'll never forgive yourself. Be bold.* But the words wouldn't come. They battled at the edge of her tongue, reticence trying, as always, to prevent her from grasping her heart's desire, fighting to squash the words back into their box of inadequacy. *Not this time. I'll be no more heartbroken if he rejects me. At least I'll have tried.* Finally, Erin forced out, "Can I start?"

Sean dipped his chin. "Of course. Ladies first."

Erin took a deep breath and let the truth spill from her lips. Once the first words passed the barrier of her shyness, the rest poured out unchecked, in a babbling gush of long-suppressed emotion. "Sean, from the night you took me to homecoming and kissed me in the parking lot until this day, the love I have for you has never wavered, never changed. I love you. You're my one and only, Sean, forever. If I can't have you, I don't want anyone. Why, when I've already found my perfect love, would I even attempt to replace you? I would rather have your memory than any other man. And to this day, I still want you as much as I ever did."

* * *

Her sweet words, her familiar scent, deluged Sean's senses as Erin's love poured over him like rain. *It's always felt that way, and you've always loved it.* She sat so close to him, and the temptation proved overwhelming. He kissed her, rewarding her words with a tender, wet touch of his lips. "Are you telling me, Erin, that you've never... dated anyone, not in all these years?"

"Why would I have?" She touched his cheek. "No one can compare. Now you, Sean. Tell me what you feel."

He looked into her soft brown eyes, shining with love. *Surely it can't be wrong to love her back.* She'd had years to think about this and her feelings hadn't changed. After everything that had happened, she still wanted him. His resistance shattered. Taking her hand in his, he answered her. "I love you. I see you the way I always saw you... as the woman I want to marry. I told you that a long time ago. I don't see you as boring, or a baby. I never did, even when you were eighteen and in high school. It scares the hell out of me, though, to think that one day you might wake up beside me and realize I'm the man who took away all your choices, and I would see that regret in your eyes."

Erin's hand slipped out of his. For a moment his breath caught, and then he exhaled in a whoosh as she slid her arms around his neck, whispering into this ear, "Silly man, you *are* my choice. You were my choice four years ago and I have never doubted or regretted it."

How did you not know that? The realization dawned on him that he *did* know, that he always had, only his rational mind had overruled what his instincts had always understood. *You'll never find a love as pure, deep and real as this one. You'll never find another person who loves you more.* But even as the sensation of her perfect affection washed over him, those rational thoughts took over his mouth and spilled out an inane comment. "I don't understand how you knew at such a young age exactly what you wanted in life."

Erin didn't release him but pulled back a fraction to meet his eyes again, pursing her lips even as she answered his words. "It's just the way I am. I know what I want. It's not hard for me to make decisions about really important things. Did I ever tell you about the first time I played the oboe?"

"No. Tell me," he urged. *This is something I need to understand. If Erin is comparing our relationship to her lifelong passion for music, I have to get it.*

"It was in sixth grade," she began. "Everyone was trying out different instruments to see what they wanted to play in the band. I had been fooling around with a clarinet, and I liked it, but it wasn't quite right. Clarinet has this cheerful quality that really didn't suit me." She teased the back of his neck with her fingertips, making him shiver. "But I thought it had potential. Then the director handed me a double reed. I blew it and it made a sound like a duck call. I hated it. I couldn't imagine what on earth would make anyone want to use such a thing." A grin spread over her face. "Then she showed me their loaner oboe. It was a mess, covered in fingerprints, the keys tarnished. It even had a big crack in the wood. It was so ugly. I put the reed in it and blew, and it quacked like you can't even imagine. It was horrible."

Sean returned the smile. *I can easily imagine the sound.*

"Then she told me something. She said I had to be gentle with it, not blow so hard. So, I took it easy and it came alive in my hands. That day I knew there was nothing else I would ever want to do." He watched her closely, waiting for her to make the connection. *Even as a kid, I recall how clear-thinking she was. She never rambled. She chose her words with care. What are you trying to tell me, baby?*

Erin continued. "Falling in love with you was the same. I just knew you were it, that there would never be anyone else. That's why I was in such a hurry to go to bed with you."

Sean remembered that night, how eager she'd been, how tenderly they'd made love. She'd given him everything she had, without reservation, even though she had not expected him to love her back or to keep loving her. His remaining doubts about whether his love would ultimately satisfy her burst under undeniable reality. "Oh, Erin, sweet baby. I'm sorry. I should have listened to you."

"Yes, you should have," she scolded gently. "But it was as much my fault. I didn't trust you would want me long-term, and it kind of became a self-fulfilling prophecy. That's why I didn't fight for you. I didn't think I was good enough to hold you anyway."

"I always felt that you were too good for me, or at least for the kind of life we would have together," he admitted. *And I actually thought she wouldn't be able to make her own decisions. She knew what she wanted all along.*

* * *

Erin tilted her head, considering how to phrase what she wanted to say. "It's sort of an issue of trust, isn't it?"

"What do you mean?" Sean's passionate expression turned puzzled.

She elaborated. "I have to trust that you want me, even though I don't see myself as desirable. You say you love me, and it won't change or fade. I have to choose to believe it. You have to trust me too, that I love you as much as I love my oboe, and being with you is really what I want, more than being a high-powered musician."

"Are you sure, Erin, that a small-town life with me would be enough for you?"

He still sounds so tentative. How did we love each other so intensely without me realizing his insecurities? Was I really that self-centered, that I could only see my own? "Yes, absolutely. Are you willing to trust me on this?"

He looked at her, his eyes filled with longing, and then he nodded slowly.

"Sean, I've been away for three years. I want to go home. Will you be my home?"

The worried expression melted from his face, and his lips pulled back into a smile, revealing those crooked front teeth she'd always found so appealing. "If that's what you want, baby."

"It is," she said, firmly and without doubt.

"So, we're back together then, just like that?"

Oh, he likes that idea. "Just like that. It was always meant to be, I think. I know I haven't felt right for one single day since then."

"Me either," he said thoughtfully, "but you still have another semester of school. You need to finish."

"I will. I have to. But what are we going to do? How will we handle it?"

"Do, Erin?" Sean's voice suddenly turned dark with passion. His eyes glowed. "I have an idea about what we should do. Shall I tell you what it is?"

"Yes." Eagerness flared. *I think I'm going to like this idea too.*

"First, I'm going to take you to my hotel room, right now, and make love to you in ways you can't even imagine, all night long, and hold you until morning."

The suggestion put a little smile on her face. "Yes, please."

One corner of his mouth turned upward as he continued. "Then, tomorrow, when the stores open, I'm going to take you to a jeweler and you can pick out a ring. I'll put it on your finger, so everyone knows, for the rest of your time here, that you're mine. And then, this summer, baby, we're getting married."

Erin shivered. "Sounds perfect. Let's get started right now."

"Come on."

Sean took her hand and led her to his car, driving quickly through the busy city traffic to a small and unassuming hotel near the interstate. Though clean and respectable, the room lacked pretension. A brown carpet covered the floor, with golden spirals decorating the lush pile. The king-sized bed had been simply dressed in white sheets and a matching coverlet. A fat, old-fashioned television rested on the built-in dresser. A small round table stood in the corner by the window. But when Sean opened the room impatiently with his key card, they didn't see any of it.

He pulled Erin through the door, kissing her before he could even get it closed. She worked the buttons on his shirt eagerly, pushing it to the floor. Sean released Erin's mouth to pull her sweater over her head. She unhooked her bra and dropped it before throwing her arms around his neck again. He took one breast in his hand, caressing it tenderly and then teasing the sensitive nipple.

Erin gasped as pleasure shot through her. She had always loved to have Sean touch her breasts. Even better would be if he took her nipples in his mouth. She cupped the little globe in her hand and raised it, pulling Sean's head down so he could take the tender peak. He did, sucking it into his mouth and nipping gently. Erin could feel herself going all liquid as he repeated the process on the other side.

"Let's get on the bed," he murmured. "But leave your clothes behind. You won't need them."

Erin stripped off her jeans and panties eagerly and pulled back the white cotton coverlet, stretching herself out on the sheets. Sean pounced in an instant, nude, pressing his body hard against hers. She enjoyed the strength of his muscles, the size of his erection as it compressed her belly. He took her jaw in his hand and touched his mouth to hers again. She wrapped her legs around his waist.

It was too soon, but passion had destroyed them both, and Sean took the invitation thoughtlessly, finding her wet entrance with his sex and thrusting deep. Erin made a soft protesting sound. Her fingers tightened on his shoulders.

***

"What's wrong, baby?" Sean asked, freezing his forward motion.

"You're too big," she gritted through clenched teeth.

"Did that hurt?"

"Yes."

Oops, didn't mean to do that. "Little girl, have you forgotten how to take me?" he asked in mock reproof.

Erin tried to smile. "I guess I did."

"You're so tight. I can't imagine. It's like your first time all over again." He leaned up on one arm and with his free hand smoothed her hair back from his face.

"Well, you know, I haven't had sex in almost three years," she said.

"Three years?" *Can she mean...*

"My one and only, remember?"

He hadn't dared to hope that she had been chaste all that time. He would have wanted her regardless, *but to know she's still mine, all mine... well, that's magnificent.*

He didn't want to hurt her, however, so he stayed still inside her, giving her resisting body a chance to adjust to his size. Meanwhile, he aroused her with passionate kisses, caressing her breasts again. He chafed one straining nipple and then the other. Erin hummed, and he could feel her growing wetter. Her sex clenched around him. He leaned up further, wanting to see their bodies joined before working his hand down her belly to her intimate folds. *She's so wet for me.* He found the delicate point of her clitoris, swollen with need, and began to stroke it gently. *Once she comes, she should be more relaxed, better able to let me move.*

* * *

Erin moaned as Sean brought her higher and higher. She was so full of him, not just his sex in her body, but full of love, overflowing with it. She had let go of this dream, and miraculously it had come true anyway. The pleasure built to an explosion, making her scream as her body tightened around his even more.

Sean began to move carefully in a gentle glide. It didn't take him long before he joined her in oblivion.

When they surfaced from the deep, beautiful place their passion had thrown them, both Sean and Erin felt a little stunned. Sean withdrew gently from Erin's body and lay down beside her, pulling her close with her head cradled on his shoulder.

"I love you, Sean," she told him softly, trailing ticklish lines across his chest with her fingertip. "I'm so glad we found each other, but why were you here?"

"Danny asked me to visit. I didn't realize she was trying to set us up again. I got a little mad at her," he admitted.

"I know. She talks about you all the time. It was driving me crazy."

"Me too. She was right though."

"She usually is."

Sean toyed with the ends of Erin's hair, making her tingle. "Baby, how is she doing, really? She says she's better, but you see her every day. Is she really doing all right?"

"She is, thankfully. I don't think I could have handled another year like that first one."

"What was it like?" he wanted to know.

"Freshman year?" Erin shook her head at the memory. "Oh, she was a mess. It was all I could do to get her to go to class, do her homework, and study. She used to have nightmares, wake up screaming, break down crying at odd moments. I didn't want anyone to know how destroyed she was, but it was really difficult."

"Wow. Poor Erin, and all without any help." He cupped her cheek in his hand. "How did you manage?"

"Well, I just did my best, you know?" She shrugged. "I felt like, other freshmen were handling college without needing to rely on anyone, but part of me wanted to call you all the time. Like, I had to audition for the freshman woodwind ensemble. It's an elite group on campus, only one musician per instrument. I was so nervous, and I just wanted to hear your voice, hear you tell me it would be okay, and then, after I made it, I wanted to call you again and tell you how happy I was."

Sean gave her a lopsided grin. "Erin, you could have done that. That's what people do when they love each other."

Erin tried to explain, reasoning what at the time had seemed unequivocal. "It just seemed so mundane, like such a bother. Later, after you stopped calling me, I felt like I had pestered you too much. I was too dependent on you, and you were sick of it."

A little of that low self-esteem that had plagued her through her whole life bled into the words. His arm tightened around her.

"No, that isn't what happened," Sean protested. "I was so worried about holding you back that I forgot how much strain you were under. Erin, I bet you none of those other freshmen went a single week without calling their parents at least three times to tell them how everything was going. That's normal. I called my dad just about every day for a while. You were doing more than any of them. How did you stay sane?"

"I practiced a lot," she replied with a telling shrug. "In fact, there really wasn't time for anything else. I practiced and studied and took care of Sheridan. That was it. If she hadn't started to heal, I think I might have cracked under it."

"So, what happened?" he asked. "She was pretty bad over that first summer, so what changed? And where were you? You didn't come home." He trailed a finger over her skin, eliciting delicious tingles.

Erin snuggled closer into Sean's naked body. *Just where I want to be.* "Me? I took classes and then I traveled around for various summer music series in different towns, starting in Des Moines."

"You did?" Sean's eyes widened. His tickling fingers stilled.

"Yes. There are lots of playing jobs for young musicians in the summer. I've been to the Ozarks, Omaha, New Mexico, Bismarck, and Moorhead. Oh, and I finally got to Texas too. I played a two-week opera run in Fort Worth." Erin winked.

He laughed. "Did you like it?"

A frown creased Erin's features. "I liked the music, but the other musicians were often … difficult. Unkind, competitive, and just kind of snarky. They were usually okay to us. We were just kids and no threat, but to each other … it got brutal pretty often." She shook her head. "I don't know how they can be a team and make music together when they're always cutting each other down. It made me miss that little symphony back home even more. The people there are so nice."

"So, you've played all over, have you?" he asked. His fingers twined in her hair again.

"Yes." She settled closer to him, enjoying the sensation of smooth skin, coarse hair and bulky muscle under her cheek.

"And what about during the year?" His fingertips left her hair to trace grapevines on her bare back.

All these touches are starting to turn me on again. "Well, I play with the university orchestra, the senior woodwind ensemble, and the chamber orchestra, but the metropolitan symphony doesn't need any oboes right now."

"Their loss."

"Thank you." She kissed him where his shoulder met his neck. "Wait, I think we got off topic."

He responded to her tickling kiss with a squeeze. "We did. I was wondering how it was that Danny suddenly got so much better."

"Believe it or not, she met someone."

Sean turned his head sharply in Erin's direction, meeting her eyes again. "She did? Who?"

Erin sighed. "Her English professor, Dr. Burke. To this day, I don't understand what she sees in him. I had a class with him and I dropped it. He must be the harshest, strictest, pickiest man in the whole academic world. I hated his class. Somehow, though, working with him brought Sheridan back to life. Since the beginning of sophomore year, she's taken a class from him every semester. She's in love with him. The more she relies on him, the less she needs from me. It was kind of a relief."

Awareness sparked in the depths of Sean's eyes. "Wait, I think I saw him. Is he really tall with black hair?"

"Yes. Did his clothes look like they came out of the rag bag?" Erin asked, rolling her eyes at Dr. Burke's famously terrible wardrobe.

"Uh huh."

"That's the one."

Sean's eyebrows drew together as he considered. "I wondered if there was something going on there. The way he looked at her... protective, and even a little possessive. Are they... involved?" Oddly, for being an overprotective big brother, Sean seemed curious and not in the least disapproving.

"I don't exactly know," Erin replied. "They have the strangest relationship. He does these crazy, romantic things for her, and I know what you mean about the way he looks at her. They spend huge amounts of time together, but as far as I know, they're not actually dating. I'm pretty sure he wants her, but he won't make a move, and she's still too shy and hurt to approach him. It's like the love affair of two porcupines."

"Sheridan, shy? I never would have imagined it." Sean's lips twisted. "Well, I guess it's up to them, isn't it? If she's even interested in someone, that's progress."

I've always thought so. "It is. So, while Sheridan was finding a way to fall in love in spite of everything, I was able to get back into living my life a little. She doesn't need my encouragement so much because she gets it from him. Without that pressure, I was able to move forward myself."

"Move forward academically," Sean guessed.

"And musically," Erin added. "After what we shared, going out with anyone else would have been a step backwards."

* * *

Erin's sweet words, made even more powerful in light of how badly he'd messed up their relationship, blew Sean away. "I don't deserve you, Erin."

"Of course, you do!" she exclaimed. *Admit it, man, her enthusiastic affection is something you've missed these last few years.* "You're my anchor. You made it possible for me to get through high school. All the happiest moments in my life were because of you."

Sean scoffed. *Now she's just exaggerating.* "How? Your achievements had nothing to do with me. I didn't get you into that All-State band, for instance, you did that yourself."

She sighed as though in mild exasperation. "Sean, I made All-State twice before we got together. It was nice, but having you there to hear me play was what made it great. No one else has ever come to a concert just to hear me before."

"Your parents?"

Erin shook her head.

"How can someone as wonderful as you come from such useless, selfish people?"

"I don't know. Sometimes I hate them both," she admitted.

"You're entitled. Don't let them convince you, though, that you're worthless." His trailing fingers headed to more and more interesting places, enjoying her baby-soft skin and sexy curves. "You are precious and valuable. The way they treated you was like throwing a treasure in the trash. It doesn't reflect badly on you, only on them."

Erin smiled, pressing a gentle kiss on Sean's shoulder. "You're the only one who sees me that way."

I see we still have a ways to go, baby girl. Don't we? "It's not true, but at any rate, if the person who admires you most is going to be your husband, I think that's rather appropriate, don't you?"

"Yes. You're right. Do you think you might have recovered enough to… admire me some more?" She arched against him, showing him what she meant.

Hot damn. More sex. What a great idea! "Let's find out."

He rolled to his side, pulling her close. They leaned together, touching their mouths to each other for a tender, arousing kiss, tongues tangling and mating as they ran their hands over each other's bodies, preparing each other for another round of loving.

The more they touched and caressed and kissed each other, the more the years of hurt and misunderstanding fell away until their love shone as pure and uncomplicated as it had once been. Better, because they no longer felt responsible for Sheridan. Her pain had ceased to overlay their relationship. She had moved on, survived, and now they could focus entirely on each other. It was selfish and greedy and decadent and wonderful, the way they devoured each other. It went on and on, a single endless loving in many acts, with interludes for showering – together, of course – and ordering and eating pizza. And when the last powerful orgasms faded away, they cuddled up together and fell asleep.

Chapter 16

In the morning, reality struck Erin. She had come away with Sean without anything but the clothes she was wearing. She had no clean panties, no toothbrush, not even her purse. It was all locked in her dorm room and she didn't have the key. *I completely forgot that the reason I went to the English building was because I locked myself out of the room again. And now I'm stuck here with nothing but dirty clothes to put on.* That simply wouldn't do. While she listened to Sean's soft, even breathing, she picked his pocket for change, trying hard to muffle the clanking of coins so as not to disturb his rest. Then she crept down the hall and bought a toothbrush from the vending machine, and then returned to the room to put it to use.

By the time she had cleaned up and turned on the coffee pot, Sean began stirring.

"Morning, baby," he said sleepily, his hair rumpled.

The sight of him made her heart turn over. *Every time I look at him, I see my forever.* "Good morning," she replied, her voice low and husky. She poured a mug of the coffee and brought it to him.

"Thanks." He sat up against the pillows and took a sip. She snuggled in beside him. He slipped his arm behind her back and kissed her temple. "You ready to go ring shopping?"

"Sure, in a little bit," she replied.

"What's the hold-up? I don't want to take a minute longer to claim this." He grabbed her hand and kissed her bare ring finger.

"I know, but, Sean, these clothes are dirty," she whined.

"So?" He raised one eyebrow.

"So, I'm not going to the mall in dirty underwear," she explained in teasing irony. *Duh, silly guy.* "We need to go back to my dorm, so I can get dressed."

"Girls." He snorted.

"Easy for you to say," she retorted. "Your clean clothes are right there." She pointed to his suitcase.

He shrugged, glancing at the clock. "It's only 7:30. I guess that's okay, since the stores won't open for a while anyway."

"Finish your coffee, darling, and let's go. I hope Sheridan is there. I don't have my key."

Ten minutes later they climbed into the Mustang and hurried back to the university. Hand in hand, they approached the room that had been Erin's home for the last three years. She knocked.

"Who is it?" Sheridan called.

"It's me, Danny. Let me in please," Erin replied, turning the locked doorknob.

"Where the hell have you been?" Sheridan's angry voice filtered through the door. "And, damn it, stop calling me Danny!"

I never can remember that. "I got locked out again," Erin explained.

"When?"

She cringed, and that cringing showed in her tone. "Yesterday afternoon."

"And after that?" Sheridan demanded, giving no quarter.

"I ran into someone. We went on a date."

Silence, and then Sheridan responded with, "Erin, since when do you go on all-night dates?"

Her face flamed. "Sorry. Look, I'll tell you everything, but can you please let me in?"

"Fine." Sheridan wrenched open door and froze to see her roommate holding hands with her brother. They stepped into the room, Sean looking as sheepish as Erin felt. *We've been busted big time. Thank goodness it was only Danny.*

"Oh," Sheridan said, her expression suddenly blank, "I see you found Sean. Well, that's okay then. I wish you had called and told me, though. I was worried about you."

"I completely forgot," Erin replied, giving her friend a hug with one arm while her other hand remained firmly in Sean's calloused grasp. "As you can see, I've never been so safe in my life."

"Sis, I'm sorry I yelled at you yesterday," Sean told his sister earnestly. "You were right."

"Of course I was," Sheridan replied, not the least bit mollified. "I'm not stupid you know."

"No, you're brilliant, and we were both too stubborn to realize it," he said in deep contrition. Then he squeezed Erin's hand.

"So, is everything all right between you now? I guess it must be if you're back to spending the night together."

"Everything is wonderful!" Erin beamed. "We're engaged. We're going to get a ring today."

Sheridan considered this in silence for a moment. "Well, getting you two hitched up should make my life easier. Okay, let me ask an awkward question. Sean, you didn't come up here planning to sleep with Erin, right??"

"No, of course not." A dull red stained his chiseled cheekbones.

"Which means you weren't prepared. Erin, when did you go off the pill?"

Erin also blushed. "A couple of years ago. I didn't think I would need it."

"I doubt it's still working. So, you're back to unprotected sex again? Remember what happened the last time?" She quirked one golden eyebrow at them.

Erin's breath caught as the previously unconsidered thought bloomed to vibrant hope. "I would like that," she said softly.

"Not while you're still in school, baby." Sean protested.

"Nine months from now I'll be done," she pointed out.

"Erin…"

Don't take this joy away. Not now. "You promised me," she reminded him. He fell silent.

"Erin," Sheridan said, "I'm not going to be happy with you if you get pregnant again before you're married."

"It may already be too late." Saying the words caused a curious sensation that was only partially a thrill of nerves. *Please, God, if I mean anything at all to you, let it be so.*

Sheridan spoke, interrupting her ruminations. "Well then, why don't you guys forget about getting engaged and just get married."

It took a moment for the unexpected suggestion to sink in, but when it did, Erin whipped her head around to meet bright blue eyes that mirrored the thoughts in her own mind. *Get married? Be married? No question about who belongs with whom, no question about when it will end.*

Erin took a deep breath. "Her idea has merit."

"It does." Sean pulled her into a loose embrace and rested his chin on the top of her head. "I can't imagine anything more appealing. But can it be done?"

"Only one way to find out," Erin said.

"Yes. Get dressed. I'll work on the details."

Erin hurriedly grabbed clean clothes and dragged them into the bathroom while Sean scoured the phone book. She could hear his muffled voice through the door.

When she stepped out, casually attired in blue jeans and a navy sweater, he informed her of what he had discovered. "They issue licenses at the county courthouse, which opens at nine."

"What will they need for documentation?" she asked as she ran a brush through her hair.

"Birth certificates and driver's licenses," he replied. "Do you have all that handy?"

"Yes," she informed him. "Of course, my license is in my purse." She indicated the small black satchel on the bedside table. "And my birth certificate is in a box in my closet, but what about you? You don't carry that around, do you?"

"Not normally," he said, "but I needed to renew my passport."

"Are you going somewhere?" she asked.

He shrugged. "Not a firm plan, but I was considering it. So, at any rate, I didn't get around to taking it out of my wallet yet. Weird coincidence."

"That was divine intervention," Sheridan said. "I think even God wants you two married before you can get into any more mischief."

Erin rolled her eyes and Sean laughed. "Okay, sis." He turned to Erin. "Come on, baby, let's go. They open up shortly, and I want to be first in line." He extended his hand.

Wow. He must want this as much as I do...Married to Sean. I can't wait. "Yes, let's." She grasped his hand.

* * *

Nervous, still clutching hands that had grown increasingly sweaty, they entered a tile-floored room with white walls studded with service windows. Over each, a small plastic box displayed a number in red lights. They collected a number slip from a dispenser near the door and searched the room, wondering which of the benches embedded in the wall they should sit in to wait.

Before they could find a seat, a mechanical voice called their number to window seven, where a kind, grandmotherly-looking woman waited to help them from behind a cheap veneer counter.

"Hi," Erin said, "we'd like to purchase a marriage license."

"Of course," the woman replied. "Here's the paperwork, my dears. You did know there was a five-day waiting period, right?"

Erin's face fell. "I didn't know. We were hoping to do it today."

The woman's smiling wrinkles transformed into a mask of consternation. "Why? Is there a reason for your hurry?"

"I have to be at work Monday, and I live three hours away," Sean told her.

"And I'm a student here and I have classes. I can't just leave," Erin added.

"Oh." The clerk blinked, and in an instant, her encouraging smile reappeared. "If you want, you can apply for a waiver. Here's the form. Go fill it out quickly, okay?" They nodded, accepting the clipboard holding the stack of papers that would transform their future. "Good. Listen, I don't know if I can get this approved, but I'll try. It's a pretty quiet time of year. I'm going to attempt to push it through, but it might be a lengthy wait. In the meanwhile, here's a list of people who officiate weddings. We don't have justices of the peace in this state. Try calling some of them, to see if anyone can work with you, if we can get the paperwork approved."

"Thank you," Erin told the woman earnestly.

"Baby," Sean said as they took their seats on the bench nearest the window, "I think you need to make the calls. If I do it, it's going to seem like I'm pressuring you. I'll work on this paperwork."

"Okay." Erin pulled out her cell phone and started dialing. At the first number, no one answered. The second woman told her she needed at least two weeks' notice, and they would never get their paperwork approved anyway. The third was only an answering machine.

"No luck," she told Sean, frowning.

"Keep trying," he urged her, glancing up from his clipboard.

The fourth person on the list, one Rick Williams, answered the phone.

"Hello, my name is Erin," she said quickly, trying to push out her request before he interrupted with a refusal. "I'm trying to find someone who would be willing to officiate a wedding."

"That's my job," he replied in a loud, jovial voice. "What do you have in mind?"

"Nothing fancy," she replied. "We just want to get it done. The thing is, we want it done today."

The line went silent for a moment. Then the man on the other end inhaled audibly and boomed, "Yikes, that's fast. Do you have the license?"

"We're working on it. They're trying to push it through," she explained.

Another silence seemed to indicate him thinking. "Well, if you can get it, I don't have any plans for this afternoon. No one much really gets married in November. If what you want is a barebones legal ceremony, I have a budget option for $150.00. Do you have a venue in mind?"

A venue? I never thought of such a thing. Looks like even a tiny wedding takes some planning. "No."

"Would my office be okay?"

"Sure. That's fine." *Whew. That was easy.*

"Any guests?"

"I think one."

"You'll need two witnesses. Do you mind if my secretary signs your license?"

Oh Lord, how many details do we need to work out? "That will be great."

"All right. Let's say four o'clock. If you can't get the license approved today, call and let me know, and we'll reschedule something later, okay?" he suggested.

"Awesome. Thank you so much." Erin sagged with relief.

Sean's stomach growled loud enough for her to hear it.

"Think we can step out for lunch?" he suggested.

Erin glanced at the clock and stared. *12:47? Where did the morning go? I wonder how long it will take to find out what's happening.*

Erin opened her mouth to agree, when, "Murphy," rang out over the intercom.

Trembling, stomach churning, she clung to Sean as they walked back to the counter, certain their waiver had been denied. *It's too much to hope I'll ever really get to be his wife.*

"Well, my dears," the clerk said, waving the pile of papers in front of her crinkled smile, "this would never have happened in June, but here you go. Good luck. Here's your approved license and waiver."

She handed Sean the sheaf. Erin was on the phone with Rick about half a second later, confirming the arrangement to meet in his office at four. Her trembling threatened to turn to outright shaking as they approached the car.

"Erin," Sean said as they walked, "don't you have classes today?"

Gracious, how did I forget? "Yes, actually. I have a bassoon lesson scheduled for about half an hour from now. Thanks for reminding me."

Tugging out her phone and frowning at the low battery, she pressed the speed dial.

"This is Dr. Yamamoto," the accented voice she recognized answered.

"Um, this is Erin James, I need to reschedule this week's lesson, please. Something has come up."

"You, Erin?" he asked, sounding surprised. "Ah, well. I guess I get the day off after all. Happy Thanksgiving."

"You too," she replied. *I am happy, and thankful doesn't even come close.*

"Bassoon?" Sean asked as she hung up.

"Yes. I'm a double reed major. I have to be proficient in all the oboe variations: English horn, bassoon, and contra, as well as piano. I've even been working a little with the flute. The more I know, the more lessons I can teach later. Anyway, my other class today is Political Science, which I hate. We're allowed three no-shows per semester. I've never missed once, so it's okay."

"I kind of liked that class," Sean admitted.

"Well, run for mayor, if you want," she replied in disgust. "I can't stand it. It's hard to imagine anything worse than politics."

"To each his own, baby. I think I just want to major in you for a while."

Erin couldn't help melting. "Now that sounds lovely. So, what's next?"

"Let's get something to eat." She grinned at the hint of a whine in Sean's voice.

"Hungry?"

"Very. I had this insatiable wench trying to ride me all afternoon and evening," he quipped.

"I don't remember you complaining," she said, arching her eyebrow.

"Nope. There's nothing wrong with a wife who really likes sex." He spoke in a sexy tone that made her insides curl.

"Or a husband either." They treated each other to a long, smoldering assessment before Erin turned the conversation back to the practical. "You know, if we go to the mall to eat, there's a little jewelry store right there. We could shop for some wedding rings."

His teeth flashed in a grin that set her heart pounding. "Sure. Sounds good."

* * *

Arriving at the mall, they strolled to the food court. Erin bought herself a small roast beef sandwich and a side salad while Sean piled into an enormous burger.

"Take human bites," she urged, watching him wolf down the oversized patty.

"I'm starving," he mumbled into his napkin.

"I think once we're married, I'm going to have to keep a close eye on your nutrition."

He swallowed. "And make sure I get plenty of exercise," he replied, leering.

"No sweat," she replied. *I guess I really am an insatiable wench. How wonderful.*

They finished about the same time, and, dumping their trash, made their way down the hall to the jewelry store. The small space formed the location, not of a chain, but a local business owned by a well-respected local jeweler.

Looking at one price tag, she winced. *$200 for a gold band? $1800 for a solitaire? Who has that kind of money? At least there's no need for the expensive diamond. A set of simple gold bands should do the trick.*

Except that so many gold bands lay inside those cases, Erin didn't know where to begin. Some had diamond chips or other inset stones, others had silver accents. Some were thick, and others were thin.

"Hello, sir, ma'am, how can I help you?" The owner, a dapper elderly gentleman, emerged from a back room to assist his bewildered clients.

"Well," Sean told him, "we're getting married – today, actually – and we'd like some rings."

"Yes, I have rings." He stated the obvious with a wry smile. "What kind do you like?"

"I don't know," Erin said, shaking her head. "I don't wear jewelry. I'm a musician and most rings just get in the way."

"I imagine something smooth would get in the way less," he pointed out.

"Okay, but that doesn't really narrow things down much does it?" She waved her hand at the crowded cases.

"Do you want them to match?" the man asked, hoping to narrow the selection.

Match... each other? Of course. "Yes."

He opened his mouth to speak again, when a soft exclamation from across the room interrupted the interrogation.

"Erin," Sean called, "come here a minute."

She drifted over and gasped. Tucked into the back, behind some chunky jewelry that made Erin think of old ladies with hair like meringue, lay a forgotten ring set, dusty from having been ignored so long. The man's ring was massive, the woman's dainty, and they consisted of flat, broad gold bands featuring a running pattern of Celtic knots all the way around. The heavy black antiquing made the shining twists of that ancient symbol of eternity stand out brightly. *They're perfect.*

"Sir, can we see these please?" Sean asked.

"Those? Why those?"

"We're Irish," Erin replied.

He glanced at their dark hair and fair completions as he pulled the box out onto the counter. "Of course you are. Here you go."

Erin slid the small band onto her finger. It fit perfectly. She struggled to restrain her tears, but one escaped anyway. Sean brushed it away, softly caressing her cheek. Then he tried on the larger one. Despite its size, it wouldn't quite go onto his work-roughened finger. "It's too small," he complained.

"Normally, it would take me a few days to fix it," the jeweler explained, "but we're a little dead right now, as most of the customers are at work. Friday will be a different story. I can have it fixed for you by three."

"Great," Sean replied. "The wedding is at four, so that should work."

The jeweler tried a series of blank rings onto Sean's finger until he found just the right fit. "All right then," he said, putting both rings into a tiny manila envelope and making a note on the outside. "See you at four." He disappeared into the back room.

"Well, now what?" Erin asked as they left the store.

"I don't know. Do you want to shop for anything else, like a dress?"

"Hmmm, maybe so," she replied. "The only dress I own is a black one I wear to performances."

"That's not too festive," Sean concurred.

"I'm not sure I'm entitled to white. I'm not exactly a virgin," Erin commented, thinking of the previous night's endless passion, not to mention their nearly year-long affair.

"You don't have to be a virgin to be perfect, you know," he pointed out, making her shiver with another of those passionate, smoldering looks that promised to do further damage to her non-existent virginity later. "To me you're an angel. Wear whatever color you want."

Not hardly an angel, Erin thought, but she appreciated the sentiment. "I have an idea." She took out her phone and called Sheridan again. A few minutes later she hung up and turned to him.

"Two hours isn't much time, really. Why don't you go back to the hotel and get ready? Sheridan is going to drive my car over and meet me here. We'll pick out some dresses. If you come back to the jewelry store at three, we can head over to Rick's together."

"Oh, okay," Sean agreed. A little frown creased his forehead. "I hate leaving you though."

And I love the blue fire in your eyes that shows me how much. "I know." She trailed her fingers down his cheek. "But just think, this time tomorrow, no distance on earth can separate us."

Sean scooped Erin into his arms and kissed her. "I love you, Erin."

"I love you too."

Erin couldn't help watching his backside as he walked away. *He looks so fine in his jeans. I can't wait to get him out of them again, only next time it will be as his wife.*

* * *

Back at the hotel, Sean considered what lay ahead of him. He felt strangely calm. *Taking one of the most momentous steps in adult life is not bothering me at all.* Despite giving up, for all time, the opportunity to be with anyone but Erin, he felt no nerves. In fact, the thought of having her all to himself for the rest of his life soothed an ache he'd nursed far too long.

For three agonizing years, he had tried to forget her, to move on. It had been an abject failure.

He'd tried to force himself to get out there, but he couldn't do it. No one had been able to compare. To this day no one could. Last night, holding Erin – his Erin – had only confirmed what he'd known all along. *She's the one, and we're getting married in a couple of hours. Perfect.*

Sean considered calling his parents – the relationship had been kept too much a secret already and the reckoning would be terrible – but he decided against it. They might try to talk him out of it, and that just wouldn't do. *I finally have the opportunity to do what I've always wanted, what I've dreamed of these last few years. Better to let them know when it's done.*

* * *

At four o'clock exactly, the bride and groom and their guest arrived at the office of Rick Williams, wedding officiator.

Erin's knees trembled under her touchably soft silver dress, but her fingers, laced through Sean's, remained steady. *He looks good enough to eat in that blue Sunday shirt. It matches his eyes.*

Though she knew she looked her best, Erin felt a momentary pang realizing that, no matter what, this bride would always be outshone by her best friend. Sheridan simply glowed in everything she wore. Turning back to Sean, seeing the tender heat in his eyes as he regarded... *Me – his future wife. He only looks at me like that* – more than compensated.

"Hello there," boomed a loud voice from behind the desk. Rick turned out to be a heavyset man of middle years with a pleasant face and sparkling eyes. The sight of him made Erin smile. He resembled everyone's favorite uncle. "Okay, ladies, which of you is Erin?"

"I am." She stepped forward.

He looked her over and smiled kindly. "Nice to meet you. I take it this is your intended."

"Yes. This is Sean." The men shook hands. "And this is my best friend, Sheridan."

"Well, I'm glad to be able to help you today. Do you have your paperwork?" he asked. They handed him the stack and he examined it carefully. "Looks good. So, did you two have any requests?"

"To get it done? This has been a long time coming, and I can't wait another minute," Erin told him seriously.

"So, just a no-frills, legal wedding?" he guessed.

"Yes."

Rick considered them for a moment. "Forgive me, but something about you all says Catholic. Are you sure this is what you want? Would it really be so bad to wait for a church wedding?"

"This is exactly what we want," Sean said firmly, "I'm sure my mother will drag us to the church later."

The man's pondering expression changed to a broad, eye-twinkling grin. "Ah. Well, all right then. Come over here to the fireplace. Let's get you two married."

Chapter 17

𝄞

Monday evening, after work, Sean sought out his parents at their home, feeling nervous. *I have no idea how they will take what I'm about to tell them.*

Still, it had naturally been a wonderful weekend. He had never felt so content and satisfied in his life. His only regret was that, having slept five nights with Erin in his arms, last night he had been alone again. The knowledge that she would come to him at Christmas, so they could spend the month-long break together helped some, but he still missed his wife. *Wife. That sounds so good.*

Sean deliberately arrived a little early and met Ellen and Roger in the kitchen. "Hi, Dad. Hi, Mom, how are you?"

"I'm well, dear," Ellen said, "how are you? Did you have a nice visit with your sister? How is she doing?"

"Danny is doing so much better, I can't even believe it. She's practically back to her old self. I've never been so happy to be teased in my life. As for me, well, I'm great. I have something I need to talk to you about though. Would you please take a seat?" He indicated the barstools.

Roger sat, but Ellen, sensing something up with her son, gave him a long appraisal. "Sean, what on earth are you wearing? That looks like a wedding ring!" she exclaimed.

He pulled out a stool for his mother and gently slid it up to the bar. "Mom, Dad, the reason this looks like a wedding ring is that... it's a wedding ring."

Roger nodded as though this didn't surprise him in the least. Ellen, however, gawked, aghast. "Why exactly are you wearing a wedding ring?" she demanded.

"There's no exotic and mysterious reason for it. The reason I'm wearing a wedding ring is that, well, I'm married." He couldn't prevent a sheepish smile from spreading across his face. *I must look like an idiot.*

"Married!?" Ellen stared, open-mouthed at her son. "When did you get married?"

Sean considered for a moment. "Wednesday." *After making love to Erin all Tuesday night... Stop it!* He tucked his hands into his jeans pockets and discreetly adjusted himself so as to avoid the zipper.

Ellen's eyebrows came together. "But you were down visiting your sister on Wednesday."

"Yes."

"So, whom did you marry?"

"Isn't it obvious, Ellen?" Roger asked his wife. "He's married Erin James."

"Erin? Sheridan's Erin?" She turned to Sean. "Is that right, son?"

"Yes, although I think it's safe to say she's more mine than Danny's now." A little voice inside his head couldn't seem to stop cheering.

"Why?"

For a thousand reasons I could never explain "It wasn't a spur of the moment thing," he replied, "or rather the timing was, but Erin and I have been together for four years and we just didn't want to wait anymore."

"I beg your pardon? You've been together four months?" Ellen demanded, looking more like a storm cloud with every word.

"No, Mom. Four years," he explained. "Erin has been my girlfriend since her senior year of high school."

Ellen gave her son a hard stare. Then she turned to her husband. "Did you know about this?"

"I suspected," Roger admitted cheerfully. He didn't seem perturbed. "Since we work together, we talk a lot. I was aware he was seeing someone, even though he didn't ever say who. But he asked a couple of pointed questions about age differences that got me thinking, and since Erin was pretty much a constant part of our lives, she seemed a likely candidate." Roger addressed his son. "She's a lovely girl. Congratulations."

"Thank you, Dad." Sean felt like a lit Christmas tree. *Dad approves. Thank you, Lord!*

"But, son, why didn't you ever say anything?" Ellen wanted to know.

Well, we're fifty percent there. Got to keep working on Mom. "We got together at homecoming. I don't have to remind you what a dark time that was. With poor Danny and everything that happened to her, we didn't want to add to the upset by flaunting our controversial relationship. Honestly, even though Erin was young at the time, she's so mature it was like dating someone my own age. It has never been an issue between us." Each word sounded more aggressive than the last.

"Don't be defensive, son," Roger admonished. "It's years past."

"I know, but at the time, would you have approved of us being together?"

"Probably not," Ellen commented, her voice every bit as hard as Sean's had been.

"And that's another reason we didn't say anything. Erin absolutely needed me in order to get through that year. I couldn't risk her losing my support. She was on the brink most of the time already."

"Why is that?"

Come on, Mom, enough. Why do you have to argue on and on? Her endless questioning tightened his shoulders and stiffened his spine. He squirmed. *Knock that off. You look like a guilty kid.*

"Well apart from the fact that she appointed herself Danny's champion and shield, and took as many of her problems on herself as she could, her own parents were going through a divorce right then. It was a hard year for both of them."

"All right," Ellen conceded. "But what about after? There was no need to keep it a secret so long."

"You're right," Sean agreed. "It was a mistake, but at the time, we didn't know what was best to do. It was confusing. For one thing, we decided to take it easy for a while, so she could concentrate on college. Remember, Dad, you told me not to let her give up her dreams for me?" He and Erin had discussed how they wanted to describe their ill-advised separation, and that was the best explanation they could come up with, since neither of their feelings had wavered for a moment. He continued. "Maybe we got into the habit of keeping our relationship private. I regret that because it made Erin think I wasn't proud to be her boyfriend, which I absolutely was. That's why I'm telling you now. I love my wife. I'm so thankful to have her. Oh, and there's something else."

"What?" Ellen's hand fluttered on her chest, as though she couldn't take another shock.

"She's coming up for Christmas, naturally. I know you two haven't seen her in a while. The thing is, Erin has never had a loving family. You know what her parents are like. I absolutely intend for the Murphy clan to embrace her with open arms and make her one of us. She deserves it after all she's done for us and I won't accept anything less."

"Of course, Sean," Roger told his son. "She's your wife. She already is one of us. Besides, Erin has been a member of this family for years."

Bingo. Thank you, Dad. "I think so too."

"Well," Ellen said a little stiffly, "There really isn't anything to be said to that, is there? It's done. But I have a couple of questions that need to be cleared up first."

Uh oh. I don't like the sound of that. "I'll answer any question you ask, Mom. Be sure you really want to know."

"Oh, I do." Ellen's eyes narrowed to suspicious slits. "Just before the girls left for college, Erin took off to spend the night with her boyfriend. She was quite blunt with me about what she was doing. Was that you then?"

Boy, Mom doesn't hold back, does she? The burn in his cheeks told him she already knew the answer. "What's worse, Mom? To think she was sleeping with me, or with someone else while she was dating me? Yes, of course it was me."

"And she also told me that wasn't the first time. That she gave her virginity to her boyfriend a long time ago."

He closed his eyes. *She said that? To Mom?* "Yes."

"Why?"

At least that question had a simple answer. "So we could be as close as possible. Erin and I knew we were it for each other. She's never been with anyone else. Since I got together with her, I haven't either. I don't think that's so bad, but are you sure you need this information? How does it benefit you to know?"

"I'm trying to understand exactly what kind of girl you're bringing into the family."

Now that's going too far. Sean glared.

"Ellen," Roger said sharply, "don't say anything more. I know you're upset by the surprise of this, but we already know what kind of person Erin is. She's the best, most loving, most selfless person any of us has ever known. She gave unselfishly to our family for years, almost to the point of damaging herself. If what she wants in exchange is a place at our table, it's a small enough thing to ask."

"I didn't think the cost of that help would be our firstborn son," Ellen groused.

"Don't be melodramatic, Mother," Sean said sarcastically. "She's hardly going to take me away from you. You know she has no family. If you could get past being upset, you'd see that

Erin will make you a fine daughter. You're going to need one. Sheridan's never coming back. She's going to graduate school, and she wants to stay at the university and teach, so if you want to continue having a daughter in your life, it's going to have to be Erin. I suggest you make peace with it. She wants to be part of the family, so the only person who can take me away is you, if you refuse to accept my wife."

Ellen slumped on the barstool. "I can see that. Let me process this for a while. I'm sure once the shock wears off, it will be fine."

I hope that's true.

* * *

About the time Sean was having his white-knuckled conversation with his parents, Erin arrived at the music department's recital hall for the rehearsal of the senior woodwind group. She entered a few minutes early. She hadn't even opened her oboe case since Tuesday, and she felt a little rusty after so many days. Crossing the wooden floor of the stage, she plunked herself down in one of the uncomfortable orange plastic chairs, set her music on the stand, and began putting the pieces of her instrument together. She glanced over the rows of seats anchored to the floor. *How many classes, concerts and recitals have I attended in this space? How many performances have I given? It's as familiar as my dorm room.*

Just as she slipped her double reed into the top of the oboe, a couple of her friends came in. This woodwind group, calling itself The Young Bohemians, had grown really close, almost like family, and Erin felt quite sure that no matter where everyone ended up, they would always stay in touch.

Tory and Justin arrived first, hand in hand. Erin deliberately blew hard into her oboe and greeted them with a raucous quack. This was a game these young musicians played. All of them were far too accomplished for their instruments to make such ugly noises unless it was on purpose, but all were young enough to remember when this had not been the case.

"Hi, Erin," Tory greeted her with a one-sided hug around the shoulders.

"Hey, guys. How's it going? Did you have a good break?"

"Oh yes," the black-haired girl said, waggling her eyebrows, "I took Justin to meet my parents."

"How nerve-wracking. Justin, did you survive intact? I don't think it will help your clarinet playing to have pieces missing from your hide."

"It was fine." Justin – a quiet man with a nose almost too large for his thin face and dark hair that stood out in all directions – rarely said a word. He let his instrument do most of the communicating for him.

Tory giggled. "Yeah, except when they almost caught us in bed together."

"Really?" Erin laughed. "Then I'm doubly glad you're still alive."

Justin blushed and sat down assemble his instrument. He gave the embarrassing situation the raspberry through his clarinet, making it squeal horrendously, just as Ilona, Marisol, and Marcus came into the room.

"My God, Justin," Marcus sneered teasingly, his aristocratic features wrinkling in disgust at the horrible noise, "if that's all the better you can play that thing, we'll have to move you to percussion." He lugged his bassoon case over to a chair and opened it.

"What about you, Erin?" Tory asked. "What did you do? Did you go anywhere?"

"I had a wonderful Thanksgiving," Erin said simply. *There's nothing better than a honeymoon, after all.*

"I'll say you had a wonderful time, Erin," Marisol said, tossing her dyed red hair. "Just what the hell is that on your neck? Don't tell me it's from a curling iron. I know a hickey when I see one."

Erin put her hand to her throat. "Oh God, did he leave a mark?" Her pale face felt flushed and she knew it had turned scarlet.

"My, my, my, Erin, what *did* you do over Thanksgiving?" Ilona drawled. "Did you finally lose your virginity?"

"Uh, no." Her cheeks burned hotter than ever.

"Liar," the redhead teased.

"Seriously. There was nothing to lose. Can we drop it please?" She shuffled her music.

"Nothing to lose?" Tory asked, surprised. "You've never dated that I'm aware of."

Erin took a deep breath. "Actually, you've never known me when I was a virgin. I've had a boyfriend all along, since high school. I had a great weekend, but well, like I said, we've been together for years. It was not even close to being the first time."

Everyone stared at her.

"Um, if that's the case, why didn't you ever say anything?" Ilona asked.

"Well, uh, I... I mean..." Erin stammered, trying to recall the story they'd concocted. "We kind of decided to take it easy while I was away at college, so I would have time to study, you know? But he came up for a visit, and it was... just too much. We were both about ready to burst. So, we decided to just... get married." She held up her left hand, displaying the pretty ring.

After a moment of stunned silence, all the girls began to scream, making noises no one would have expected a group of serious musicians to make. They descended on Erin, hugging her.

After a moment, Tory said, "You know, my roommate said she saw you on Tuesday, in the courtyard outside the English building, making out with some hot guy. I told her she was crazy. Was that true?"

"Yes." The heat in Erin's cheeks faded into a happy glow.

"So that's your husband? What's his name?"

"Sean." Erin sighed the name like a lovesick puppy. "He's actually my roommate's older brother. We've known each other forever."

"How nice. Sean what?" Tory asked.

"Murphy."

"Hmmm. Erin Murphy," Marisol tried it out.

Erin had never heard her name transformed this way, and it sounded so great she almost went to pieces and cried.

At that moment, the director came in. "Hey, what's this? Why aren't your instruments put together? What's going on?"

"Sorry, Dr. Johnson. It's just... we've had some amazing news and we lost track of time," Ilona said.

"What news?"

"Erin just got married!"

Dr. Johnson's bushy salt and pepper eyebrows met. *That is not a promising look.* "Erin, please come with me right now. The rest of you, I want those instruments assembled and warmed up in the next five minutes."

Erin set her oboe on the music stand and followed Dr. Johnson down the hallway and into his messy, music-laden office, her heart pounding. "Is something wrong, sir?" she asked as she leaned the threshold.

"Well, not wrong exactly," he replied, but his voice sounded no less stern. "I was wondering what this would mean for you professionally. I've been talking to recruiters from symphonies all over about you. They want to hear you play. There's one in particular in Omaha that I thought would be a good place for you to start."

"Sir, I've never asked for any of that," Erin protested. "It has always been my intention, after I finished my degree, to go home."

"Why? You're good enough to play anywhere." Perplexed, he raked his fingers through his nimbus of silver hair.

"Thank you, but there are more important things than professional accolades."

"Like what?"

"Like being loved." It was a personal thing to admit to a professor, but Dr. Johnson had been her mentor from the beginning and she owed him the truth.

"I see. Well, what are you planning to do then?"

"Play in the symphony, and probably teach some lessons," she explained, as the future, the beautiful future she almost had given up on dreaming about, played like a film behind her eyes. "My hometown doesn't really have a dedicated double reed specialist. I could fill in that spot. Help other kids achieve, you know?"

"Hmmm. I think that's a pretty small ambition for someone of your talents."

The images shattered. *You too, professor? Jeez.* Erin, having heard far too much of this argument, lost her cool a little. "Why does everyone take it upon themselves to belittle my dreams? I'm just as capable as anyone else of deciding what I want to do with my life, and it is *my* life, damn it."

Dr. Johnson raised his hands in apology. "Sorry, you're right. I don't mean to put you down, Erin. You have every right to make your own choices. It's just kind of surprising. Usually, people who are very talented have big professional ambitions."

"Well, I don't. The most ambitious, unlikely thing I've ever wanted was to be part of a family. Nothing has ever come close to that in my heart," she blurted.

Dr. Johnson leveled an understanding look at Erin, one that made her cheeks hot. *Oops. Might have overdone it a bit.* But he didn't speak. Instead, he gave her a gentle hug and sent her back to the recital hall to warm up her oboe.

* * *

Later that night, Erin stretched out in her bed. Without Sean, the cold nipped at her, as did her loneliness. *It will be a month before my husband will be able to hold me again.* She didn't want to disturb Sheridan, in the bed across the room, but she couldn't help sniffling.

"Erin, are you okay?" Sheridan asked.

"I'm fine," she said in a gloomy voice.

Sheridan hopped out of the bed, kneeling beside her friend and giving her a warm hug. Erin's control cracked a little more, but she tried hard to hang on.

"Poor Erin. This must be really difficult." Sheridan smoothed her hair away from her forehead.

"You have no idea." A tear escaped, and she dashed it away.

"Why don't you call him, sweetie."

"I can't do that. How silly."

"It isn't either," Sheridan insisted. "It's fine. I'm sure he would love to hear your voice. He misses you too, you know."

"I don't want to bother him."

"Erin," Sheridan said sharply, "why do you put yourself down this way? It's not wrong or a bother for you to call your husband and talk to him. No one would say that's a bad thing. Here. Take the phone. Do it."

Erin grasped the device. *I really don't want to be annoying, but the thought of hearing Sean's voice is so appealing.* Torn, she looked at her friend.

"I promise he'll be glad. Just dial the number, Erin. You'll feel so much better if you talk to him."

Erin dialed. She counted the rings with a pounding heart, holding her breath.

"Hello?"

Oh, that voice. I could wrap myself up in it like a blanket. "Hi, Sean."

"Hey. I was wondering if you would call," he replied, sounding… happy.

"Is this a good time?"

"Sure. I've got nothing going on. Is anything up?"

"No. I just missed you. I wanted to talk to you for a while." *Damn it, voice. Don't waver. Sound confident, you baby.*

"I miss you, too. This is a really weird situation, isn't it?"

"It is. Good thing it's temporary. What's going on with you?"

"I talked to my parents today."

She winced. "Are they mad?"

"Mom's a little hurt that we didn't tell her sooner. Dad's actually great with it."

"Oh, good." *Thank heaven one of them is okay.*

"Is Danny right there?" His voice took on a lascivious tone.

"Yes."

"If she weren't, I would make love to you right now."

From this distance? "How?"

"Oh Erin, there's so much you have to learn. It's called phone sex."

Erin's cheeks heated. "Sounds interesting."

"Hmmm. At least let me hold you for a while. Close your eyes, baby, and imagine you're here. Can you visualize it in your mind?"

The warmth of Sean's affection did seem to wrap around her. "Yes."

"Good. You're lying on your side in bed with me. I'm pressed up against your back, spooning you, with my arm around your waist. Can you feel me there?"

"Almost."

"Try hard. I can almost feel you too. Now, I sweep your hair away from the side of your neck and kiss you there."

Erin giggled.

"What is it?"

"You left a hickey on my neck. I was so busted with my woodwind ensemble this evening."

"I did? I didn't even realize." He laughed, and the sound warmed her right down to her toes.

"Me either."

"Well anyway, I would kiss you right there. And I would hold you close while you fell asleep. I love you, Erin."

"I love you too."

"Good night, baby."

"Good night."

"You see," Sheridan said softly as the phone beeped, signaling the end of the call, "he loves you and he wants to talk to you. Just plan to call him every night at bedtime, okay, and save yourself worrying about it."

From the hazy warmth of her husband's imaginary embrace, anything seemed possible. "Okay. I'll do that."

* * *

The next day, when Erin was at her oboe lesson, Sheridan called her mother.

"Hi, Mom."

"Hello, darling. How are you doing?" Ellen asked.

"I'm great. I just finished reading some amazing poetry. Would you like to hear it?" she teased.

"Um…" Mrs. Murphy was not a great lover of poetry, as Sheridan well knew.

"I'm just kidding, Mom. Listen, did Sean talk to you yesterday?"

Ellen didn't even pretend not to know what her daughter was talking about. "He did. I simply can't imagine what came over them. Couldn't you have talked them out of it?"

Uh oh. That doesn't bode well. "Actually, it was my idea."

"What?" Ellen sounded stunned even over the phone. "Why?"

"I've always known those two belonged together. I set them up in high school too. They're a great couple."

"So, you've known about them all along?" Ellen griped, "Why does no one tell me anything?"

"It wasn't the right time then. You know that. Our family, wonderful though it is, was strained to its limits. Who knows what might have happened if there had been a fight over a girlfriend. And even though Erin was only eighteen, she's always been more mature than the calendar admits, and was perfectly marvelous with Sean. Now she's twenty-two, I'm all better, and it's time for those two to come out of hiding and be a couple. It's the perfect timing."

"I just don't understand it at all," Ellen continued to complain. "Why Erin for Sean?"

"Why not?" Sheridan shot back, unintimidated by her mother's anger. "We all know what a wonderful person she is. Mom, the question isn't 'why Erin?' It's why do you have a problem with her?"

"I'm not really sure. Something about it just feels wrong," Ellen groused.

"It's not wrong for them to be together. It's ideal," Sheridan protested. "You know, if you're saying, after everything that Erin has done for all of us, that she's not good enough to marry your son... well, it's like she's a servant or something."

"What? I don't appreciate that comment at all."

Sheridan could visualize her mother's scowl as though the woman were sitting across the room, but she refused to back down. "No, seriously, think about it. Erin's good enough to cook our Thanksgiving dinner, play her instrument for us, babysit me until her own life nearly passes her by, but not good enough to be Sean's wife? Even though they love each other like nothing I've ever seen? What sense does that make? Mom, you need to get over whatever is bothering you and let this be."

"That's what everyone keeps telling me." Ellen sighed dramatically. "I'm not going to order her out of the house."

"But will you welcome her into it?" Sheridan pressed.

Mrs. Murphy didn't answer, and the conversation ended without any further resolution.

Chapter 18

On the last Friday afternoon of the semester, the day before winter break began, Sean's phone rang. Caller ID revealed Erin's cell "What's up, baby?" he asked as he scrolled through his emails. *Sweetest sound ever, your voice. I can't wait to hold you.*

"You know how I said I would be there by evening?" She sounded just shy of frantic.

The tone of her voice broke through his amused distraction. He sat up taller in his chair. "Yes."

"Well, there's no way. I've been delayed on one of my finals, and I have to take it tonight. If I don't, I'll fail the class and put my scholarship at risk. I don't know how long it's going to take, but I won't be there until late."

"That's okay," he soothed her. *Damn, I don't want a delay either, but it's not that bad.* "Don't be upset. It's fine. Take your test. Do your best. I'll wait up for you."

"No, don't wait, Sean," she urged. "It could be after midnight before I get there. Go to sleep. When you wake up in the morning, I'll be there beside you."

"Okay. Good luck. I love you, Erin."

"I love you too."

Sean did try to wait up for his wife, but he had been so busy working on the surprise he was giving her for Christmas that by eleven he simply couldn't stay awake anymore.

About four hours later, Erin entered the apartment quietly. It had been terrible trying to drive so far in the dark, especially after such a difficult week, but she'd managed it. She set her bag quietly on top of the dresser and approached the bed. *Sean, beautiful sexy Sean, my husband.* He lay on his side, deeply asleep and relaxed, the blanket riding low to reveal his powerful shoulder and chest. He had left a little space for her beside him. *I must be the luckiest woman on earth.* She slid into the bed beside him and snuggled her body against his, her back to his front, the way they always talked about on the phone.

He didn't wake up, but stirred, cuddling closer to her, his arm falling over the soft curve of her waist. She pulled the covers over them both and closed her eyes. *It's so wonderful to be home.*

* * *

Sean woke up the next morning feeling warm and comfortable. He opened his eyes to find his wife close in front of him. His arms tightened around her waist. *She must have arrived very late for me not even to be aware of it. Silly girl. I hope she was able to drive safely.* Not wanting to wake her, he kissed the top of her head and carefully lifted his arm from her waist before rising from the bed.

He admired her beautiful face. *Lovely woman. I'm going to do such decadent things to you today.* Smiling, Sean walked into the kitchen to make some coffee.

Around nine, he returned to the bedroom and knelt beside the bed, stroking Erin's hair and leaning down to kiss her on the lips. She stirred and made a little humming noise.

"Wake up, baby," he said, trailing his fingers over her cheek, more to tickle than to stroke.

"Ugh," Erin groaned. "What time is it?"

"Time to get up," he replied. "Listen, I know you haven't had enough sleep, but if you sleep all day you'll be mixed up tomorrow too. How late did you get in?"

"Around three."

"Oh wow, that's really late. Well, there's some coffee for you if you want it, and you need to have some breakfast, too."

"Why?" she whined, still resisting waking fully.

"I'm sure you can guess. I intend to put you through your paces today, little girl, and it won't do to have you getting faint from lack of nourishment."

The suggestion brought Erin the rest of the way up, and she sat in the bed, arms around her knees. "That sounds pretty intense. I can't wait. Can't we just get started?"

"Nope. Food first."

Erin stretched. The blanket fell away from her body. Sean pressed a soft kiss to each of her breasts before extending a hand and helping her to her feet. She stepped into the cradle of his arms for a long, welcoming hug, and then headed into the kitchen in search of that coffee. Sean trailed after her. *Nothing can go wrong now that my Erin is finally here with me.*

She sipped her hot drink as she poured cereal into a bowl and splashed milk on it, and then sat down at the table.

Sean joined her. "What happened yesterday? Why did your test go so late?"

"It was the weirdest thing," she replied between bites. "That test was supposed to be Wednesday, first thing in the morning. I got there, all ready to be done with political science forever, and sat down, but after I had barely started, I got really sick. I actually had to go to the bathroom and throw up. It was so embarrassing. I guess the cafeteria food wasn't too good or something." She paused and swallowed hard, as though the memory of vomiting had nauseated her. "The professor could see I wasn't up to working on it, and he said I could take it later. He would email me the questions and I could work on them at my own pace, but that they were due by midnight Friday or it would be a zero." Erin shrugged. "That sounded fine. I spent the rest of the morning throwing up, but I was okay after that." Sean stroked her hand in sympathy and she continued. "He never sent me the questions though. I called and left messages, emailed him, and looked in at his office, but I couldn't find him. Finally, on

Friday, I just waited for him. It was two hours before he showed up. He had forgotten completely. So, I stood there while he sent the email, but then I had to go and take a final in one of my music classes. That was supposed to be the last one. I finished around six, had some dinner, and then started the test. It was so hard, and my grade in there isn't good. If I aced the final, I could possibly get an A, but I still had to do really well for a B. I don't want to end up with a C, so I worked my butt off on it."

"One C is not the end of the world," Sean commented. *I got more than one, and I still graduated no problem.*

"I know, but I don't like it. I don't even like getting a B, and I've only had three of them so far: both semesters of chemistry and algebra."

"You're such a good student."

Erin beamed, the way she always did when someone praised her. "Thanks. I do try hard. Anyway, I finished the test about ten and spent another hour looking it over. Then I submitted it electronically, but I wasn't about to go until I got confirmation that he had received it. He didn't do that until midnight, and that's when I was finally able to leave."

"You probably should have waited and come down in the morning," he told her seriously.

"Sean, I don't want to sleep away from you one more night than I have to."

"That's sweet, but please don't risk your safety. We have a lifetime of nights to spend together."

"It's not enough."

Sean kissed her forehead. "So, you're feeling okay now?" *Please, don't be sick. I have plans for you.*

"I think so. I do feel a little funny, but that's probably just fatigue."

"No doubt." He eyed her figure with interest. *Good.*

"Um, would it be okay for me to take a quick shower before we get started? I feel kind of grungy."

"Okay. Don't bother getting dressed, though." He winked at her.

Erin shivered with delight and hurried into the shower. While she cleaned up, Sean deliberately lowered the temperature in the apartment. It was freezing outside, and the small adjustment made a big difference. He grinned. *This is going to be fun.*

* * *

Soon, Erin emerged, dripping. She dried off quickly and ran a comb through her wet hair before searching for her husband. She found him on the sofa, flipping mindlessly through the television channels, so she intentionally stepped between him and the screen. He lifted his eyes to see Erin completely naked. She smirked at his stunned expression. Between her damp skin and the coldness of the room, her nipples stood out harder than she could remember them ever having been, exactly level with his face. He wrapped both arms around her waist and pulled her closer to kneel, straddling his lap.

"Sean, what did you do?" she demanded. "It's so cold in here."

"Don't worry, baby, I'll keep you warm," he replied with a wicked grin. "Besides, you look so hot like this."

"I've gained weight." She waved at her offending curves.

"I know. In all the right places." He cupped one breast in his hand and teased her nipple with work-roughened fingers. Erin hummed with pleasure. "You do like that, don't you?"

"Oh yes. I always have." Her voice already sounded slurred, and no wonder. *Sean sure knows how to touch me the right way.* He leaned down and took first one straining peak in his mouth and then the other.

Erin began to squirm with the stimulation, grinding herself against Sean, so she could feel his erection through his clothing.

Sean held his wife with his arm behind her back while the other hand snaked around her body to open and caress her intimate folds, spreading the copious moisture before stroking her softly in her most sensitive place.

Erin was so turned on, it only took a moment for her pleasure to build and burst. She came hard, moaning deep in her throat. *It's a little disappointing that it happened so quickly*, she thought. Oh, but Sean wasn't finished with her. Not even close. He scooped her into his arms and laid her down on the sofa, positioning one of her legs on the back, lowering the other to the floor, so she was completely open for him. Then he stripped off his own clothing.

For some reason, Erin had never been modest where Sean was concerned, and the fact that she lay spread out before him with her legs parted, far from embarrassing her, actually turned her on more. She watched him watch her, his blue eyes dark with desire. Then he moved, rubbing her wet sex again before sliding two fingers into her. Erin made a soft sound of pleasure and arched her hips as he penetrated her, wanting him deeper. He gave her what she wanted, burying his fingers to the palm inside her snug womanhood.

"Do you know what I'm going to do to you now, baby?" his asked, pure fire dripping from his voice.

She looked up at him.

"I'm going to go down on you. This time there's no way you're going to be able to come silently. I want you to scream."

Erin drew a shaky breath. They gazed into each other's eyes for a wordless moment, and then Sean leaned down and delivered on his promise, licking her, sucking, teasing her clitoris with the tip of his tongue, and all the while his fingers flexed and tickled in the deepest part of her, teasing a spot she had never known existed. Every time Erin's orgasm began building, he backed off, driving her higher than she realized she was capable of going, until her whole body grew hot and tingly and her sex burned like fire. Only then did he give her that last critical lick that drove her over the edge. As he'd promised, she couldn't remain silent in her climax. Her cry of pleasure nearly was a scream. Her whole body rose from the sofa with the force of the spasm, her back arching, her head tilting back. At last, the final moment passed, and Erin lay, limp and sated, quite sure she would never move again.

"Poor Erin," Sean teased her, sliding his wet fingers out.

"Why?" she whispered; her lips would barely form the word.

"I'm going to take you so hard. It's a good thing you're ready for it."

"Be gentle," she urged.

"No. Not this time. You can take it."

He lifted her hips and lined up the tip of his sex with her opening. Her orgasms had left her relaxed and drenched, ready for his entry. He thrust hard, driving all the way to the hilt inside her in one powerful surge. He immediately began to pound her, not giving her time to adapt, just making her take it all. At first, she wanted to protest that he was too much, too big. But then she realized he was right. *I can take it. Take every inch.* She could feel each ridge and vein rubbing inside her. Suddenly discomfort became pleasure, the kind that rode the edge of pain; powerful, undeniable and wild. Sean thrust hard until he dragged a true scream from Erin's laboring lungs and left her ground under with overwhelming passion. She fell limp while he finished inside her with a shout.

A long moment later, Sean rose from the sofa, scooped his wife into his arms and carried her back to the bed. He tucked her under the blankets and slipped in beside her, pulling her flush against his body. Despite being wrung out from that intense loving, she felt cherished. *He knows how much I love sex and gave me one for the record books, a beautiful memory to sustain me during our next separation.* She smiled. "Damn, you're good, honey."

"You're not too bad yourself."

Erin rolled over and slid her arms around her husband's neck. "I love you. Let's just stay in bed together forever, okay?"

Sean grinned. "We can for a while, but we've been invited to my parents' house for dinner tonight."

Erin made a face.

"I thought you liked my parents."

Erin bit her lip. "I do. I just haven't seen them since way before we got married, and I feel a little funny about going to them now, knowing how I've misled them all these years. It probably wasn't the best idea."

"True, but it's done. What can we do about it now?" he asked.

"Nothing, but I still feel kind of bad."

"I know. It'll be okay though."

I hope he's right.

* * *

Later that evening, Sean escorted his wife to his childhood home. After spending a large portion of the day naked in bed, she now wore a demure pair of black slacks and a Christmas sweater. She had her oboe case in one hand and a folder of music in the other. Nerves worse than her wedding day set her knees knocking.

They entered the formal living room where, in the bay window, a large real tree – strung with lights but not yet decorated – perfumed the air. The fireplace sparkled with burning logs, making the room cozy and cheerful.

Roger and Ellen rose to greet the arrivals. Roger approached first and engulfed Erin in a massive bear hug. "It's so good to see you," he said. "Welcome to the family."

Erin's eyes stung. It appeared that at least from this man, all was forgiven. She hugged him back, unable to speak. *This is more than I ever expected.* When he released her, she gifted him with a sweet smile. He smiled back before turning to greet his son.

Erin faced her mother-in-law.

"Erin," Ellen said coolly.

"Hello, Mrs. Murphy. Thank you for inviting me."

Ellen nodded. Erin swallowed hard. *She looks furious. This is going to be awkward. I do not want to be the cause of problems between Sean and his amazing family. Somehow, I'm going to have to fix this. It's necessary, not least of all because my own mother is a dud, and I'd really rather keep Sean and Danny's. I hope the secrecy hasn't ruined that possibility for good.* The two women regarded each other, Erin with longing, Ellen with barely suppressed disapproval. Then Erin set her case and folder on the table and cautiously extended her hand. Ellen took it briefly. Erin remembered when Ellen had been willing to hug her and grieved.

Apparently sensing the tension, Roger intervened, offering Erin a glass of wine, which she took and sipped gratefully. Sean approached and slid his arm around his wife's waist, making a demonstration of his affection. He escorted her to a loveseat, where he sat beside her, still holding her. He gave his mother a hard look. She looked back steadily. The unpleasant silence stretched on.

"So, Erin," Roger said finally, "how's school going?"

"Very well." Erin smiled, perhaps a little wider than was necessary, in reaction to the thick tension in the room. "I'm so glad to have finished that semester. It was a pretty tough one."

"The next one is your last, right?" he continued.

"Yes. I can't wait to be done," she replied eagerly. *Come home and live with Sean. That will be so amazing, especially now that we don't have to hide it anymore.*

"How have you enjoyed studying music?" Roger asked, a hint of intensity touching his voice.

"It's been great. I love it. I've learned so much." *Erin, you're gushing like an idiot. Tone it down, girl.*

"I see you've brought your oboe with you," Roger commented.

"Yes. I remember that you've liked to hear me play before. I thought if you wanted to this time... well, I'm ready." *What if they don't? What if I've been presuming?* She didn't want to show off, so she quickly added, "If not, no big deal."

"I would love to hear you again," Roger reassured her. "After dinner?"

"Sure, if that's what everyone wants."

Nerves and frustration caused the wine to churn in Erin's stomach. She found a coaster and set the glass aside. *Hmmm. I've been awfully uncertain in my stomach for the last week or so. Interesting.*

"Erin, there's a little left to do in the kitchen before we can eat. Would you please come with me?" Ellen requested.

Erin sighed. She didn't know what Mrs. Murphy was going to say to her, but she suspected it was going to be hard.

Sean's hand tightened on his wife's. She squeezed back. *I deserve to be told off, and there's no point in trying to prevent it.* She tried to send the message through the fingers they'd laced together but had no idea if Sean understood.

"Sure. Of course." She ran the back of one finger lovingly over her husband's cheek before following her host into the kitchen.

* * *

Sean moved as though to follow.

"Let them go, son," Roger told him. "They have to work it out for themselves."

Sean shook his head, not denying his father's words, but worried nonetheless. "I know. I just don't want Erin to be hurt. Her life has been painful enough."

"It's going to be all right," Roger reassured his son. "Let your mother say her piece. I'm sure she'll feel better afterward."

Sean's every instinct screamed at him to go, to protect Erin, but he heeded his father's advice… *advice, that reminds me…* "Dad?"

"Yes?" Roger stopped staring at the door through which the women had just left and turned to face Sean.

"Why did you change your mind?"

"About what?"

Sean explained. "You remember, years ago, I asked you about whether it was wrong for me to be with her? You said I shouldn't let her give up her life for me. In a sense, that's what she's doing, but now you seem fine with it. Why is that?"

"You did your part, son," Roger said with an intensity that didn't seem to fit the situation. "You gave her the choice and the time. Four years later, she's still with you. She's made her decision. She wanted you more. I'm glad she still has an outlet for her art. Now it's up to you to give her the best life possible."

That makes perfect sense. "Right. It's what I aim to do."

* * *

In the kitchen, Ellen gave her young daughter-in-law the task of making a tossed salad. Though Erin lacked the skill and practice the Murphys had, she could manage this. She knew exactly how Ellen liked salads to be made, and carefully replicated all the instructions she had been given during that long-ago Thanksgiving season.

"Erin," Ellen said as she whisked flour into a pan of succulent roast beef drippings to make gravy.

"Yes, ma'am?" Erin kept her eyes focused on the knife she was using to chop a tomato, but she listened attentively to her mother-in-law's words.

"I have to tell you something. I'm not happy with you or Sean about the way you have handled this relationship. It was *wrong* of you both to keep it a secret for so long." The whisk clanked loudly against the sides of the roasting pan, jangling Erin's shredded nerves further.

"You're right. I'm sorry," Erin answered gently. She made no attempt to defend herself.

"And I'm especially upset that you two actually got married without telling anyone about it. That courthouse wedding isn't valid, I hope you realize."

Erin set the knife on the cutting board and turned her head to see Ellen glaring at her. "What do you mean?"

"I mean, my dear," and the sarcasm in her usual endearment stabbed into Erin's heart like the knife had just stabbed into a head of romaine, "that you and Sean are both Catholic. A civil wedding doesn't create a spiritual marriage. You two must have your marriage sanctified by the church, and until you do, you're living in sin."

Sean warned me about this. "I understand. How does one go about it?"

"I have the number of a priest you can call. He's willing to take you through a series of marriage preparation classes after Christmas. I believe you can manage to do all of them before you go back to school. Are you willing?" The implication of '*woe betide you if you're not*' echoed unspoken in the cavernous room.

"Yes. Of course. Thank you for looking into that for us. I appreciate it."

* * *

Erin's soft answers were disarming Ellen. She had been spoiling for a fight, but Erin provided her no ammunition. "And when you do that, when you say your vows properly, in front of the priest, I expect to be invited to witness it," she proclaimed in righteous anger.

"Of course. I wouldn't have it any other way." Erin tipped shredded romaine into a bowl and retrieved a couple of carrots.

Ellen pressed on, hoping for a reaction. "I want to know one thing, though. Just why exactly did you want to keep everyone from knowing you were with Sean?"

"Didn't he tell you?" The girl turned haunted brown eyes Ellen's direction.

For a moment, the older woman felt her will to argue soften in the face of Erin's distress, but then she remembered. *She stole your son right out from under your nose, without even a word of warning.* "He did. I want to hear your side of it though."

Erin merely repeated the same story Sean had told her. "There was no time between us getting together and that horrible attack on Danny. Everyone was so upset. I knew no one would approve of me and I didn't want to add to the problem. I realize that it was a poorly thought out plan, I just don't know what would have been a good time. Secrets have a way of perpetuating themselves. The longer you keep one, the harder it is to come clean later. The thing is, I needed Sean. The situation with Danny was so horrifying, I couldn't cope without his support."

Nothing new in that story. And it's all too reasonable. Irritated by Erin's continued meekness, Ellen blurted without reflection, "I'm not sure why that is. You weren't attacked. You were just on the sidelines. What on earth did you need support for?"

* * *

The question struck a blow to Erin's heart. *It's exactly what I always feared. They never saw me as part of the situation or the family.* Just like her mother said, she hadn't been needed. She didn't answer right away, as she struggled to maintain her composure. She didn't succeed. The unkind words stuck her in a weak place, and her calm collapsed. "Because I'm weak. Weak and selfish." A tear ran down Erin's cheek.

* * *

It had been a mean thing to say and Ellen knew it, but she wanted to get a reaction. Now she realized she had gone too far. "Selfish? No one said you were selfish, dear. You were a good friend to Sheridan during that dark time," she said, trying to soothe Erin.

"I know. I did everything I could. I only wish I could have taken her pain away completely. I tried so hard to help her." The girl's voice broke on every word. She set the knife down again and gripped the countertop until her fingers turned white.

"You did help her, dear."

Erin drew in a ragged breath. It seemed her own dark thoughts had taken over and were now running the conversation. "Yes, but I *was* selfish though. I gave everything I had to Danny because she's my friend and I love her, but the whole time I was being greedy because I was so jealous of this family. I wanted a little piece of it for myself. I wanted you and Roger to be my parents, not my own mom and dad. They don't love me the way you love your children. They wish I'd never been born, but when I came over here, I knew what love meant. I could see it, like a homeless child watching a holiday feast through the window. I wanted a place in this family, and I wanted Sean, so I took him, and kept him. You don't have to tell me I'm not good enough to be part of this family. I know that. I don't deserve to be a Murphy." Erin sucked in a noisy breath.

"Erin, dear, don't cry. I didn't mean it." Ellen tried to backpedal, but it was too late. A flood of misery poured from Erin.

"No, you're right. You're absolutely right. I was wrong to do what I did, to marry Sean. He deserves so much better than me. I should have let him go. I tried, but I couldn't do it. I love him too much. I'm sorry, Ellen. I'm sorry to have pushed myself in where I'm not wanted."

Erin fled the room, weeping. She ran up the stairs to Sean's old bedroom, where she had lived out her last months of high school and threw herself on the bed. Ellen could hear the thump right through the floor. *Oh heavens, what have I done?*

* * *

The soft sound of sobs filtered down into the living room. Sean leaped to his feet, pounding up the stairs after his wife. He found her face down on the bed, weeping, and he scooped her onto his lap, holding her tight and stroking her hair. "What's wrong?" *As if I don't know. Damn it, Mom.*

"Nothing. I'm fine. Please, just leave me alone for a little while, Sean."

"Leave you alone while you're hurting? Not a chance, baby." He cuddled her against his chest, rubbing her back in soothing circles while she poured out a lifetime of suppressed misery. She mumbled despairing, heartbroken words under her breath. "I'll never belong anywhere. It's hopeless. I should let Sean go. He does deserve a better wife."

"Erin," Sean said sternly, "I don't know what she said to you, but it doesn't matter. I love you. You're my wife. I'm glad to be married to you, and I'm not letting you go. This is it for us, you know. Remember how we promised? For better, for worse, for richer, for poorer, in sickness and in health until death do us part? I meant that. I'll never release you from those vows, so put your old demons of inadequacy away. They don't tell you the truth, they only torment you. There's nothing wrong with you, Erin. Nothing."

"I can't stand to come between you and your family..." she choked.

"You *are* my family," Sean interrupted, grasping her hand and holding it in front of her face. "From the day I put this ring on your finger, you were as much my family as anyone else in this house. You are no less important to me than my own parents, and don't forget that."

"I don't deserve it." She wiped her eyes on her sleeve and sniffled.

"Of course, you do." He dropped her hand and lifted her wet face, kissing her tenderly over and over, caressing her lips with his to show her he loved her. After a while, she began to calm. "Do you believe me?" he asked.

She squeezed red, watery eyes and lowered her face in assent he didn't believe.

"Go wash your face, baby. It's supper time soon."

She tilted her chin in a weak agreement. He lifted her to her feet. Leaning down, he murmured, "I love you no matter what anyone says – even you." Sean wrapped his arms around her in a tight hug and then patted her bottom, sending her to the bathroom. Then he headed downstairs, straight to the kitchen.

"Mother, what did you do?" he demanded, his jaw clenched in anger.

Ellen turned to face him, leaning on the stove. She looked stunned, not at Sean's question, but at the explosion she had just caused. She didn't answer him.

"Come on, Mom. Why was Erin crying? What did you say to her?"

She took a deep breath and swallowed hard before speaking. "I just told her I didn't like you two keeping secrets, that I wasn't happy about it, and that a civil ceremony wouldn't do."

He didn't believe it for a second, but rather than call his mother a liar, he went on. "Why did you do that? I asked you not to."

"I had no idea she was so... fragile."

Sean rolled his eyes. "I told you she was. She's wanted to be part of this family from the beginning, and frankly, Mother, she's earned it."

Ellen lowered her gaze to the floor. "I know."

Unmoved by her contrition, Sean gave vent to his fury. "I can hardly believe that my own wife would be made to feel unwelcome. We're supposed to be this great, supportive family that clings together in times of trouble. You know how Erin grew up. You know her parents have always made her feel like an unwanted burden, and it's crap, Mom. She's amazing." He narrowed his eyes. "If you've also made her feel unwanted, I don't think I'll ever forgive you. She was starting to come around, to believe that maybe she was okay, but now I'm going to have to start over again building her up. It's not right."

"I'm sorry," Ellen cried. "I didn't mean to hurt her."

Sean glared, unmoved. "Don't tell me you're sorry."

His mother lowered her head. "You're right. Somehow I'll make this up to her."

"You had better. If she doesn't feel comfortable being with you, we won't visit anymore." He turned on his heel and stalked away.

* * *

Sean's harsh words struck Ellen like a hammer blow. *It's perfectly clear that whatever issues I have with Erin's behavior, I'm going to have to let them go or risk losing my son for good.* She began to brainstorm how to repair the damage.

* * *

Not surprisingly, a sensation of strain and discomfort hung over them all through dinner. Erin remained silent, eyes on her plate, pushing her food around without eating it. Sean hovered protectively near her, holding her free hand and trying to lend her comfort and support. It didn't help. The deep wound inflicted on Erin's soul from her early childhood had been ripped open, leaving her suffering in ways none of those well-adjusted people could understand. Her misery pulsed like a heartbeat in the room.

If Erin had known everyone could see what she was feeling, she would have tried to suppress it – hers was a private grief – but she didn't look up, so she couldn't see the concern in their faces.

Neither of the Murphy parents had ever realized how desperately damaged Erin was. They had seen her as strong, capable, and she had been when dealing with someone else's pain. Her love for Sheridan had given her strength. Maybe, if she could help her friend enough, she would finally be worthy. Maybe she could earn the right to be with Sean. Not that she had helped for that reason exactly. She had helped because there was no other choice. She loved her friend and had to be there for her.

Knowing her attempt to integrate herself into the family had been an utter failure made her feel even worse. *I'll never belong anywhere. I should have gone to Omaha. At least there, my music would have been appreciated.*

* * *

When enough of the food had been consumed to be able to say legitimately that dinner was over, Erin rose without being asked and cleared away the dishes. Ellen remembered Sheridan telling her that she saw Erin as a kind of servant. It had been a hurtful thing to say, but maybe not an entirely inaccurate one. She went to help, silently.

As they placed the dishes in the dishwasher, Ellen made her first attempt to rectify the situation. "Erin, love, would you please play for us this evening? I've missed your music."

Erin smiled gravely and nodded. She retrieved the music stand she had left years ago in Sean's bedroom, and moments later, the Murphys took seats around the formal living room; Sean and his father on the sofa, Ellen on an armchair nearby, while Erin set up her sheet music and put her instrument together.

Soon Christmas carols filled the house. Erin had carefully chosen ones that sounded best in the oboe's melancholy voice: "*O Come, O Come Emmanuel*," "*What Child is This*," "*Silent Night*," and "*The Coventry Carol*." If the atmosphere had been less strained, it would have been an enjoyable evening. As it was, the music did help somewhat.

As he watched his wife play, Sean leaned over to his father and whispered, "Look at her, Dad, just look at her. Have you ever seen anything so beautiful in your life?"

"She's a wonderful girl, son. I'm glad you have her," Roger replied.

From her seat across the room, Ellen could see her son's face as he watched Erin play. She had never witnessed such an expression of adoration and pride. *So, this is truly not a whim, this romance. It's love of the deepest, truest kind, based on selfless dedication. No one will be able to come between them.* It was something she had needed to know.

When the music ended, Sean pulled his wife down to sit beside him on the couch and put his arm around her, declaring his loyalties. She cuddled against his side, laying her cheek on his chest. She seemed so tiny against his size, delicate and lovely but still fragile. *How did I miss seeing that fragility all these years? How did I not notice the wounded heart behind the brave face?* Ellen's guilt intensified.

She's exhausted, Ellen realized, watching Erin suppress a yawn. Sean seemed to notice, even though he wasn't looking at his wife the way Ellen was. "Well, we'd better go," he told his parents, rising and helping Erin to her feet.

"Will you come to Mass tomorrow?" Ellen asked.

"Of course," Erin said softly. "It will give me a chance to talk to them about... what we said."

"What's that, baby?" Sean glanced from his wife to his mother and back.

"Having our vows recognized by the church. It's an important thing to do," Erin explained.

Sean nodded. "Oh, sure. We can do that."

"Will you both please come and see us for Christmas?" Ellen urged. "We would love to have you."

Erin tried to smile at her mother-in-law. "If you want us here, we'll be here."

Okay, Ellen. Make the effort. "Then please be here, Erin."

Much was said in those simple words, and everyone understood it. It would take effort to make this mess back into a family, but if everyone did their part, it would be possible.

As they were leaving, Ellen pulled Erin into a hug. "I'm sorry," she said softly.

Erin nodded. "It's okay. Thank you for inviting me."

She tried harder. "I need you to know you're always welcome here."

This time, Erin really smiled. "Thank you."

* * *

And then Sean took his wife home and pulled her into bed with him. Even though they had made love already that day, she needed more, and as usual, he seemed to know it without her having to say a word. He undressed Erin tenderly, kissing her body as he revealed it, showing her how much he adored her. Finally, he pulled her on top of him and slid into her, so they could be one. Erin could not deny his beautiful expression of love. It soothed her hurt and reminded her she was not alone or unlovable. *I love you*, Sean told her with his embracing arms, his clinging lips, his thrusting sex. Erin felt the undeniable message and understood. *Even if no one else ever does, it will be enough.*

* * *

Roger and Ellen undressed and climbed into bed in silence. She reached for the lamp, but he took her hand, restraining her. She turned towards him.

"What is your *problem*, Ellen?"

"I don't know." She felt no surprise at his confrontation. "I'm really sorry about what happened. I didn't mean to upset her so."

"But why do you have such issues with her? She's a sweet girl."

He isn't going to budge. I know that stubborn jut of the jaw all too well. Ellen struggled to put her vague feelings of unease and distress into words. "She is. I just hate the secrecy."

"It's over." His voice remained flat.

"I know. I know. I didn't think –"

"No, you didn't," he interrupted.

Thank goodness. I have no idea what I was trying to say.

Roger continued in a softly-voiced but no less intense tirade. "It's not like you to be so insensitive. What is it about Erin that makes you so uncomfortable? You never used to be that way with her."

"I never realized she loved Sean," Ellen said, again fighting for the words.

"I know. But is it really so bad that she does?" Roger demanded. "She's going to be good to him. I mean, I'm glad our son is married to a woman capable of that level of selfless love and devotion. You can't imagine how terrible that year was for her, and yet she rose to the occasion over and over, beyond what anyone could have asked for or expected. It's no surprise she needed some help."

His comment reminded her of a question she'd been meaning to ask. "That's another thing I don't understand. Everyone keeps talking about how terrible that year was for Erin, but it was Sheridan who was raped, who became pregnant, and who had to give up her baby. She was the one who had the terrible year."

All of us did. How horrible to watch your child suffer endlessly and be unable to help.

"She did, but there was a lot going on behind the scenes that we didn't know." Roger paused, considering. "If I share this with you, you must keep it in complete confidence. Don't mention to Erin that I've told you. You'll upset her again."

"I promise." *Goodness knows I'm not going to make things worse.*

"Do you remember when Erin made our Thanksgiving dinner?"

"Yes…" She gave her husband a questioning glance.

"She was pregnant at the time."

Ellen gasped.

"Sean told me, and this was just the other day mind you, that he probably made Erin pregnant the night Sheridan was assaulted, just before you called him from the hospital."

Stunned by the revelation, long minutes passed while Ellen struggled to wrap her mind around it. "But what happened then?" A terrible suspicion dawned on her. "Wait, she was encouraging Sheridan to have an abortion. She didn't do that did she?" *If that little…*

"Calm down Ellen." Roger interrupted her runaway thoughts again. "No, of course not. Sean told me that once they got over the shock, they were both happy. It meant they would stay together, get married. He hated that she wouldn't be able to go away to school, but he wanted to keep Erin with him, and this made it possible."

"So, what happened then? Where is this baby?"

"Erin miscarried the next day, when we were out shopping. Sean was there, and so was Sheridan. She lost her baby right here in the upstairs bathroom. Sean said it was literally the most terrible day of his life. Apparently, the baby looked perfectly fine and normal. They had to take it to the hospital to have it examined. They were devastated."

"Oh my God. How awful." Now Ellen really felt guilty. She could picture the scene in her mind. *That poor girl, and here I am, making it worse.*

"Do you remember what it's like, Ellen, to lose a baby?"

"Do you think I can ever forget? I remember exactly what it's like." Her voice wavered. "Poor Erin. That must have been heartbreaking." *And Erin shouldered that pain nearly alone. No mother to help her. Only Sean, grieving beside her, and Sheridan, already stressed beyond her ability to cope. It's a miracle she came through it as well as she did, and no one ever said a word.* Ellen's defensive reaction began to crumble.

"It was," Roger agreed, "but she concealed it. She didn't want anyone to know that she was suffering as badly as Sheridan. She needed to be there for her friend. And let's not forget, my love, why we married exactly when we did." His stern mouth turned upward in one corner.

"I know. It's a good thing Sean has never added up the numbers." Even all these years later, the embarrassment of being the good little Catholic girl who got pregnant out of wedlock brought a hint of color to her cheeks. *I have not one stone to throw at Erin.*

"Would it be so bad if he knew?" Roger pressed.

"I don't know. I would be embarrassed if he found out." Ellen bit her lip.

"What, that a passionate nature runs in the family? Why do you think the Murphys are so loyal? It's because we love so deeply." He kissed her temple, making her smile.

Her swirling thoughts gelled into a desire for action. *It's time to stop fussing about what's already done and get busy being a family again.* "You're right. Listen, Roger, I have an idea about how to make this right with Erin."

"Tell me."

Chapter 19

Erin and Sean spent much of Sunday doing very little. After Mass they returned to the apartment and passed the afternoon alone together, talking, catching up, and making love.

By Monday, Erin began to feel better. The ache of her lacerated heart faded in the wake of Sean's tender affection, just in time for him to go back to work.

"Do you have to go?" Erin whined playfully, clinging to Sean's neck. "Isn't it your Christmas holiday too?"

He chuckled. "No, baby. Not until Thursday. Christmas isn't until Sunday, and we have a few houses we're restoring downtown."

"Restoring houses in December?" she asked, lifting one eyebrow.

"We're not painting exteriors, but there's no reason we can't lay flooring, tear down unnecessary walls and replace wiring."

"Sounds like business is good for Murphy Construction and Renovation," Erin commented.

"It's booming," he agreed. "All those home improvement shows on television have given people the itch to spruce up dated spaces, so that's why I have to go. Lots to get done before Christmas." Sean kissed his wife goodbye. "I'm glad you're in better spirits." He smiled. "I love you, Erin. I'll see you tonight."

"I love you too. Have a good day."

Left to her own devices, Erin rummaged around the apartment, looking for something to do. While not a huge fan of cleaning, it would pass the time, so she washed dishes, vacuumed, and dusted. It only took about two hours. As she began contemplating what to do next, and whether the neighbors would object to the sounds of the oboe filtering through the walls and floor, the telephone rang.

"Hello?" she said, wondering who it could be.

"Oh hello, Erin," Ellen said. "I'm glad I found you."

"What can I do for you?" Erin asked, still feeling a little wary.

"I wanted to invite you over today. I'm making Christmas ornaments, and I was wondering if you would be interested in joining me."

Making ornaments? How on earth do you do that? I thought they came in packages at the store. Though she had not put up a tree in years, or even attempted to celebrate, the idea nonetheless appealed to her. *Remember how homey the Murphys are... and how much you like it.* "Sure. I've never made ornaments before. When should I come?"

"Right away."

I don't dare refuse. Good thing she sounds more relaxed. "I'll get there in half an hour or so."

"Perfect. See you then."

This time, when Ellen met Erin, her altered demeanor confused Erin even more. Her mother-in-law greeted her with a warm hug and pressed a cup of cocoa into her hands. Erin sipped it, grateful for the warmth on such a cold day, and found it rich with vanilla and cream. *Delicious.*

Ellen escorted her into the kitchen, where the table had been spread with newspaper. On one side, a lump of some kind of strange, brown dough sat on a cutting board. Across the table, she saw a box of colorful glass balls, the ones that could be purchased cheaply at any discount store. Beside them lay a set of poster paints and some brushes.

Erin considered the scene but didn't know what to make of it. "What should I do?"

"Why don't you start by rolling out the cinnamon dough? Then you can cut it with the cookie cutters and we'll bake them for a long time until they're hard. They make lovely smelling ornaments."

"Oh, sure. I can do that." Erin grabbed the rolling pin. "How thick?"

"About a quarter inch."

She got to work and soon had a baking sheet full of stars, bells and little reindeer ready to be baked. Ellen, in the meanwhile, appeared to be painting designs on the balls.

Erin peeked at what she was doing and gasped. Ellen had painstakingly crafted a traditional Madonna in a blue headdress, sitting in a stable with a cow on one side and a donkey on the other, gazing adoringly at a stone manger filled with hay, where a baby lay wrapped in a blanket.

"Did you really paint that? It's amazing. I had no idea you were such an artist."

"I'm not," Ellen replied, her cheeks growing pink. "I went to art school for a while, but I dropped out."

Dropped out? With talent like that? "Why?"

"Well," Ellen's blush darkened. "I had been seeing Roger for a while, and I... became pregnant."

Erin raised her eyebrows. "Really?"

"Yes. With Sean. I was nineteen at the time."

Erin squinted at her mother-in-law. "Why are you telling me this?"

Ellen turned to face Erin, a sheepish smile pulling her lips. "I'm trying to make things better between us. I said some unkind things and I regret them. I'm not happy you two felt compelled to keep your relationship a secret, but I'm not so perfect either. I want you to know that I forgive you. Also, I have never for a moment thought you were selfish. You need to know that. I was thankful and grateful for all your help."

"Thank you." Encouraged, Erin decided to take a chance. "You know, I got pregnant once too."

"You did?" Ellen blinked.

"Yes. At the same time as Danny. I had a miscarriage."

Ellen set down the paintbrush and rested a hand on Erin's arm. "I'm so sorry. I had a miscarriage between Jason and Sheridan. It hurts, doesn't it? But you know what, having a baby helps a lot. Now that you and Sean are married..."

If only. I'm so ready. "That's good to know."

"Those look good, dear. Why don't you pop them in the oven? It's already on."

Erin carried the cookie sheet away and considered what she had been told. *I'm not sure why Ellen's being so nice, but I appreciate it.* Not to mention sharing those difficult memories created a bond of empathy between the women. *Now we know each other's secret pain. It makes a difference.*

While the cinnamon ornaments perfumed the kitchen, Erin sat down next to Ellen and watched her paint.

"Would you like to try one, dear?" the older woman suggested.

Oops, I was staring over her shoulder. That must be annoying. "I don't know how. What if I mess it up?"

Ellen gestured at the supplies. "It's not a problem if you do. The paint washes off until it's dried, and even if it's hopeless, so what? Both the paint and the balls are cheap. If you have to throw it away it's no great loss. Give it a try."

Erin carefully selected a ball in a warm gold tone and picked up a brush. *What to paint?* Concentrating intensely, she began to work on the decoration... and messed up. Rolling her eyes, she washed off the paint and tried again, and messed up again. "This is hard," she complained, setting the ball on the table.

"Don't give up, dear," Ellen urged, sensing Erin's frustration, "new things are always difficult." She began to sing softly. Erin listened to the quiet melody. *Away in a Manger.* The soothing lullaby in her mother-in-law's delicate voice released some of Erin's nervous tension.

She nodded and tried again, and gradually began to sing along. *I don't have the best voice, but this is a Christmas carol, so who cares?* The two women sang while they painted. This time Erin made progress. By being very careful, she managed to paint the ball without messing it up again. She painted a simplified but recognizable version of the Murphy family homestead, with its snowy yard on each side, and fireplace smoke pouring from the chimney. She used the end of the brush handle to dot snowflakes on the scene. Underneath she painstakingly traced the word 'home'. *It's nothing like what Ellen's doing, but for a first attempt, I'm happy with it.* She showed it to her mother-in-law.

"Oh, that's good, dear. When it dries, I'll add it to the ornaments we'll put on the tree. Our family has a tradition of decorating together, as you might recall. I'd like to do it Wednesday, when Sheridan gets home. Will you and Sean be able to come?"

"I think so, but I'll have to check with him."

Ellen smiled.

This is the woman I remember. The one I always wished was my mother. Now she sort of is.

"Oh good. By the way, I have something to ask of you. Everyone in this family has an ornament made specifically for them. Would you be willing to let me make one for you?"

Erin drew in a slow breath. *Oh, wow!* "Why would I not be willing?"

"Well, normally I put a strand of hair inside it. It's a transparent ball you see. For each of my children, I took a curl from their first haircut and put it inside, along with their name, their birth date, and some kind of decoration. In order to make one for you, I would need a piece of your hair."

"Oh, that's fine." Erin tried to sound nonchalant, even as her eyes swam. She blinked away the tears and focused on her next project, a shiny silver ball.

Immediately, Ellen left the room and returned with a manicure kit. Taking out a pair of minuscule scissors, she lifted Erin's hair and cut off a tiny section from underneath. Then she threaded the hair into a hollow glass ball and capped it with a gold ornament hanger before returning to painting as though nothing had happened. "Erin," she said a couple of minutes later, "how is my daughter? Sean says she's better, and she sounds like it on the phone, but I still worry. Is she really improving?"

"Yes," Erin said. "Almost back to normal."

"Oh, that's good." Ellen smiled, then her lips pursed, and she added, "Have you met Dr. Burke?"

Here we go. Erin resisted the urge to roll her eyes. "Yes. She told you about him, did she?"

"She mentions him often. I'm not really clear on what kind of relationship they have though. Is this just a professor she has a crush on, or are they involved?" Ellen peered at Erin, as though the secret to understanding Sheridan's feelings lay in her friend's eyes.

Erin tapped the end of the paintbrush on her front teeth. "Honestly, I don't know. I think it's somewhere in between. It's as if they like each other but neither is able to make a move yet."

"What kind of man is he?" Ellen pressed.

"Hard to say." Erin pondered her words. "What Sheridan tells me doesn't fit with my observations during the small amount of time I spent in his class. To me, he seemed grumpy and withdrawn, but he might just be really shy. He's sweet with her, and the way he looks at her is intense."

"How old is he? Whenever I ask Sheridan, she changes the subject."

Erin could see visions of an elderly man with a bent back and big glasses floating in front of her mother-in-law's eyes and hastened to reassure her. "I don't think he's particularly old." She placed her second completed ornament on the table and debating whether to take another. *This is interesting, but I'm not sure*

I want to start again. "I would be surprised if he's much more than thirty. He may be younger than that. He must be one of those genius types. Maybe that's why he sometimes seems so awkward. But he sure is crazy about her. I don't know if anything will ever come of it. I am glad, though, that she's able to be attracted to a man again."

Ellen's face expressed relief. "Yes. So am I. For her sake, I hope he comes around." She set aside her supplies and retrieved the paint water cup. "All right, that's enough ornaments for this year. Would you like some lunch? I've been thinking about soup and a sandwich."

Perfect timing. "Thank you. I would like that." She followed her host into the business part of the kitchen. Ellen dumped the paint water while Erin retrieved plates, bowls and cups. *All these years later, I still know where everything goes, and now that Ellen has settled down, this kitchen feels as much like home to me as any place I've ever been. Thank God.* "Let me give you a hand. What can I do?"

Ellen gave her a considering look and said, "There's some chicken and some pesto mayonnaise in the refrigerator. Could you make the sandwiches, please?"

"Of course." Erin opened the door and found the items. "Shall we use these little buns, or are they for something else?"

"Those would be fine," Ellen agreed. "Can you hand me that container in front of you?"

Erin located a glass bowl filled with green-flecked red liquid and carefully passed it to her host, who popped it in the microwave. Erin constructed the sandwiches, taking the initiative to add a slice of lettuce to each. *I hope that's okay. I really crave something crunchy.* Her mouth watered as the smell of tomatoes and basil wafted through the room.

The microwave beeped, and Ellen ladled the soup into the two bowls and placed them on the bar side of the island, adding glasses of ice water to counter the dryness of the blasting heater. Erin brought two plates of sandwiches and they both took a seat.

"Thank you for inviting me today, Mrs. Murphy," Erin said between bites. "I've had a really good time."

"You're welcome. It was nice to have you." Ellen smiled. "But you don't have to call me Mrs. Murphy. Ellen will do, though if you wanted – and I understand if you don't, dear – I would be glad for you to call me Mom."

Erin blinked. Then she reached over and grabbed the older woman in a tight hug.

"Goodness!" Mrs. Murphy exclaimed, startled.

Erin kissed her on the cheek. Then they both returned to their lunch in companionable silence.

Chapter 20

Christmas morning dawned bright and cheerful under a blanket of new-fallen snow, and the young Murphys woke up early, snuggled in Sean's old bed in his parents' house, where they had spent the night after attending evening Mass.

Sleeping over was fun. Especially when we recreated that one special night... I don't think I was nearly as quiet this time... hope Sean's parents didn't hear. Erin pulled on her pajamas and exited the room to find Sheridan in the hallway. Her friend gave her a knowing glance, which sent a bolt of embarrassed heat to her cheeks. *Guess someone heard. Damn, she busts us all the time.*

"So much for a silent night," Sheridan teased, and Erin giggled.

Sean emerged from the room, and slid his arm around Erin's waist, escorting her down the stairs. "Quiet, sis," he called over his shoulder. "You're as innocent as new-fallen snow and didn't hear a thing."

"Of course."

Laughing, they padded down the hall to the kitchen, where Ellen stood, bleary-eyed in her blue bathrobe, standing guard over the coffee pot. The enticing aroma teased Erin's nose. They formed a line like schoolchildren, eager to claim a cup of the rich brew.

Sean's arm around Erin kept her from feeling the chill quite as strongly as they shuffled to the formal living room, where the tree twinkled in the bay window. He led her to the loveseat, where they snuggled together. Roger had already sprawled on the sofa with his mug, eyes half-open.

So, this is what a family Christmas is like. I remember, but I've never felt like part of it quite this much before. Erin leaned her head on her husband's shoulder. *And what a gift I have for Sean. I hope he likes it.*

Ellen and Sheridan entered side by side, and Ellen perched on the sofa beside her husband.

"Hey," Sheridan protested. "Where do I sit?"

"You're the kid," Sean replied. "You get to hand out the presents. Don't tell me you're too good for it now."

Sheridan rolled her eyes and retrieved a narrow box wrapped in silver paper. She seemed to be suppressing giggles as she handed it to her dad.

He tore the wrapping to shreds immediately and opened the box... and then burst out laughing. "Thank you, Danny," he chortled, holding up a dark blue necktie with Snoopy and Woodstock on it. "I'll be sure to wear it to the next client meeting." He quickly wrapped it around his neck, where it created a bizarre effect against his dark green pajamas. The odd pairing sent everyone into gales of laughter.

"What's next, sis?" Sean demanded, pretending to be in charge.

"Something for anyone other than you," she replied. "You're going last."

Sean pouted. Erin's belly ached from holding in laughter as her friend rummaged through the little pile and produced another box in the same paper. "Here, Mom. From me."

Ellen smiled and gently pried the tape from the edges of the shiny wrap, revealing a box in which a lavender silk blouse rested. "Oh, that's lovely, dear. Thank you."

One by one, Sheridan dispersed the presents, and one by one they opened them.

Roger's wife had given him homemade fudge, the same as every year, and he ate a piece immediately. Erin had heard about his sweet tooth and when he opened her gift to reveal a box of chocolate liqueurs, he beamed enough to entice a shy smile from her. From his son, he received a new socket wrench. "Hey, I needed this!" he exclaimed. "Thank you, all. This Christmas is perfect." He sank back on the sofa and ate another piece of fudge.

Ellen received from her husband a set of pearl earrings. Sean gave his mother a necklace with a single pearl dangling from a delicate gold chain. Erin, having seen all the pieces ahead of time, had contributed a blazer in a daring print that featured a complementary but darker purple than the blouse. As Ellen pulled the jacket from the box, an object rolled into her lap. She lifted a glass ball, like the ones she and Erin had made: pearlescent white and covered in lavender dots. Wavy lines in purple, gold and pale green encircled the top and bottom. In a careful script, the word *'Mom'* repeated around the middle. Ellen gave her daughter-in-law a teary smile and rose to hang the ornament on the tree.

"Sheridan," Ellen said as she returned to her seat, "Our gift can't be wrapped, but we wanted you to know that your father and I have found an apartment near the university and we've signed a lease for two years. You won't need to worry about housing while you work on your master's."

"Oh, my goodness!" Sheridan exclaimed. "That's the best idea ever. Thank you, Mom. Thank you, Dad." She beamed.

"Open mine, Danny," Sean urged.

She grabbed a familiar-shaped object, papered in green, and gave it a little shake. "Looks like a book," she commented.

"Well, duh," he replied. "What else for the family bookworm?"

Sheridan rolled her eyes and tore open the paper. "Oooooh," she exclaimed, holding up the volume. "How did you know I would like a book of Victorian poetry?" She regarded her brother with curiosity.

"A nerd like you? I figured."

"I told him," Erin added. "I said you really liked the Victorian poetry class you took, but that textbooks aren't so pretty on your bookshelf. This one has a nice cover and some of the poems you said you loved, so..."

"So, good choice, Sean, letting your wife choose," Sheridan teased.

"Hey, I'm a smart guy," he replied, buffing his nails on his shirt.

"You're smart enough to marry Erin is all," Sheridan replied. "Now you, Erin. What do you have?"

Erin tore into her package. "This one is from Mom," she said, indicating Ellen. Removing the lid from a box that had once contained coffee mugs, she saw it held three glass balls, ones that Erin had not seen her make. The first was her own, with her strand of dark hair inside. Her name, Erin James Murphy, was painted on it, along with her birth date and the date of her marriage to Sean. She smiled at the sight of it. The second was even more poignant. It said First Christmas Together and was circled at the top and bottom with black bands and yellow Celtic knots that mimicked their wedding rings. A tiny and stylized but recognizable oboe crossed with a carpenter's hammer formed a small X in the middle. Her name and Sean's had been painted above the design. The space below remained blank.

"We'll put the date of your church wedding there," Ellen said mildly.

The third glass ball was transparent, empty, and blank. Erin looked at her mother-in-law questioningly.

"For later, dear," Ellen said, and Erin choked, swallowing hard as she rose from her seat to hang the two completed balls on the tree.

Sean dug into his pile. First Sheridan's gift: a framed picture of the couple's wedding. They stood in front of the fireplace in Rick's office, holding hands and gazing at each other with expressions of deep love as Sean placed Erin's ring on her finger.

"Thanks, Danny." His voice turned gruff as he passed the picture around.

When Sheridan opened Erin's package, she squeaked. Taking a great risk, Erin had photographed her friend when Sheridan and Dr. Burke stood close together. She was gazing up at him with soft adoring eyes. He stared back, intense and passionate, and since the shot showed them only from the shoulders up, his ugly clothes didn't distract from the image. Erin had printed the photo and framed it.

"Oh, Erin," Sheridan said, "thank you."

"I know how important it is to have a picture of someone you care about," Erin said softly.

"Now you," Sheridan insisted. "Sean, where's your present for Erin?"

"Oh, I don't need anything," she replied, squeezing his hand. *Being with him is gift enough.*

"Don't be silly," he said, lifting her fingers to his lips. "Of course I have something for you. It's just a little hard to wrap. I'll show it to you later."

"Okay, honey. What did you get?"

Only a card remained. Sean opened it and read, and then froze as the paper slipped from his fingers. "You don't have to do that."

"You've earned it," Roger said firmly.

Erin picked up the card. Inside, she discovered a briefly scrawled note proclaiming Sean a partner in his father's company. She squealed with delight and squeezed her husband tight. "Congratulations," she told him.

"Do you know what this means to me?" he asked in a choked voice.

"Of course, honey," Erin replied.

"She'd have to be deaf not to," Sheridan pointed out. "You talk about it all the time."

Erin crossed the room to Roger and hugged him too, kissing his cheek.

"You're a wonderful father," she said sincerely.

"Thank you, Erin," he replied.

"But Erin, you didn't give Sean anything either."

"Oh, I have something for him all right, but it's going to take me a minute to get it ready. If everyone would excuse me, please." She struggled to her feet, wishing she could remain in her husband's embrace even as she grinned with excitement. *This is going to be great.*

* * *

"I wonder what she's up to," Sean mused. "Do you know, Danny?"

"No clue."

He shrugged. "I guess I'll find out. Anyway, thanks, all of you. You did a great job. And thanks for making Erin feel so welcome, especially you, Mom. You really turned this around."

"You're welcome, my dear," Ellen replied, admiring the pearl jewelry her husband and son had given her.

"Sean," Erin called, "could you please come here?"

"Better go see, son," Roger said.

Sean followed the sound of his wife's voice and found her in the bathroom. "What's up, Erin?"

"Your gift." She held out a small object to him.

He looked at it, not sure what it was... a small white plastic stick. She turned it over to reveal a little oval-shaped depression with a blue plus sign in it. "What is this?"

"It's a pregnancy test, Sean. We're going to have a baby."

Sean drew in a deep breath. *It's no surprise, really. We haven't bothered with birth control since we got back together.* Though aware how fertile they seemed to be together, he still found the realization momentous; exciting, scary and overwhelming. Erin's smile lit up the room. *She wanted this so bad.*

He reached out to her, gathering her into his arms and pulling her close. "I love you, little girl," he told her simply.

"I love you too. Shall we go let everyone know?" she suggested. "No more secrets, right?"

"Right." He slipped his arm around her waist and walked her back to the family room.

"Um, everyone?" Three heads popped up. Sean glanced at his wife. Her normally reserved smile turned more dazzling by the moment, until it rivaled his sister's for sheer impact. "Erin's pregnant."

There was a moment of stunned silence.

Sheridan recovered first. Squealing, she dashed to her friend and threw her arms around her. "Congratulations, Erin. I'm so happy for you. How far along are you?"

"Not very," Erin replied. "Probably about six weeks. I only figured it out a couple of nights ago. Of course, we can pretty much guess when this happened."

"Yes," Sheridan said firmly, "on your wedding night."

It's a good answer, and as likely as not to be true.

Roger and Ellen approached, hugging Erin congratulating her. Sean still felt rather stunned, and he accepted his parents' hugs numbly.

"Don't worry, son," Roger told him. "You'll get used to it."

Sean nodded.

"Are you feeling all right, dear?" Ellen wanted to know.

"Yes," Erin replied, "for the most part. I did have one bad day during finals. That's when I got to thinking."

"I see."

No doubt she does, and more than anyone's comfortable with.

* * *

Later, around noon, bored with the football game and worn out from a busy evening and early morning, Erin excused herself to take a nap. Sheridan watched her friend trudge off to bed. She could remember the overwhelming fatigue of early pregnancy. *It's so wonderful one of us will finally be able to have a baby and it be a joy and a blessing instead of a crisis. What a sweet Christmas present. I may have gotten them back together, but God is blessing them, even if Erin does have to go back to school. Wait, school!* Concerned by her sudden realization, Sheridan began to track down her family.

She found her father asleep in front of the game. *Well, he won't really be part of this process anyway, at least not by doing anything different than being kind, generous, and welcoming as he's always been.* Leaving Roger to his nap, Sheridan padded down the hall to the kitchen. Inside, Ellen was busy preparing a batch of dinner roll dough. Sean stared into the refrigerator.

"Hey, guys," she said to capture their attention.

"Oh, there you are, dear. Come and help me, won't you?" Ellen urged.

"In a minute, Mom. Can I talk to you two quickly first?"

Ellen and Sean looked at each other. Then Sean closed the fridge, Ellen dusted her floury hands on a towel and they followed Sheridan into the den.

Sheridan took a breath, leaning against the wall beside the television as her mother and brother claimed the recliners. "Sean, Mom, listen. I'm so happy Erin's going to have a baby. She wants one so bad, has ever since…" Sheridan trailed off, not sure how much to reveal to her mother.

"Ever since she lost the last one?" Ellen finished for her daughter. They both stared at her. "Erin told me the other day."

Wow, they really have turned things around. "Yes, since then. Anyway, this is going to be really hard on her. She's facing one of the most difficult parts of pregnancy – the beginning – during her last semester of college. It's going to be a doozy. She has some really hard music classes, not to mention her last English class and a philosophy credit. She also has to do her senior recital, which is basically the culmination of her entire course of study. If it doesn't go well, she won't graduate."

"It'll go well," Sean said, dismissing the worry with a wave of his hand. "She's too good for it not to."

Sheridan rolled her eyes. *Listen, smarty pants.* "I know, but this is Erin we're talking about. Do you think she will believe that? She's already stressed about it. And she's going to have to do all of it, alone and *pregnant,* without you, Sean."

Sean grimaced. He obviously hadn't thought of that part.

Sheridan spelled it out for him. "She's going to leave in the middle of January to finish school and won't be back to stay until the middle of May. That's a long separation during a pregnancy."

"Crap." Sean frowned. "She'll only be a couple of months from delivery when she gets back, won't she?"

Sheridan counted up. "Not many at all. She'll probably deliver at the end of summer."

Ellen shook her head. "Not the best timing, but there's nothing to be done about it, really. What point are you trying to make, Sheridan?"

"Just this. When I was going through a crisis pregnancy, everyone closed ranks around me and showered me with love and affection and support, Erin most of all. I appreciate what all of you did for me, but Erin was the one who went to school with me, defended me from the other students, and made them leave me alone. She was the one who went to college with me when I was devastated by grief and made sure I didn't give up on life. I owe her more than I can ever repay."

"Danny, it's not a debt. Erin wanted to help you because she loves you," Sean reminded his sister.

"I know. I love her too and I want to help her. The bulk of the burden for getting her through this semester is going to fall on me, since I'm the one who lives with her, and that's fine. I'm ready for it. But I think it's time for the Murphy clan to close ranks around one of its own again. Erin gave and gave to this family until it almost broke her. It's time we all gave something back. Sean, it's second nature to you to be there for Erin, but I think you need to do more. She's not one to ask for anything, so you might want to press her a little, give more than you think she needs. Big gestures will almost certainly be appreciated."

"Of course. Do you think you might be willing to...clue me in from time to time? I'm not really all that intuitive, especially over distances," he requested.

"Of course. Now Mom –"

"I've been trying," Ellen protested.

"You've been great," Sheridan hurried to reassure her. "I can't believe the change. Well done. But just always remember how fragile she is. The Murphy bluntness doesn't go over well."

"I realize that now." Ellen looked at her children sheepishly. "Don't worry. Erin is one of us, and I intend to be as much a mother to her as I am to you."

Sheridan gifted her mother with one of her breathtaking smiles and the conference broke up, the women trailing back into the kitchen to continue preparing the supper feast.

* * *

That afternoon, Erin woke up from her nap around three. She descended the stairs to discover her husband sitting on the living room sofa, nibbling on a cookie.

"Hey, baby," he called. "Get your coat."

"Are we going somewhere?" she asked, rubbing her eyes.

"A little drive," he replied, and then winked ostentatiously.

Erin giggled, though she had no idea what he was up to. Still, she retrieved her coat and snow boots from the entry hall and followed her husband outside. The sun shone on the snow, making it glitter. As they approached the car they noticed, on the limbs of a heavily dusted pine, a little red cardinal that chirped pleasantly at them.

"Where are we going?" Erin asked softly, reluctant to break the silence of the muffling snow.

"It's a surprise."

Sean drove his wife through town to a pretty neighborhood near the hospital, one filled with old, beautifully maintained houses on large lots. He pulled to a stop in front of one that didn't match its neighbors at all. *What an eyesore,* Erin thought, frowning at the peeling paint, the half rotten front porch pillars, the badly decayed steps. The only good thing about the appearance of the house was the massive maple tree, nude and sleeping now, but waiting in breathless anticipation for spring. *When the leaves appear, it will be glorious.*

Erin regarded Sean questioningly. He didn't say a word, just helped her out of the car and escorted her to the front door, showing her the safest path up the crumbling stairs and across the sagging porch. He pulled out a key and let them into a house that appeared to be in the last stages of decomposition. Dust billowed from a wrinkled and stained gray industrial carpet. Flypaper, already completely covered in dead insects, hung from the sagging, water stained ceiling. The walls sported rags of peeling wallpaper in several different patterns. Erin looked at the devastation and finally said, "Sean, what is this place?"

"This, Erin, is our home," he announced with pride.

"Is this a joke?" she demanded, squeezing her eyes shut to block out the sight. When she opened them, and the ugliness had not disappeared, she frowned.

"No, baby. It's ours. I've already bought it, and I'm restoring it." I know it's a little shabby now, but by the time you're done with school, it will be ready.

"You are?" She scanned the wreckage, frowning. "Can you fix something that's such a mess?"

He laughed. "Sure. It's what I do. I've worked on places worse than this. Most of what you see is actually cosmetic. This place has excellent bones, and under all the muck, some great details as well. Just wait and see how it comes to life."

"I trust you, Sean," she said, taking a step toward her husband. Dust billowed from the ugly carpet and set her coughing. She waved her hand in front of her face, "but it's a little hard to picture."

"No harder than it is for me to look at a piece of sheet music and understand how the instrument will sound," he pointed out, reaching out to help her make her way off the dusty carpet and onto a patch of torn linoleum in the hallway.

"Good analogy." She grinned. "That I get."

"Okay, let me show you the parts I've already finished." He indicated a hallway full of open doors.

"Show me everything," she urged. "I want to understand."

Sean gave his wife a dazzling Murphy smile, proving the family charm hadn't all gone to his sister, and escorted her out to the rest of the house.

Chapter 21

The young couple thoroughly enjoyed the rest of their holiday together. The week after Christmas they began meeting with the priest twice a week to have their marriage sanctified by the Church. This pleased Sean's mother. Erin still didn't want to bother with a big wedding, especially not as she had been married for over a month and was already pregnant. They did choose a date, about a week before she had to leave to return to school, to say their vows before the priest and those family members who cared to attend.

Erin sent a card to Motley, inviting her mother, but received no reply of any kind. She didn't want to call, because her mother could be so caustic, and she didn't feel like listening to any ugly comments. Her father seemed marginally better. Though still selfish and obsessively absorbed in his work, he hadn't been particularly mean.

She called him. "Daddy? This is Erin. How are you?"

"Hi, pumpkin," he replied, though she could tell she didn't have his full attention. "I haven't heard from you in a while. I'm great. I just landed an investment job in the Cities that's going to bring in some really good figures."

It's always work. I wonder if he actually cares about anything or anyone else. "That's great, Dad. Good job. Um, I wanted to ask you something."

"What's up?" he asked in a tepid, distracted tone, and she suspected from the tapping sound in the background that he was typing an email while he talked to her.

"I'm getting married," she said simply. *He hates long conversations when he's at work, and explaining how I'm both already married and getting married would take far too much time out of his day.*

"Really?" That got his undivided attention, and Erin couldn't help smirking. "Congratulations. To whom?"

"Do you know Murphy Construction and Renovation?"

"Sure, I've done investing for them. Roger Murphy is a good guy."

"He is," Erin agreed. The thought of her father-in-law made her smile. "Do you know his son, Sean? Well, that's who I'm marrying."

"Sean Murphy?" He sounded impressed. "Well done, pumpkin. I've worked with him too. He's loaded. He'll really be able to take good care of you."

"Sean is loaded?" *I know Roger earns a good income, but Sean himself is also wealthy?*

"Oh sure," he replied, and she believed it. *If there's one thing Daniel James understands, it's finance.* "I've invested a ton for both of them. Sean's in really good shape. He's also a nice kid. You did good."

Sean's money is not what I love. I'd love him if we lived in his tiny apartment forever. "Thank you. He is nice. Anyway, we're getting married next Saturday evening at seven, at St. Michael's. It's going to be really small, just us, the priest, and Sean's family, but I would like it a lot if you would come too. Can you do that, Daddy?"

"Next Saturday? Hmmm." A rustling of pages suggested him leafing through a planner. "I think I have a meeting with some representatives from a real estate firm in Japan. I'm not sure I can get away, but I'll see."

Erin tried not to feel disappointed. *That's as clear a rejection as I ever get from my father. I didn't expect he would make time for me.* It didn't matter really, but she still dared to hope, occasionally, that one of her parents would actually care enough to stand by her.

She didn't cry but was still staring glumly at the phone when Sean arrived home from work a few minutes later.

He took one look at his wife's gloomy face and scooped her into his arms for a long and thorough kiss, complete with wandering hands, which cheered her up considerably.

"So, I take it he's not coming?" Sean asked.

"Nope. I didn't really think that he would." Her insouciance didn't fool her husband.

He replied in his usual, comforting way. "You know something, Erin? You look like a girl who needs to be made love to."

"Oh, yes please," Erin replied eagerly. "Just let me get the casserole out of the oven before it burns."

The casserole didn't burn. The Murphys did get a little scorched, however, in the best possible way.

* * *

"Dad?" Sean said as he walked into the small office space that housed MC&R's company headquarters.

Roger rose from a filing cabinet where he crouched, thumbing through manila folders.

"Erin called her dad yesterday." He shook his head.

"He didn't refuse to come," Roger demanded, stunned.

"He did." Sean sighed. "What kind of father refuses to come to his own daughter's wedding?"

"A lousy one," Roger replied promptly. "I suggest you not let this go."

"I should interfere?" Sean raised his eyebrows. "Isn't that meddling?"

Roger shrugged. "Your wife would like her father at your wedding. By all rights, he ought to be there. You're a partner in this company. Make an executive decision."

Sean pondered... pondered... and grinned. Then he called Daniel James at work.

"Hello, this is Sean Murphy," he said to his father-in-law.

"Sean, how are you?" Daniel replied in the hearty, jovial voice he used with clients.

"I'm great. I guess you heard yesterday that your daughter and I are getting married?"

"Yes. Congratulations." The buoyant tone went flat.

Strange reaction. I wonder what that means. "Thank you. Don't you think it would be nice for you to be there? You only have one child, and a wedding is kind of a big deal."

"It is, and I'm really sorry, but I just can't get away from work. It will be fine though. She understands." Now Daniel sounded distracted, as though he'd stopped paying attention to the conversation and moved on to more important things.

Nothing is more important than family. "Oh, she understands all right," Sean shot back. "She understands that your work is more important to you than she is, and that's not fine at all."

"I don't think that's fair to say," Daniel protested, his focus back on Sean's words. *Gotcha, buddy.* "I care about Erin."

"Do you?" Sean asked, anger and sarcasm bleeding into his tone, drop by scathing drop. "When have you shown it? When did you attend her concerts, her high school graduation, or anything? Are you going to go to her senior recital or her college graduation in the spring?" Sean paused to let his words sink in before going in for the kill. "Based on what evidence is Erin supposed to know that you care about her? She has no idea. In fact, from observing you, she thinks she's a burden and a nuisance. Is that really how you see her?"

"Of course not," Daniel replied, sounding angry.

Sean attempted a conciliatory approach. "She's very much like you, you know, driven, an achiever, and smart."

"I know. I wish she would have invested her energy in something worthwhile."

What? Is he insane? "She has. Her music is amazing."

Daniel continued as though he hadn't heard. "I guess if she has you to support her, she can just play around with that oboe and not worry about getting a real career."

There's nothing to be said to that *insensitive comment.* Sean returned to the subject at hand. "Anyway, I want you to come to the wedding. It would mean a lot to Erin. She needs her father there."

"I'm sorry. There's just no way."

Sean closed his eyes in frustration. *I had hoped it wouldn't come to this.* When he spoke again, his voice turned hard and cold. "I suggest you make a way. You're not the only investor in town you know."

"What does that mean?" Daniel demanded, now sounding alarmed.

"It means," Sean said bluntly, "that family is important to the Murphys, and if you show such disrespect to yours, Murphy Construction and Renovation will never work with you again."

Silence. The building company had worked heavily with Daniel's investment firm, so that they could provide retirement benefits and mutual funds for their employees. If MC&R went to one of his competitors, Daniel would lose a substantial commission for himself and a massive investment for his company. "Does your father know about this?" he asked at last.

"He does," Sean replied. "Oh, and just so you know, I'm a partner in this company now. How people treat my wife really matters to me. Keep that in mind, Daniel. I'll leave it up to you to decide what you want to do, but in case you forgot, the wedding is Saturday at seven at St. Michael's. I suggest you be there, but either way, this conversation is never to be mentioned to Erin. Let her think you love her enough to support her, just this once."

He hung up.

"Will he come?" Roger asked, looking up from his desk.

"I think so. I hated doing that. How stupid." Sean rubbed his hand over his forehead.

"I hate to say this, but both of the Jameses are pretty stupid," Roger replied, stamping an invoice in bright blue ink and setting it aside to dry.

"Erin was lucky to have gotten the best parts of their personalities without all the selfishness and greed." As Sean spoke, images of his beautiful, dark-eyed bride danced in his mind. *Erin deserves to be happy, and bullying her father into attending her wedding is well worth it to see the joy in her eyes. I hope it works.*

"You're right," Roger agreed.

* * *

On Saturday, Erin tugged on her silver dress again and she and Sean drove to St. Michael's Catholic Church to have their marriage sanctified. All the Murphys joined them except for Jason, who was in a state of rebellion against both marriage and the church. Erin didn't mind. She had always been a little afraid of Jason anyway. Even though he was closer to her age, it was kinder, friendlier Sean she had fallen in love with. *And now I'm marrying him... again. Lovely.*

They gathered at the front of the chapel and the long wedding Mass began. Erin tried to listen to the words that would turn their marriage from a legal to a spiritual one, but found it impossible to concentrate. Despite their years of closeness and intimacy, Sean still captured her attention like no one else. Just before they spoke their vows, the door at the back of the room opened and closed quietly. Erin, facing forward, didn't turn around. Her attention remained focused on her husband, whom she vowed, again, to love, honor, and cherish until death did them part. This time they were promising to God, not just to the laws of the land, and that made it all the more serious, solemn, and beautiful. Erin's shy smile turned breathtaking as

Sean, his voice confident, promised to love his wife for the rest of his life.

Sean kissed his bride gently on the lips and turned her around to face their small entourage. As the priest presented them, Erin took in the beaming faces before her. Ellen, Roger, and Sheridan all looked on approvingly. A little apart from them, a tall, dark-haired man sat in a pew, nodding. Her lips parted in surprise.

The wedding over, the priest dismissed the couple and Erin rushed straight to her father.

"Oh, Daddy, you came. Thank you!" She hugged Daniel tight as tears of happiness blurred her vision.

"Congratulations, pumpkin," he told her gently. He released her with a kiss on the forehead and turned to shake Sean's hand.

* * *

Sean regarded his father-in-law with approval as he retrieved his wife with an arm around her waist. *Although it required nothing short of blackmail to get Daniel here, something about his expression and demeanor says he finally understands a few things about his daughter and his own responsibilities. The past can't be changed, but perhaps the future can.*

"Well, Daniel," Roger said, shaking the man's hand. "I haven't seen you in a while. Glad you could make it. We're heading back to the house for some wine and dessert. Would you like to join us?"

Daniel met his eyes, and then Sean's. "Yes," he said. "Thank you. That would be nice."

"Erin," Sheridan said sternly, "You're not having wine, are you?"

"Of course not," she replied, blushing. Her dad turned his gaze on her, one eyebrow raised in a question.

"We've actually been married a while," Sean told him. "This is just the church ceremony."

"Ah, okay," he said, and then cocked his head to the side. "Wait, what? No, never mind. You can explain it to me at the house. By the way, pumpkin, you're glowing like an angel. I'm glad to see you so happy."

"Yes," Erin said. "I have a lot to be thankful for."

"No more than I do, baby," Sean said as they walked to the door of the church and gathered up their coats. While the love in the room sufficed to warm the coldest hearts, outside, a Minnesota blizzard turned the landscape into a frozen wasteland.

* * *

With many kisses and a few tears, Erin returned to the university with Sheridan to complete their last semester of undergraduate studies. As Sheridan had predicted, it was a doozy. Erin had begun preparations for her senior recital at the beginning of the year, but there was so much left to do that she quickly became completely overwhelmed. And that was not all she was working on, either. Music majors have so many extra classes that she had a full schedule of coursework and studying as well.

With everything she had going on, Erin had to spend long hours in the music building late at night, practicing. Sheridan grew increasingly alarmed at how little sleep Erin was getting, but there simply weren't enough hours in the day to get everything done. It would have been a strain on anyone, but Erin's pregnancy made it worse.

A couple of weeks later, Sheridan returned to her dorm room to find Erin lying on her side on the bed, tears streaking down her cheek, her hand on her belly.

"What's wrong?" she asked, alarmed.

"I'm cramping." Erin gagged, and then swallowed hard.

"Are you bleeding?"

"No, not that."

"Have you been throwing up?"

"Yes." The expectant mother shot her friend a hysterical look.

"Oh Lord. Did you call your midwife?"

Erin shook her head. She'd clearly been too panicked even to think of it, remembering the trauma of her previous miscarriage, so Sheridan grabbed the business card from the bulletin board beside the computer desk and dialed. She talked to the midwife for a few minutes and then walked into the bathroom, scooping up a big plastic cup from the desk as she went by. She emerged with the cup brimming with water.

"The midwife said you're probably exhausted and dehydrated. She said you should drink a bunch of water and then lie down and rest. If the cramping doesn't subside after a couple of hours, go to the clinic."

Erin sat up, took the cup and sipped. Once she had downed all the water, she returned to her side and tried to rest. Sheridan pulled up a chair beside her and distracted her from obsessing about her condition by telling a long story about Dr. Burke. About an hour later, the cramping stopped, and the nausea subsided. Erin sighed with relief.

"Now listen, Mrs. Murphy," Sheridan said sternly, "you need to take better care of yourself. No more of this staying up half the night practicing, and you be *darn sure* you have water with you all the time."

"Yes, ma'am," Erin replied weakly. "You're going to be a great professor someday."

Sheridan ignored the quip. "And you had better plan to stay in bed for a few days and get your strength back."

"I can't. I have too much to do," Erin wailed.

"Erin, sweetie, your baby is more important. I'll help you out, but please, you have to rest."

Clearly, permission to rest was what Erin had been seeking. She submitted instantly. "Okay."

As Erin had done for her in high school, Sheridan went to her friend's professors and explained the situation, collecting homework so she could stay current with her studies.

The rest did Erin a world of good. The following week she was able, cautiously, to resume her schedule.

* * *

As winter passed into spring, all the pieces of Erin's life began to come together. She finalized her plans for her senior recital, made and confirmed all the arrangements, chose the pieces, and she passed her preliminary jury. In her senior music theory class, she put the finishing touches on one special arrangement she would use to finish the concert. All that remained was to keep up with her coursework and practice like a fiend. That, and talk to Sean. As the big event neared, she told him more and more how scary it was.

"I just don't know how I'm going to get through it. The music is too hard. I'm going to mess up and not graduate. Why did I have to push it so much?"

"Because you're Erin," he replied. "You wouldn't be my baby if you let yourself settle. Remember how it was in high school? You weren't satisfied until you were first chair oboe in All-State, accepted to every college you wanted to go to, and dating an older man. You have always gone for what you wanted and gotten it. What you want now is a spectacular senior recital, and you're going to do it. Do you want me to come up for it?"

Funny how he puts such a positive spin on everything. That year was a mess. How did he drag so much good out of it? "Oh, that's okay, Sean," she replied. "It's really mostly technical music, and not especially pretty. I doubt you would enjoy it. It's kind of a concert for music teachers, you know?"

"Are you sure?" he asked, disbelieving.

"Sure. I'll see you next week at spring break and tell you exactly how it went, okay?"

"Okay. Hey, is my sister there? Can I talk to her?"

Erin handed the phone to Sheridan and walked into the bathroom. She needed to pee, as usual, and she felt really tired. *When the conversation is over, I'm going to go right to bed, so I might as well brush my teeth.*

* * *

"Danny," Sean said, "something feels funny. Erin tells me I don't need to come up for her recital, but that can't be right. Should I plan to be there anyway?"

"Sean, you absolutely *have to* come to this!" Sheridan exclaimed, pitching her voice softly, but not losing one iota of intensity. "It's the culmination of ... well, of her whole life, really. You know Erin. She never asks for anything, especially if it seems like a bother to someone. This is one of those big gestures I was talking about over Christmas. She needs you to be there, even if you don't actually enjoy the music, and to be honest, some of it is pretty out there. The point is that you need to be there for her."

"That's what I thought. What about if I ask Mom and Dad to come too?" Sean suggested.

Now you're thinking, buddy. "Great. And see if you can bully Erin's dad into making it."

"Good idea. I'll see what I can do."

Sheridan glanced at the bathroom door. She could hear water running inside. "There's something else."

"What?"

"Erin needs new clothes. She's not fitting well into her regular stuff anymore, and she's really uncomfortable. Plus, her concert dress is so fitted, if she tries to fasten it, she'll rip out all the seams," Sheridan explained.

"Is she really that big already? It's only been a few weeks since she was up for that appointment, and she seemed comfortable enough then."

"I know, but a few weeks in pregnancy make a big difference. She's about halfway through now. And she's not huge, but she's showing. She has a little belly, and her jeans don't fasten anymore, but she doesn't have money."

"I can afford new clothes for my wife," Sean protested.

"I know," Sheridan replied, "but does she? I know you two have talked about your feelings, but have you ever talked about your finances?"

"Not really," he admitted, "but listen, I'll take care of this. I can get another credit card on my account in her name and send it to her. I can't believe I didn't think of it sooner. I must be brain dead. Can you take her shopping? Make her buy what she needs?"

"I can try. Send me the card though or she might send it back," Sheridan suggested. "This is Erin we're talking about, after all."

"Good thinking."

* * *

Erin walked out of the bathroom in her Tweetie Bird sweatpants and an oversized tee shirt with an oboe on it. Sheridan handed her the phone. "Hi again, love," she said.

"Hey, sexy baby," Sean said, and she could just imagine his eyebrows waggling. "What are you wearing?"

Erin looked down at her sloppy pajamas and laughed. "Nothing special."

"Good. Save that hot stuff for when we're together."

"I won't be able to wear it. I'm too fat." She laid a hand on her lower belly, enjoying the curve. *I'll take you over sexy panties any day, little baby.*

"You're not fat, you're pregnant. You're still hot though."

"Thanks, Sean." She smiled. *I have the sweetest husband ever.*

"Hey, listen, I've been thinking. You're going to need maternity clothes, aren't you?"

"No," she said automatically.

"Yes, you are. Don't be silly. I'm going to send you a credit card and I want you to buy yourself some comfortable things and wear them. No more squeezing into regular jeans, okay?"

How could he have known? "You don't need to do that."

"Yes, I do. You're my wife. I love you. You're also carrying my baby. The least I can do is make sure you've got something to wear."

"Well, that's very generous. I'll try not to spend too much," she promised.

"Spend as much as you want, baby. I can afford it," he said.

"Famous last words."

"I doubt it. Good night, Erin. I love you."

"I love you. Talk to you tomorrow. Bye."

Chapter 22

Three days later, the promised credit card arrived in the mail, addressed to Sheridan, who made her friend put her oboe away and go to the mall. Saturday afternoon meant an uncomfortable number of pregnant women and their entourages crowded the maternity wear store when the girls arrived, so they browsed for a while.

"What do you need? Sheridan asked. "And be sure you don't cheap out, or I'll have my brother come up and shop with you."

"That's cheating," Erin laughed.

"Here, look at this! Isn't it nice?" Sheridan held up a lovely long sweater in a raspberry color.

"That's awfully pretty," Erin agreed, "but I'm mostly going to be pregnant in the summer. Do I really need something that warm?"

"Yes. It won't heat up until May," her friend reminded her. "That's a long time to be cold. Besides, it's on sale. At least try it on."

In the end, Sheridan bullied her friend into trying on a huge number of clothes, including jeans and sweaters for everyday use, Sunday dresses, shorts (last summer's on clearance), tee shirts and tank tops, and some lovely flowing black trousers that could go with anything, but particularly with a ruched and stretchy black lace top. *Those two pieces would work well for the concert,* Erin realized.

The first time she stepped into a pair of wide legged jeans with a soft blue elastic waistband, she sighed with relief. They felt so good. No pressure on her baby bump. She pulled the sweater over her head and stared at her reflection in the mirror. *Funny how maternity clothes make a person both look and feel more pregnant.*

Sheridan walked up beside her. "Isn't that better?"

"Yes. It's better. I think I'll get both pieces."

"I think you'll get the lot," Sheridan replied.

"That's too much money," Erin protested.

"Don't worry, Erin. Sean can afford it. He wants you to be as comfortable as possible." She scooped up the clothes and laid them on the counter.

"Ma'am," the clerk said to Erin, "I wonder if you would be interested in these?" She handed her a couple of bras.

Erin eyed them; one was bright blue, the other resembled a rusty nail. "What are they?"

"Nursing bras." The woman tucked a strand of long, graying hair behind her ear. "Are you planning to breastfeed your baby?"

No doubt about it. "Of course."

"Nursing bras can be expensive, and I know you're trying to keep the cost down. These are on clearance because no one liked the colors, but the design is really good. They're quality pieces."

It makes sense, but the expense is getting ridiculous. On the other hand, they're practical. The clerk rang up the sale while Erin waffled back and forth.

"That will be four hundred ninety-seven dollars and fifty cents, please."

Erin gasped. "Oh, I can't spend that much. I have to put something back." She began digging through the pile.

"Erin, no. Don't put anything back," Sheridan insisted. "There's nothing extravagant here. You've been conservative. With these pieces, you'll be all set for the rest of your pregnancy. Come on."

"It's too much, Danny," Erin protested.

"It isn't," her friend insisted.

Erin frowned at her stubbornly.

"I know." Sheridan pulled out her cell phone.

"Murphy Construction and Renovation." Erin could hear Sean's voice through the phone. *She cheated after all.*

"Sean, it's Sheridan. I'm at the store with your wife. She's balking at paying for these clothes. Talk to her."

She handed Erin the phone.

"What's wrong, baby?" he asked.

"I have too much," she whined.

Sean's chuckle made her heart melt. "I doubt it."

"There's no way I can spend this much of your money," she explained.

"How much?" he asked.

"Almost five hundred dollars."

"Is that all?" He laughed. "I thought you would get stuff for the whole pregnancy, not just the rest of winter."

Wha...? "I did."

"Sounds like you did well."

"Sean..." she complained.

"Erin, pay the bill. Just hand the nice cashier the credit card."

She obeyed with a frown.

"Now listen. I'm not broke. If you need something, just get it, okay? Promise me."

Sean, you never cease to amaze me. At last, she began to relax and understand that he really did want her to be generous with herself. *What a novel concept.* "I'll try."

"Okay. I have to go. I love you."

"Love you too."

She gathered up her bags and the girls made their way to the food court for some lunch.

Chapter 23

As is always the case when one would really like to slow down and do something well, the time before Erin's recital flew by. She couldn't hang onto the minutes, and her music progressed painfully slowly. She doubted all of it would be ready in time.

And then, suddenly, the afternoon of the recital arrived. All the performers waited behind the big black curtain for the show to start. Erin had already warmed up her oboe. It rested on a stand on the stage of the recital hall. Now she paced nervously from one side of the backstage area to the other, running through a messy jumble of thoughts. *Tory will accompany when I need a piano. I love her for that. Wish I needed a harpsichord, she's so good at it. Wouldn't harpsichord and oboe make a whiny pair? Like a couple of squabbling toddlers. Reminds me of the baby.* She rested her hand on her belly, and felt a responding tickle, as though her little one meant to say, "I'm okay, mama." She smiled, and then returned to her ruminations. *When Tory played her recital in the fall, she switched from piano to harpsichord and even did a piece on an electric organ. I wonder if I should have done some bassoon or English horn. I didn't think of it until this minute.* Nerves set in again, obliterating thought. Then she took a deep breath and reminded herself, *Justin only played his bassoon. Marisol did switch around, but it seems it's not necessary. Dr. Johnson would have told me if the programming was wrong a long time ago. Gosh, I'm nervous. It's making me stupid. Of course, everyone gets nervous. Ilona's performance is next weekend, and she's making herself sick worrying about how her flute is going to sound. I wonder if they're nervous today. Probably not, since this isn't their senior recital.*

They're such good friends, Erin thought as she scanned one familiar face after another. *I'm grateful to have known them. After this semester we'll scatter. At least I know now where I'll be going.*

She nervously rubbed her belly again. *Next week, during spring break, I'll have my ultrasound. I can't wait to see my little one finally. But first I have to get through today.* Her fingers began trembling, and she thought she might just throw up.

Warm arms wrapped around her from behind, pulling her back against a powerful chest. She jumped. A familiar voice murmured in her ear, "Hi, baby."

"Sean!" she squealed his name a little louder than was really appropriate for backstage right before a performance. She whirled around, hugging him tight and leaning her cheek against his chest. "You're here! Why are you here?" The warmth of his embrace seemed to chase the shadows of inadequacy right out of her.

"It's your big day. Where else would I be?" Sean breathed. "Of course, I would be here to support my wife." He leaned down and kissed her tenderly on the mouth.

"Erin," Tory whispered, "is this your husband?"

"Yes," she whispered back over her shoulder. "This is Sean Murphy. Sean, this is my woodwind group. This is Tory, Ilona, Marisol, Justin and Marcus. They're my closest friends in the music department."

"Pleased to meet you, guys," he said, still holding Erin close, his big hand circling soothingly on her back.

They returned the greeting softly and wandered back to their own corners.

"What's this?" Sean whispered in her ear, cupping the curve of her belly.

"Your baby, silly."

"Our baby, Erin. The baby we made together," he reminded her.

She beamed. "Yes."

A small movement fluttered under his hand and Sean drew in a startled breath. "Did I just feel that?"

A soft giggle escaped. "Yes. It's not butterflies."

"Wow."

"Erin, it's time," Dr. Johnson told her from the doorway.

Erin nodded. "Go find a seat, honey."

"You'll be great." He kissed her once more and ducked back behind the curtain.

Much strengthened by her husband's support, Erin took a deep breath and walked out onto the stage. The lights blinded her. She couldn't see the audience at all, only her music stand, the oboe and the piano, all sitting on a pale pine floor. A semicircle of plastic chairs and other music stands encircled the back of the stage. For now, she stood alone.

"Good afternoon. My name is Erin James Murphy. I would like to thank you all for coming to my recital. I hope you enjoy the music I have prepared. My first piece is the Sonata for Solo Oboe by Carl Phillip Emmanuel Bach.

She lifted the oboe into her hands, wetted the reed and began to play. As always, once Erin began working with her instrument, all her nerves melted away and she withdrew deep within herself to the place where pure music dwelt. All the hours of preparation meant she played largely from memory, relying on her familiarity with the notes to keep her fingers moving while passionate emotion expressed itself in the tempo and volume.

* * *

From his seat, between his parents, Sean stared in awe. He had heard his wife play many times, but he had never heard anything like this. *It's technical perfection.* Her fingers flew over the silver keys effortlessly, stroking the instrument and making it weep. The piece sounded sad and mournful, but little ribbons of hope threaded through it. *This music is amazing. Long too,* he realized as it continued on and on. For ten minutes she and her instrument worked together to make the most beautiful, most moving sounds he had ever heard. At last, she lowered the oboe from her mouth and took a deep breath. The audience applauded enthusiastically.

"For my next piece," she said when the clapping died away, "I would like to play the Oboe Concerto by Ralph Vaughn Williams. My accompanist for this piece is Victoria Alonzo. This arrangement for Oboe and Piano was prepared by Dr. Keith Johnson.

This piece evoked quite a different mood than the previous one. Much more modern, it had strange intervals and didn't really make much sense to Sean, but that didn't matter. She played flawlessly, her fingers hitting each note exactly right, with no hesitation. *It sounds a bit... cold though. Guess this is one of the not so pretty, technical works for the music teachers to appreciate. I suppose, because it's difficult, she had to include it to prove what she can do.*

The audience applauded again, but with less intensity.

During the brief pause, several other musicians emerged from behind the curtain and settled themselves in the chairs.

"My next piece is the Concerto for Two Oboes in F Major, by Tomaso Albinoni. I will be accompanied by the senior woodwind ensemble, The Young Bohemians." The audience chuckled. "The second solo oboe will be played by Marcus Davies."

Sean regarded the bony, aristocratic-looking young man clutched a slender, wooden tube. He nodded, acknowledging her comment.

They began to play. *Now, this is music I can understand.* Pretty, rich and deep, it flowed over the audience, making them smile.

On and on the concert continued, for the next forty minutes, some pieces technical and strange, others lovely and haunting, some with accompaniment, others without. *Such a broad range. I knew she was good, but I never dreamed she had this much talent.* He felt another surge of guilt over the narrow life they would be sharing after she graduated. *It's what she wants, but is it really best, when she has all this inside her?*

But that music wasn't all Erin had inside her. As she set up for her last number, fitting a fresh reed into her instrument, he saw her rub the side of her belly discreetly with her free hand. *I wonder if the baby's tickling her.* She smiled, a private smile, and he understood at last what she had tried to tell him all along; that while she was a superior musician, she was also a woman, a friend, a wife, and soon to be a mother. *She has to be all of them to be whole, and would never be satisfied with the self-centered life of a dedicated artist.*

Erin returned to center stage and addressed the audience one last time. "Let me thank you all again for coming to my recital. I hope you have enjoyed the music. My last piece is based on the pop song "I Swear," by Gary Baker and Frank G. Miles, as performed by the group All-4-One. It was arranged by me for oboe and piano in honor of my wonderful husband, Sean Murphy."

She raised the instrument to her lips. This resembled nothing she had played before. She executed the simple tune with a skill beyond technicality. Each note recalled the passion and love of their relationship. *It's the song,* he realized, *that was playing the first time we danced at homecoming; the night we kissed in the parking lot, and later went to her house and made love for the first time.* So many years had passed since that night, but for a moment, he found himself there again, holding a young Erin in his arms, kissing her soft lips, and knowing that his life would never be the same. *I'm so thankful to be here for it. I can't believe she thought I wouldn't want to.* As he listened, a few of the lyrics from the chorus flitted across his memory, invoking a promise she'd made to him that night. *I felt it then but lost my way for a while. Now she's reminding me. No, it's more than that. She's making everyone not only understand how much she loves me but feel that love along with her.* It was, without a doubt, the most meaningful gift anyone had ever given him.

The last plaintive notes died away. Erin lowered her oboe. The audience sat in stunned silence for several moments, moved to disbelief by the beauty of what they had just heard. Sean looked up at his wife, standing on that stage, and felt certain he would burst with pride for her accomplishments. He brought his hands together, breaking the ice, and the room erupted into thunderous applause. Erin bowed, indicated her pianist, who stood and bowed, and then she motioned to her woodwind group to come onto the stage to be honored. After several moments of loud appreciation, including a well-deserved standing ovation, the house lights clicked on.

* * *

At last, Erin could see the audience. Among the expected complement of music teachers, music majors, and students from the music appreciation classes trying to get their concert attendance credits, a pocket of unexpected people stood off to one side. Her eyes went there directly, of course, because Sean's tall frame drew her gaze like a magnet. Standing near him, Sheridan lit up the room with her high-voltage smile. But those two were not alone.

Roger and Ellen Murphy, their expressions startled, stood with their children. As Erin looked, her mouth dropped open in shock. Daniel James, her careless, disinterested father, had left work on a Saturday afternoon, not to golf with his buddies, not to work out at the gym, but to drive three hours so he could listen to his daughter play a recital. He approached her, carrying a large bouquet of red roses, which he extended up to her.

"Well done, pumpkin," he said, and his eyes seemed rather shiny. "I had no idea you were that good."

"Thank you, Daddy," Erin replied softly, taking the bouquet and smelling it. She set her oboe on its stand and the flowers on the piano bench and then climbed down the steps at the side of the stage to where her father waited. He wrapped his arms around her and hugged her tight.

"I'm so proud of you, Erin." Those simple, desperately longed-for words meant more to her than the applause, more than the ovation. Erin sniffled, and tears began to flow down her cheeks. The overwrought emotions of the concert, combined with the wild hormones of her pregnancy, broke apart her composure and she wept noisily in her father's embrace.

"Erin?" Tory patted her friend on the arm. "That was amazing. Are you all right?"

"She's fine." Marisol joined them. "I felt the same way after my recital. It's the adrenaline. Is this your dad, Erin?"

Erin took a deep breath. "Yes, this is my dad, Daniel James." She squeezed him once more and then stepped away. "Dad, there's going to be a reception now in the band hall. I have to pack up my instrument and then I'll be over there."

"Okay, pumpkin. I'll see you there." He patted her back and followed the crowd out of the recital hall.

Erin wiped her eyes and sat down to dismantle her instrument, placing the pieces back into the case. Then, retrieving her roses, she made her way down the hall to Dr. Johnson's office. The door stood slightly ajar, but the professor did not appear to be inside. She tucked the oboe inside, as instructed, and pulled the door shut, locking the instrument inside.

Whew. Got that taken care of. Now to the party. She walked the few steps down the courtyard to the band hall where a noisy crowd munched cookies and sipped punch and coffee. She walked straight to her husband.

He didn't say a word about her playing, but his gaze burned bright. *He understood my message. I'm so glad.* Sean slid his arm around Erin's waist and held her while people approached, complementing her performance.

All her woodwind ensemble friends hugged her, and several members of the music faculty did as well. Last was Dr. Johnson. He actually scooped her away from Sean and squeezed her.

Then he backed up, taking her arms at the elbow and exclaimed, "Bravo, Erin, you surpassed my wildest expectations. You had better send me lots and lots of double reed students from your hometown."

"I'll do that," she told him seriously, visions of her future pupils flashing across her mind.

He turned to Sean. "Hi, I'm Dr. Johnson. I teach oboe here. You must be Erin's husband."

"I am." He shook the man's hand. "Sean Murphy."

"You must be very proud."

"You can't imagine." Sean's voice turned rough with love and passion as he looked at his wife, an intense expression in his bright blue eyes.

* * *

After the reception, as the audience drifted away, the James and Murphy families walked to the courtyard. The chilly air refreshed them after the stuffy closeness of the crowded band hall. The Murphys had held back during the reception, wanting Erin to receive all the professional accolades she deserved, but now they took their turn. Roger gave her one of his signature bear hugs before handing her over to his wife, who kissed her cheek.

"That was amazing, Erin, dear. You're such an accomplished musician," Ellen told her in her usual quiet, dignified voice.

"Thank you. I'm overwhelmed that you both made it."

"We wouldn't have missed it for anything," Roger insisted.

"How did you know to be here?"

"I told them, of course," Sheridan said, "I know you hate to be a bother to anyone, but really, Erin, everyone wanted to come and see you. And you sure didn't disappoint. Wow! I really liked that last one. Did you say you arranged it yourself?"

The force of Erin's grin had long since set her cheeks to aching, but she smiled wider anyway. "Yes."

"How did you choose it?"

"It was the song," Sean told her, "that was playing the first time we danced together, at homecoming."

"You remembered!" Erin exclaimed, and tears threatened to overwhelm her again as her husband amazed her with his sweetness.

"Of course. That was a life-changing moment for both of us," he replied.

Erin nodded. "It was, in the best possible way."

"Well," Daniel said, "I'm glad to have been here for this, Erin. Be sure and let me know when your graduation is, but I have a meeting this evening with some clients who want some investment advice, and it's a long drive home."

"Sure, Daddy. Thank you so much for coming." She hugged him once more and he departed.

"Okay, Mom, Dad, how about a tour of the university? I would love to show you around the campus." Sheridan collected her parents, winked at her friend, and left.

Erin took Sean's hand and led him back to her dorm room in silence. Once there, Sean tenderly undressed his wife, noting the changes to her body; the swollen breasts, and the round belly. She felt as though her entire being must be glowing with joy. *This is as close to a perfect moment as reality will allow.* Sean pressed her to him for a long, passionate kiss before lifting her onto the bed for a private celebration that quite took Erin's breath away.

Chapter 24

On the second Saturday in May, Erin sat in the gym, robed in black and wearing a square hat, to receive her diploma. *Strangers all around me. I wish Sheridan was here, right beside me. With the same last name, we should be together.* She regarded the stage. *Still, Danny's 4.0 deserves to be celebrated. Top graduate. Introducing the keynote speaker. She's completely in her element. I wish I was sitting with the orchestra.*

The musicians at the front of the gym, in front of the stage, took up Elgar's "Pomp and Circumstance" with more enthusiasm than skill. *I wish I was playing with them. They sound like they could use the help. Anything other than sitting in this folding metal chair with twenty people on either side of me. I've completely disappeared. Magna cum laude, and I'm invisible.* The thought brought a smile to her lips. *Okay, so I got the B in PoliSci. I think I hated the class too much to do better. Still, high honors. That's an accomplishment. And my music degree. That's even better. I guess college was a success after all.* The baby tickled and squirmed inside her and she rested a hand on the wiggling bump. *Thank goodness for maternity clothes. I would never have managed anything else.*

"You okay?" the woman next to her whispered.

Erin nodded. "It tickles. Nothing to worry about."

Her neighbor shook her head and muttered, "I'm never having kids."

Erin fought down the urge to giggle. *To each her own. I'm happy with how everything turned out, especially you. The doc-*

tor says you're a healthy little boy, and as strong as you kick, I believe it. She turned to the side, seeking and finding her family just where they said they'd be. The Murphys, her parents of the heart, her beloved husband, and her father, all in a row, cameras poised. She blew Sean a kiss, not knowing if he would even see her.

He immediately returned the gesture, and her heart fluttered. *He still makes me feel like a teenager with a crush. God, I love my husband. I can't wait to leave the university forever and begin my life as Mrs. Erin Murphy, oboe player and music teacher.*

Her mind wandered as Sheridan stood and gave a short speech. *Summer music series with the orchestra. I'm looking forward to that.* Sheridan sat, and a middle-aged alumnus rose and took the mic. Of his speech, which moved people to tears all around her, Erin heard nothing.

It promised to be a long ceremony, with hundreds of graduates being honored, but finally, Erin's row stood and processed to the bottom of the stairs leading up onto the stage.

"Erin James Murphy, magna cum laude," the woman announced. Erin mounted the shaky steps carefully, her fingers trailing over the rough painted brick of the wall. The stage bounced under her feet, but she made her way to the president of the university, a man with white hair and black eyebrows. He smiled, shook her hand and handed her a paper tube. She turned her head to face the camera and cheers erupted from her entourage, mingling with the polite applause of strangers and warming her heart.

Many graduates still waited after the 'M' section, and Erin passed the time dreaming of her future while they processed. It seemed years went by, but finally, graduation ended.

The graduates rose as their families flooded onto the floor, eager to embrace them.

"Erin! Erin!" Sheridan, her face nearly lost in a smile that beamed brighter than a camera flash, ran to her and threw her arms around her. Erin tried to turn to hug her friend and sister, but her belly got in the way, bumping Sheridan's hip. She patted the swollen bulge. "And hello to you too, little one," she added. Erin bit her lip.

"This way, girls," Roger's voice cut through the roar and the girls turned, arms around each other's waists, cheek to cheek as he snapped one photo after another. Then the Murphys and Daniel swarmed around, hugging the girls.

"Um, can we get out of here?" Erin urged at last. "The noise is making my head spin."

"Of course!" Ellen agreed. "I can't abide crowds. Are you two ready to head back to your room and pack?"

"We're packed," Sheridan said, "but yes."

They threaded their way among the milling sea of bodies and waded through the bottleneck at the door, sighing with relief as warm spring air replaced the chilly air conditioning in the gym.

"I can't stay long," Daniel warned. "I have a meeting early tomorrow and I need to get home." Then his face contorted. "I hope that doesn't upset you, Erin. This is your big moment."

"It's okay, Daddy," she replied, and meant it. *I don't begrudge him his long hours, now that he's willing to make a little time for me. It makes him happy to work, so why fight it?*

He smiled and squeezed her around the shoulders. "What's next for you two?"

"Well, I'm going to be playing the summer music series with the symphony... or at least part of it. I mean, this little one is coming, in July or August," she patted her belly, "and that will take precedence, but they're letting me have a solo in the first concert."

"Letting." Sean snorted. "They practically begged you, Miss Modesty."

Erin grinned.

Daniel turned to Sheridan. "I'll go home for the summer," she explained, "but after that, I'm coming back for graduate school. I think college must be my natural habitat."

"You're obviously good at it," Daniel replied, earning himself one of her beaming smiles. "Okay, this is where I parked. Erin, don't be a stranger, okay?"

Erin threw her arms around her dad. "Of course not. Drive safely, Daddy."

He hugged her and took his leave, waving as he made his way to his Lexus, parked under a spreading oak.

"I wish you didn't have to go," Erin said to her friend. "I'll miss you so much."

"I know," Sheridan agreed. "It's hard to let life happen, but we have to. And, after all, it's not that far, and I know the way. We'll still be best friends and sisters forever."

"And you two have the rest of summer to hang out together," Sean added. "Remember, I let the lease expire on the apartment to save up for the renovation, so we'll be staying with my folks for a least a month while I wrap things up. I don't want you breathing in all those chemicals."

"I really appreciate you letting us stay with you," Erin said to Roger and Ellen.

"Think nothing of it," Ellen replied. "We wouldn't have it any other way." Roger nodded in agreement.

"Okay then," Sheridan said, "let's get this show on the road." She opened the front door of the residence hall and they funneled in.

Sure enough, boxes and bags littered the dorm room, ready to be moved out to the waiting vehicles. Erin scooped up her beloved oboe case and a satchel of sheet music. Roger and Sean hefted boxes. Ellen grabbed a sack full of bedding. Sheridan knelt and rummaged under the bed, making sure nothing had been left behind. "Ouch!" she exclaimed.

"What happened?" Roger asked, concerned.

"Erin, I swear, if I stick myself with one more piece of reed... can't you put them in the trash?" She plucked the splinter out of her finger and tossed it in the corner.

"Reed?" Sean asked.

"Get used to it, brother dear. Oboe players are obsessed with their reeds. They make them themselves, and in the process, leave splinters everywhere."

"I try, but sometimes they get away from me. Sorry, Danny," Erin said.

Sheridan rolled her eyes at the excuse... and the unwanted nickname. Stuck fingers notwithstanding, it only took a short time to pack everything up and load it into the vehicles for the three-hour drive home. Sheridan took Erin's car, which her friend was giving to her to keep. Erin rode with her husband, of course. Their long separation had ended. Their new life together was beginning.

* * *

One day in early June, Sean took Erin to the grocery store. With only two months left in her pregnancy, she was beginning to feel uncomfortably heavy. Thankfully the summer heat had not yet set in.

Sean left to use the bathroom, while Erin browsed the fruits and vegetables, her mouth watering at the smell of fresh new strawberries. *All I have to do is glance at them and my husband will buy me a box and feed them to me, kissing me after each bite. Hmmm. Maybe I should shock him and just ask for them.*

"Erin?"

She turned towards the female voice, and the sight of Valerie James' face elicited a startled gasp. Erin regarded her mother warily. They had not parted on the best of terms five years ago, and they had not spoken to or seen each other since.

"Mother," Erin replied coolly.

"It's been so long. My goodness, you've gotten fat. You almost look pregnant," Valerie blurted in her usually disapproving whine.

Erin frowned at the careless insult. "I am pregnant."

Manicured fingers flew to cover a red-lipstick mouth. "Oh, Erin, didn't I always warn you to be careful? You're too far along to do anything about it now."

Erin's hands moved protectively to her belly. "Do anything? Why would I do anything? I'm happy to be pregnant. It wasn't exactly an accident."

"What, you mean you did this to yourself on purpose?" Valerie regarded her daughter with an expression one generally reserved for unmentionable things left moldering on the sidewalk.

"More or less. It's not bad, Mom." Erin kept her tone neutral, though seeing her mother's negative reaction to what was one of the most joyous events in her life did sting.

"It is. Once you have a baby, life is never the same again."

Duh. "I'm okay with that. So is Sean."

"Who's Sean?" Valerie's eyes narrowed.

"My husband." *Good Lord, woman. Don't you pay attention to anything but yourself?*

"Husband? You're married?"

"I sent you an invitation, Mom," Erin reminded her mother, forcing herself to be gentle, "I've been married for a while."

"I never received any invitation. Don't pretend you sent one." The accusation in Valerie's voice made Erin want to grind her teeth.

"I did," she protested. "Maybe it got lost somewhere. If so, I'm sorry. But it's not a surprise, is it, that we're married? I mean we've been together since I was in high school. I used to talk to him on the phone all the time. He's Sheridan Murphy's brother."

Valerie shrugged. Clearly, she had no idea what her daughter was talking about.

257

Sean returned from the bathroom and slipped his hand into his wife's turning to face Valerie.

She looked him over thoroughly, her gaze lingering on his wide shoulders, bulky biceps and narrow waist. "Nice," she said finally. "I wish I'd been informed about the wedding."

"We sent an invitation," Sean said. "You didn't get it?"

"No, I never did." Her harsh tone mellowed and turned coy at the sight of Erin's handsome husband. "Where did you send it?"

Good grief, Mother. He's half your age. Settle down.

"To Motley. The last I heard you were living with Bill," Erin said.

"With Bill?" Valerie snorted. "I only lived with Bill for four months. I moved back to town in the middle of March four years ago."

Erin furrowed her brow at her mother. "Seriously? You dumped your husband, abandoned your child, all for a love affair that only lasted half a year?"

"Don't you dare take that disapproving voice with me, young lady," her mother said, harshness returning in force. She waved a finger in Erin's direction. "You were glad to see me go. You couldn't wait to move in with your little friend. Now I see why."

The implication, though only partially incorrect, set Erin's face burning. "You're wrong," she protested. "Sean didn't live with his parents. He had his own place."

"I'm surprised you didn't move in with him."

Erin ignored the comment.

"At any rate," Valerie continued, "you got what you wanted. You always were the meanest little girl. It was a relief to get away from you and your critical comments and your hard eyes."

Erin tensed. *I knew that, so why does hearing it voiced aloud hurt so much?*

"I beg your pardon, ma'am," Sean interjected, "but that just isn't true. Erin isn't mean at all. She's the sweetest woman I've ever known."

Leave it to Sean to know the right thing to say. Mollified by her husband's support, Erin squeezed his fingers. *You make my life worth living, my love.*

"You must have low standards," Valerie sneered.

Sean's mouth snapped shut in shock.

Valerie rushed on. "You can't imagine what she said to me before she left to move in with your parents. She told me I was selfish. Erin is the selfish one, always has been. All she cares about is playing that stupid oboe, and it's loud and annoying. I hate it."

"Erin is not selfish at all. Nothing could be further from the truth." He slid his arms around her and cradled her burgeoning belly in both hands. She leaned back against him. *This is what family truly means. Love, not blood.* "And as for her playing, I can't imagine what's wrong with you. It's amazing."

"It's all right, Sean." Erin's voice remained calm and soft, though she wanted to rage. "You don't have to defend me. It doesn't matter." *I have my husband, our baby, his family, my father and my best friend, and that's so much more important than winning the approval of this self-centered bitch,* she reminded herself.

"It does," he insisted.

Erin smiled up at him over her shoulder, a tight, unconvincing smile, but the best she could manage under the circumstances. "No. I know she's never liked me. It's fine."

"You see," Valerie insisted, "she knows she deserves it. She's just mean by nature."

Me? Mean? The unfairness of the comment finally snapped the fragile ribbon of control that held back Erin's emotions. In a tone of icy indignation, she enunciated, "If I'm mean, Mother, it's because I've learned from the best. But I'm not mean. If I were, I would tell you what I really think of you. I would tell you that you're a tramp who abandons a twenty-year marriage in favor of a six-month affair. I would say that you always were a terrible mother. I would say all those things if I were mean, but I'm not. In fact, Mom, there's nothing wrong with me. There never has been. I'm perfectly fine. Come on, honey, let's get out of here."

They turned as one and left the store, leaving Valerie, her mouth open, gawking after them. Erin had finally been provoked beyond caring, and the response had been swift, vicious, and honest.

The couple drove home in silence. Sean's lips quirked with the hint of a smile, as though impressed at how strong his wife had been. Erin, as her anger wore off, began to feel a twinge of regret. *I might, perhaps, have gone a little too far.*

Back at the house, Erin found Mrs. Murphy watching the Food Network in the family room. It appeared shepherd's pie would be on the menu soon, as she was frantically scribbling down ingredients and instructions. Erin waited for the commercial before kneeling beside the chair and giving her mother-in-law a tight hug. *It all started with this woman, who raised such an amazing son and daughter that they could see past my shyness and love me anyway. What a wonderful woman Ellen is, to put off her own righteous indignation at Sean's and my choices, which really were handled badly, and welcome me into the family.*

"I love you, Mom," Erin said softly, kissing Ellen on the cheek. Then she walked out of the room up the stairs.

* * *

"What on earth was that about?" Ellen asked her son.

"We ran into Valerie James at the store."

Ellen winced. "Oh, I'm sorry to hear that. Is Erin all right?"

"Yes. She finally stood up to her mother." Sean couldn't help smirking at the memory. *It's been a long time coming, baby.*

"Good. You'd better go and make sure she's handling it."

"Right." Sean climbed the stairs to his room to check on his wife. He found Erin lying on her side on the bed. She was not crying, nor did she look upset. She simply gazed off into the distance as though deep in thought. He slipped onto the bed beside her and wrapped his arm around her waist, placing his hand on her belly so he could feel their son moving. The little boy pressed hard against his father's touch. Sean grinned.

"I love you," Erin told him softly.

"I love you too. You know why, don't you? Say it, Erin, and believe it," he urged.

Erin glanced over her shoulder at her husband, her voice calm and sure as she told him, "You love me because I'm a good girl and I deserve it."

"That's right. You are." He trailed his fingers down her cheek.

Erin sucked in a deep breath and released it. "I think I should apologize to her."

"Why? You told the truth. She is a terrible mother and there isn't anything wrong with you."

"I know," Erin replied. "But I shouldn't have called her a tramp. That wasn't necessary."

"Send her a card," Sean suggested. "Don't call. I don't want you to talk to her anymore. Nothing good can come of it."

"You're right. I'll double check the address this time, though." Her lips bent into a humorless grin.

He kissed her temple. "So, are you all right?"

"Yes. I'm fine."

"You look a little sad."

"Do I look like a girl who needs to be made love to?" The curving of Erin's mouth increased until her parody of a smile became real.

Sean grinned at the old, often repeated comment. "Yes, you do. Turn over, baby, and let me help you with that."

His words revived Erin completely. She rolled into Sean's embrace, a little awkwardly with her big belly throwing off her balance, and wrapped her arms around his neck, pulling him over to kiss her. He didn't resist. Erin still, always, had the sweetest, most kissable mouth, and Sean was no more immune to it than he had been the night of the homecoming dance. He opened his mouth on hers and she responded in kind, letting his tongue plunge between her lips. She hummed as he plundered her deeply, loving the heat rising between them.

Sean lifted her shirt over her head, unhooking her bra to reveal her breasts. They had grown large, bigger than he had ever expected, and he lifted one in his hand, testing its weight before lowering his mouth to the tender peak. Erin pressed her husband's head closer to her, urging him to give the straining nipple a thorough tending-to, and Sean complied, tugging, sucking and nipping gently, until Erin made soft pleasure noises with every breath. Then he released it and went directly to the other to begin again.

When Erin's lay panting with desire, he pulled back and began stripping off his clothing. She wriggled awkwardly out of her pants and underwear, baring herself for another consummation of their love.

"Lie down, Sean," she told him, her voice sultry and slow. He did, and she crawled over to him, taking his sex in her hands and stroking it. He made a soft, approving sound as she worked the large shaft. "I can hardly wait to feel this inside me," she said, "but first..." She lowered her face and rubbed her cheek against the sensitive head before pressing her lips to the tip. Her dexterous little tongue snaked out and she licked him. Sean groaned. Erin took her time, teasing him all over, nibbling with her lips, before she returned to the tip and opened her mouth, taking him deep inside.

"Oh Erin," Sean moaned, "that's amazing." *I love it when she does this. She's so good at it. All those years playing the oboe have given her some excellent oral skills, and she's not even shy about it.*

Erin pleasured her husband with her mouth and hands for long moments. Her tongue and lips teased the sensitive tissues, alternating with hot, wet suction, until completion threatened.

Tempting as is it, I don't want to let go in her mouth, not this time. Not when Erin hasn't had her pleasure yet. "Stop now, baby," he told her gently, "It's time for me to be inside you."

* * *

Oh yes, Erin thought, her insides clenching in anticipation.

Erin gave her husband one last, thorough lick before releasing his sex. In the past, it had been their custom for him to be on top, but during late pregnancy, the weight of the baby had grown uncomfortable in that position, so Erin simply stayed where she was, kneeling, and Sean moved around behind her. He parted the petals of her sex and caressed her to make sure she was ready for him. Wet, relaxed and eager, she wiggled her hips. Sean took her invitation, pressing gently into her, groaning as her tight passage slowly opened around him.

Erin wanted to squeal with pleasure as Sean's big penis slid home inside her, but she feared Ellen might hear from downstairs, so she held it in.

He began to move, easing into her, pulling back and returning, making her body tighten with the pleasure of his taking. *It's so good.* Erin moaned as Sean loved her, slow and deep. Another soft sound escaped as her peak drew rapidly nearer.

* * *

Sean could feel Erin clenching as her orgasm approached. *I don't want her to come too fast. She should enjoy every second.* Her muffled squeaks and moans, and the restless way she rocked her hips, demonstrated a deep pleasure he wanted to continue, so he deliberately slowed his pace even more, but it was already too late. Erin was so aroused, so close, that even this lesser stimulation proved overpowering. One delicate thrust pressed too deep, delving fully into her and she went up in flames, pressing her face into the pillow to hide her ecstatic sobs as she squirmed and spasmed.

Sean couldn't hold out against the beautiful, sexy sight of his wife's orgasm. He thrust deep once, twice, and let go, giving her his own glorious peak. After a few moments, he gently slipped out and lowered her to the mattress on her side, joining her, face to face, and pulling her as close as her belly would allow.

"Thank you, Sean," she said sweetly. "That was just what I needed. What a wonderful husband you are."

"It's my pleasure, baby, believe me. I love you so much, Erin."

"I love you too."

They kissed tenderly.

* * *

So, the world isn't perfect, Erin thought. *It's full of bad mothers and tragic situations. Knowing I'm completely loved by this amazing, sexy man, have been loved by him for so many years, means a lot. If I can get and keep him, I must be a good girl after all.* Erin smiled. *Life's pretty good when you're a Murphy.*

Epilogue

August 2006

Sean Murphy knelt in his swimming trunks in a kiddie pool full of warm water on the newly refinished floor of their living room. *I hope the tarp I laid down will catch the splashes.*

No longer a filthy disaster area, the room now glowed with life and charm, all polished oak floors, wood framed windows, and crown molding. The walls had been painted a soft white. He and Erin had picked out a sofa and loveseat in forest green brocade, which they had arranged at right angles facing the red brick fireplace.

Erin. He stroked sweaty hair back from his wife's face and kissed her temple. She didn't seem to notice.

As the long minutes passed, he wondered just how the hell he had ended up in such a predicament. He had pictured his wife giving birth at a hospital, with pain medication. *I should have guessed she would accept nothing less than a home delivery, especially as she experienced no complications.* Actually, the labor had been fine, if slow, starting early in the morning with a few twinges, and progressing throughout the day. The contractions had intensified, but never really gotten so bad she couldn't handle them; that is, until about ten minutes ago. The midwife, a sweet woman named Sara, with decades of experience, had decided that rather than waiting a further three hours for Erin to dilate the last centimeter, she would break her water. Then all hell had broken loose. The pain had suddenly gotten intense, so Sara and her assistant Abby had helped Erin into the birthing tub, so the water could help her cope. Now Abby ladled water over Erin's back as the contraction surged, and Sean supported her, his hands on her waist, hers around his neck, her forehead on his shoulder while she moaned and squirmed, trying to find a less intense position.

I hate this. She's in so much pain. "Can't we do anything?" he asked the midwife.

"No. This is just part of it. No one can handle nine-centimeter contractions well. We just have to help her endure. It won't be long."

The contraction faded, and Erin started to sob. "I can't do this," she wept.

"You're doing it," Abby said firmly. "You're doing great. Just a few more minutes, Erin, and you'll be able to start pushing. Your baby will be here before you know it."

"Breathe, Erin," Sean told her, stroking her back gently. "Remember to breathe."

Erin took several slow, deep breaths, trying to calm herself and relax her muscles before the next contraction could begin. There was no time. Her belly tightened painfully again, and she moaned. In the middle of the contraction, the sound Erin was making changed from a groan to a growl. Sean could feel her arms tensing.

"Are you pushing, Erin?" Sara asked sharply.

"I have to," Erin panted.

"Abby, quick, check her. We don't want her to push unless she's fully dilated.

As the contraction faded, Abby gently checked Erin for dilation. Though the assistant moved gently, Erin still shrieked in pain. Sean squeezed her hips, trying to comfort her.

"She's complete, Sara, and the baby is already descending."

"Good. That should make her feel a little better."

"What's happening?" Sean wanted to know, confused by the rapid back and forth conversation of the two professionals.

"We're starting the pushing phase," Sarah replied, her attention on Erin. "This is usually easier on the mom, because it gives her something to do. Can you keep holding her?"

"I can hold her forever," Sean said.

"Good. Let's have her turn though, so she's facing me. You can hold her from behind now. Just hook your arms under hers."

Sean nodded and helped his wife change position just in time for another contraction. This time, she did seem more in control as she bore down, trying to bring their son into the world.

"Good, Erin. Push. You're doing so well. He's really coming down."

"It burns," Erin hissed through gritted teeth.

"I know it does. That's your baby being delivered. Push into the burn, Erin. Don't fight against it."

Erin pushed and then exhaled loudly, her head falling back against Sean's shoulder. "It hurts," she wailed.

"I know it hurts," he murmured. "Don't stop." Another contraction, another push. Sean supported his wife in the water, thankful for the muscles he had developed working construction for so many years. *This is hard.* Another push, another. "Is anything happening?"

"Yes, Sean" Sara reassured him. "It won't be long. The baby is much lower now. The head is crowning. Erin, do you want to feel?"

Erin shuddered. "No. I don't want to feel that."

"Okay. Sean?"

When she's about to lose it? "No thanks. Let's just get this done, okay?"

"Okay. Push. One more should get the head out."

Erin's push turned to a soft cry as the head emerged. She panted.

"Wonderful, Erin. The head is out. Just give me a little push, honey, and you'll get to meet your son."

Erin pushed one last time and the baby slithered into the midwife's hands.

"I want to sit down," Erin told Sean. He lowered her into the water, so she could position herself more comfortably. Sean took a seat behind her, pulling her back against his chest. He wrapped his arms around her. She leaned her head on his shoulder.

Sara lifted the baby out of the water and suctioned out his nose and mouth. He let out a squeak and then began to howl.

"Sean, Erin, meet your son," she said, placing the baby in Erin's arms. Erin looked down into the baby's face. He stopped crying and stared back at his mother, his eyes squinty in the light, his little lip sticking out. Sean leaned over his wife's shoulder.

"Oh, Sean," Erin breathed, "just look at him. Have you ever seen anything so beautiful in your life?"

"Only one thing," he replied, awed.

"What's that?"

"You." He kissed her temple. She smiled. There was a flash as Sara took a photo of the family.

"That was a good one," she said to Abby as the assistant began setting up equipment to weigh and clean the baby. Sara handed Sean a pair of scissors. She clamped the cord and held it up, so he cut it. Then she took the little boy from Erin and handed him to his father, so she could help Erin out of the water for a post-delivery examination.

Sean climbed out of the tub, cradling his son in his arms, and walked across the tarp over to the loveseat where Abby waited to examine the little boy.

"Congratulations, Dad," she told Sean. "What's his name?"

"Jordan. Jordan Matthew Murphy."

"He's precious."

"Yes, he is." He handed the baby to the midwife's assistant and turned to his wife. Erin lay on the couch, draped in a towel, as Sara delivered the afterbirth. Sean remembered the last time, the miscarriage. *What a tragedy that was, and we almost compounded it by losing each other not long after. But now, everything's perfect. Erin's my wife, and our son was born alive and healthy.*

Abby scrubbed the baby vigorously with a soft cloth and he began to wail again. The assistant wrapped Jordan in a blanket and handed him to Sean, who carried him over to Erin. She scooted up on the sofa and eagerly held out her arms, cradling their son and gazing down into his face with adoration. Sean smiled, placing his hand on his wife's shoulder. The circle was complete. A new branch of the Murphy family had begun, passing on the legacy of love to the next generation.

Dear Reader,

Thank you for the time you've spent with Sean and Erin. I hope you enjoyed the reading as much as I enjoyed the writing. They were a fun couple to work with. I hated for the story, and the music, to end.

But books can't go on forever. The good news is that Book 2 of The Hearts in Winter Chronicles: *When the Words are Spoken*, which is Sheridan's story, has also been published, along with a third installment, When the Heart Heals, and a fourth, Caroline's choice. Scroll down for excerpts and links.

But in the meanwhile, I would very much appreciate it if you would take a moment and leave a review of *When the Music Ends*. Thank you again.

Sincerely,
Simone Beaudelaire

Dear reader,

We hope you enjoyed reading *When The Music Ends*. Please take a moment to leave a review, even if it's a short one. Your opinion is important to us.

Discover more books by Simone Beaudelaire at https://www.nextchapter.pub/authors/simone-beaudelaire-romance-author

Want to know when one of our books is free or discounted? Join the newsletter at http://eepurl.com/bqqB3H

Best regards,

Simone Beaudelaire and the Next Chapter Team

The story continues in:

When The Words Are Spoken by Simone Beaudelaire

To read first chapter for free, head to:
https://www.nextchapter.pub/books/when-the-words-are-spoken-romance

Other Books by Simone Beaudelaire

When the Music Ends (The Hearts in Winter Chronicles Book 1)
When the Words are Spoken (The Hearts in Winter Chronicles Book 2)
Caroline's Choice (The Hearts in Winter Chronicles Book 3)
When the Heart Heals (The Hearts in Winter Chronicles Book 4)
The Naphil's Kiss
Blood Fever
Polar Heat
Xaman (with Edwin Stark)
Darkness Waits (with Edwin Stark)
Watching Over the Watcher
Baylee Breaking
Amor Maldito: Romantic Tragedies from Tejano Folklore
Keeping Katerina (The Victorians Book 1)
Devin's Dilemma (The Victorians Book 2)
High Plains Promise (Love on the High Plains Book 2)
High Plains Heartbreak (Love on the High Plains Book 3)
High Plains Passion (Love on the High Plains Book 4)
Devilfire (American Hauntings Book 1)
Saving Sam (The Wounded Warriors Book 1 with J.M. Northup)
Justifying Jack (The Wounded Warriors Book 2 with J.M. Northup)
Making Mike (The Wounded Warriors Book 3 with J.M Northup)

CPSIA information can be obtained
at www.ICGtesting.com
Printed in the USA
BVHW091315201120
593806BV00010B/669